現在就跟著老師這樣學英文句型！
先說明、後講解，最清楚易懂！

User's Guide 使用說明

完勝攻略 ❶ 先說明，再講解，觀念清晰學

針對所有句型、文法概念先簡單清晰的加以說明以後，搭配例句加以分析解說，幫助讀者強化觀念，所有例句皆附上中文翻譯，方便參照學習，在提升句型觀念同時，也無形中增強寫作能力。

完勝攻略 ❷ 隨堂測驗，學習效果立即考驗

每個主題重點學習後，皆附隨堂測驗提供即時練習，並精選大考試題收錄於各章節中，模擬測驗實力立刻展現！

完勝攻略 ❸ 習題編寫詳解，疑惑馬上解答

書中所有題目都附有詳解，幫助大家在做完題目後能夠真正釐清易混淆觀念，學習才能真正達到效果。

Preface 前言

　　筆者從事高中升大學之英語補教事業迄今近20年，教學過程中常遇到學生問到這類問題：

　　「老師，為什麼翻譯英文句子順序跟中文不一樣？」

　　「老師，為什麼有些動詞的後面只能加ing，有些要加to，有些兩種都可以用？」「老師，『他比我高』到底是 "He is taller than I." 還是 "He is taller than me."？」

　　我不知道怎麼回答你，但我努力在本書中告訴你為什麼。

　　英文文法是許多同學在學英文時遇到的最大瓶頸，遭受挫折之後，往往因此失去了學習的動力與樂趣。因襲中國數千年來的科舉制度，台灣無數莘莘學子幾乎每個人都是從小 考到大。面對地球村及國際化時代的潮流，台灣很難自絕於競賽之外。從國中 基測、高中學測、指定科目考試、全民英檢（GEPT）、托福（TOEFL）、雅思（IELTS）、多益（TOEIC）、公務人員升等考試……等等，無一不與英文學習有密切的關係。

　　教了那麼久的補習班，深深慨嘆升學考試制度僵化限制了我們學習英文的方式，連帶使得「考試引導教學」所造就的「補教名師」都清一色跟隨考試方向。對此，我頗不以為意，我堅信英文學習可以是更多樣化、更多元化的。

如果你問我，為什麼要學好文法句型呢？

● 文法是學習英文的關鍵 （an important element that determines English learning）

★文法協助我們了解句子結構 （any part of a sentence, any section of an article）
★文法協助我們解題 （to figure out the questions in a cloze test）
★文法需要實際運用 （to put them into practical use）
★文法需要不斷練習（Practice is the only key to success in mastering sentence structure.）

　　簡單來說，文法的學習目的在協助我們瞭解句子的結構、掌握句子的意義，在閱讀過程中瞭解文意，在寫作過程中幫助我們寫出正確的句子。

　　在本書之中，我們融合了語言分析學（linguistics-analysis）、語法學（syntax）、語意學（semantics）、使同學了解英文文法的來龍去脈，靈活應用，改善一般學生只是抱著文法猛K卻一竅不通的通病。

　　本書是專為高中以上學生訂作的一本句型參考書，單元編排循序漸進，條理分明，書中每個句型從基礎講解切入，在逐步累積觀念的過程中，我們針對最易出錯的部份做強化學習，搭配完整的習題演練，透過反覆練習將語言規則內化，務必使讀者在每一次自我訓練中獲得最大效果。打好文法句型基礎後，學生往後不論在閱讀各類書報雜誌、練習作文寫作，必能更加得心應手。

　　希望藉由本書，能讓您破除以往對英文句型的恐懼，打好英文文法基礎！Then I, your teacher, will dare to whisper, "I have not done in vain!"

Contents 目錄

五大句型、名詞子句與副詞子句

動詞時態

part3 分詞

part4 關係詞與形容詞子句

part5 so(such)...that/enough to/too...to 等用法及感嘆句

形容詞變化法

假設語氣

Part 1

五大句型、名詞子句與副詞子句

── Part 1 ──
五大句型、名詞子句與副詞子句

　　要學好英文，就要從基礎開始，就好像學習修理機車，你得先知道各種工具的名字。英語之句型無論多複雜，皆可歸為五大類基本句型。要看清楚句中哪一部分是主要部分，哪一部份是修飾語等，才能正確地掌握文意。本章目的即在於學習如何分辨句中要素及五大基本句型之重要動詞，並簡單介紹名詞子句和副詞子句。

一、英文句子的基本構成要素

❶ 單字（Vocabulary）

❷ 片語（Phrase）：視引導的字詞決定為何種片語

❸ 句子（Sentence）：可獨立存在的結構（有主詞＋動詞）

❹ 子句（Clause）：不可獨立存在，視引導的連接詞決定為何種子句

二、句型分類——句子依其動詞的種類，可分成五大基本句型

| Vi | (1) 主詞（S）＋不及物動詞（Vi）→Dusk deepens. |
| | (2) 主詞（S）＋不及物動詞（Vi）＋ 主詞補語（**SC**）
→She is a singer. |

Vt	(1) 主詞（S）＋及物動詞（Vt）＋ 受詞（**O**）→I hate you.
	(2) 主詞（S）＋及物動詞（Vt）＋間接受詞（**IO**）＋ 直接受詞（**DO**） →I give you money.
	(3) 主詞（S）＋及物動詞（Vt）＋ 受詞（**O**）＋ 受詞補語（**OC**） →I find it hard.

三、八大詞類

★ 詞性分類

名詞（Noun）	代名詞（Pronoun）
動詞（Verb）	介系詞（Preposition）
副詞（Adverb）	連接詞（Conjunction）
形容詞（Adjective）	冠詞（Article）

★ 詞的不定性

1. It's <u>wrong</u> to <u>wrong</u> someone.
　　　adj.　　　V

2. The bus will <u>stop</u> at the next bus <u>stop</u>.
　　　　　　V　　　　　　　　　N

3. Get some <u>water</u> from the <u>well</u>, and <u>water</u> the plants <u>well</u>.
　　　　　N　　　　　　N　　　V　　　　　　adv.

四、句型要素

❶ 句子要素中不可或缺的是主詞（Subject）與動詞（Verb）。

❷ 及物動詞（Transitive Verb）接受詞。

❸ 受詞（Object）可分為間接受詞（IO）與直接受詞（DO）。

❹ 補語（Complement）可分為主詞補語（SC）與受詞補語（OC）。

❺ 修飾語（Modifier）為形容詞（adj.）及副詞（adv.）。

五、五大句型的注意事項

1. O為<u>受格</u>→可改成被動語態（通常是N）

2. C為<u>補語</u>→非補不可（可以是adj./N/介＋N）

3. MOD為<u>修飾語</u>→可有可無（通常是adj./介＋N）

主題一｜句型：S+V

此句型為主詞＋（不及物）動詞的形式，動詞本身不需要加上受詞和補語，即能表達完整意思，也常與地方副詞、時間副詞、情狀副詞等連用，使句意更加完整。

• **It** **rained** **very hard** **in eastern Taiwan** **last night**.
　S　　Vi　　情狀副詞　　　地方副詞　　　時間副詞
昨天晚上東台灣雨下得很大。

• **The sun** **shines** **brightly** **in the sky**.
　　S　　　Vi　　情狀副詞　地方副詞
太陽在天空中閃耀著。

• **Time** **flies** **like an arrow** and **waits for** **no man**.
　S　　Vi　　情狀副詞　　　　　Vi　　受詞
光陰似箭，歲月不饒人。

• **You** **must get** up **very early** to see the sun rise **tomorrow morning**.
　S　助動詞 Vi　　情狀副詞　　　　　　　　　　時間副詞
為了要看日出你明天早上必須要非常早起床。

• **The little** **girl cries loudly**.
　　S.　Vi.　　情狀副詞
那個小女孩哭得很大聲。

• **She** **dyed** **her hair** **in the salon**.
　　S.　　V.　　　　地方副詞
她去髮廊染了頭髮。

 **隨堂測驗**

( ) 1.下列何者為S＋V的句型？

(A) Still water runs deep.
(B) Every dog has its day.
(C) A good medicine tastes bitter.
(D) Light blue can make people feel more patient and loving.

( ) 2.下列何者不是S＋V的句型？

(A) She is a doctor.
(B) He cried.
(C) What makes you think that you can win the contest?
(D) How about going mountain climbing?

( ) 3.下列何者不是S＋V的句型？

(A) It had rained heavily the night before.
(B) Money talks.
(C) The tragedy nearly drove him mad.
(D) Jacky Wu showed up at Taipei's Core Pacific City Mall last Sunday.

( ) 4.下列何者不是S+V的句型？

(A) He is flying a kite.
(B) They lay down.
(C) Nobody cares.
(D) Accidents happen.

解答：1. (A) 2. (B) 3. (C) 4. (A)

解析：① (B) S+V+O (C) S+V+adj. (D) S+V+O
　　　　② (B) S+V 　　③ (C) S+情狀副詞+V+O+adj.
　　　　④ (A) S+V+O

主題二 | 句型：S＋V＋SC

　　此為主詞＋（不及物）動詞＋主詞補語的結構；用來補充說明主詞狀態者，稱為主詞補語（SC），形式有名詞、形容詞、分詞、片語、子句……等。此句型有兩大適用的動詞類別：

 例句講解

1. be 動詞：

- **He is an engineer.** 他是一位工程師。
- **To see is to believe.** 百聞不如一見／眼見為憑。

2. 各類連綴動詞

似乎動詞	seem, look, appear
保持動詞	keep, remain, stay, continue
來去動詞	go, come, return
站坐動詞	sit, lie, stand
轉變動詞	go, run, get, turn, grow, fall, become
感官動詞	see, look, sound, smell, taste, feel

- **The teacher seems very satisfied.** 老師似乎很滿意。
- **The weather stayed warm all week.** 整個星期天氣都很暖和。
- **The well ran dry.** 井枯了。
- **A good medicine tastes bitter.** 良藥苦口。

- **The clock is running.**
      S   V   SC（→SC 為現在分詞）

  時間流逝。

- **The question is how to keep the naughty boy in line.**
      S   V   SC（→SC 為名詞片語）

  問題在於如何讓調皮的小男孩守規矩。

- **The best way to court a girl is to establish friendly relations with her.**
            S   V   SC（→SC 為不定詞片語）

  追求一個女孩的最好方法就是跟她建立友善的友誼。

- **Messages more than seven days will be deleted from the inbox folder.**
                S   V   SC（→SC 為過去分詞）

  超過七天的信件會從收件夾裡被刪除。

隨堂測驗

(   ) 1.下列何者為S＋V＋SC的句型？

  (A) Let me buy you a drink.
  (B) Can you keep it a secret?
  (C) His remark is hitting the nail on the head.
  (D) Light blue can make people feel more patient and loving.

(   ) 2.下列何者不是S＋V＋SC的句型？

  (A) The old man lay dying on the stretcher.
  (B) Birds sing above the roofs.
  (C) The teacher seems very satisfied.
  (D) Children's poetry is not just for children.

解答： 1. (C) 2. (B)

解析： ① (A) S+V+O　(B)+V+O　(D) +V+O
　　　　 ② (B) S+V+地方副詞

主題三 | 句型：S＋V＋O

此為**主詞＋（及物）動詞＋受詞**的結構。此句型的動詞可為「不及物動詞」加「介副詞」形成的「雙字動詞片語」，而形成及物動詞。例如：call up, call at, call on, call for, put off, get on, turn on, turn off等。

- **James calls on me every morning.**
  = **James visits me every morning.**
  每天早上都會拜訪我。

- **We thought of having a picnic.**
  = **We considered having a picnic.**
  我們想要辦個野餐。

例句講解

- **She doesn't know what to do.**
  　S　　　　V　　　　O（→受詞為名詞片語）
  她不知道該如何是好。

- **He enjoys taking a walk.**
  　S　　V　　　　O　（→受詞為動名詞）
  他很喜歡散步。

- **I regret having made such a careless mistake.**
  S　V　　　　　　O（→受詞為動名詞）
  我後悔犯了這個粗心的錯誤。

- **We are going to visit the wounded and the dying.**
  　S　　　V　　　　　　O（→受詞為複數名詞）
  我們要去探視傷者及垂死者。

 隨堂測驗

( ) 1.下列何者為 S＋V＋O 的句型？

(A) That man that told you that was a liar.
(B) I appointed him assistant professor.
(C) The best way to court a girl is to establish friendly relations with her.
(D) She usually put off carrying out what she should do until the last moment.

( ) 2.下列何者不是 S＋V＋O 的句型？

(A) The penguins jump in and out of the water like dolphins.
(B) Diamond cuts diamond.
(C) Some people in Taiwan speak English with a strong Taiwanese accent.
(D) In the severity of winter, all things patiently wait for the coming of spring.

( ) 3.下列何者為 S+V+O 的句型？

(A) She made me the class leader.
(B) Jack visits me every week.
(C) The lady walking that dog is kind.
(D) I did awful on the test.

解答： 1. (D) 2. (A) 3. (B)

解析：

① (A) S+SC+V+O　(B) S+V+O+OC　(C) S+ SC+V+O
② (A) S+V+地方副詞+O
③ (A) S+V+O+OC　(C) S+ SC+V+O　(D) S+V+O+情狀副詞

主題四 | 句型：S＋V＋IO＋DO

此為**主詞＋（及物）動詞＋間接受詞＋直接受詞**的結構，為授與動詞用法，其後需接兩個受詞：一為直接受詞（DO），通常為物，另一為間接受詞（IO），通常為人。**若間接受詞（IO）與直接受詞（DO）對調，則應加上適當的介系詞。**

授與動詞	介系詞
pay（付）tell（告訴）bring（帶來）give（給）sell（賣）deliver（遞送）lend（借給）teach（教）show（指示）send（寄給）write（寫）offer（提供）	to
buy（買）order（訂購）choose（選擇）make（做）get（取得）leave（留給）sing（唱）	for
ask（要求、問）inquire（要求）make（做）	of
play（開玩笑）	on

- **He played me a trick. = He played a trick on me.**
  他擺了我一道。

- **Let's not make this a mess. = Let's not make a mess of this.**
  我們別讓這裡變得成一團糟。

- **He sang me a song. = He sang a song for me.**
  他唱了首歌給我。

- **He did me good. = He did good to me.**
  他對我不錯。

- **Let me buy you a drink. = Let me buy a drink for you.**
  讓我請你喝杯飲料。

- **He asked me a strange question. = He asked a strange question of me.**
  他問了我一個奇怪的問題。

• Please send **her these photographs**.

= Please send **these photographs** to **her**.

請把這些照片寄給她。

 **例句講解**

• <u>**The old man**</u> <u>**told**</u> <u>**me**</u> <u>**that gray hair is a sign of age, not of wisdom.**</u>
　　S　　　V　　IO　　　　　　　DO（→DO 為名詞子句）

那位老人告訴我頭髮變灰白是歲月的象徵，而不是智慧的象徵。

• <u>**The aborigines**</u> <u>**taught**</u> <u>**the settlers**</u> <u>**how to fish in the frozen river.**</u>
　　S　　　　V　　　　IO　　　　DO（→DO 為名詞片語）

原住民教移民者如何在冰凍的河裡釣魚。

 **隨堂測驗**

(　) 1.下列何者為S＋V＋IO＋DO的句型？

　　(A) I caught the ball.

　　(B) Wet weather brought sickness to the neighborhood where the two women lived.

　　(C) He is proud to be on the team.

　　(D) He died a few days ago.

(　) 2.下列何者不是S＋V＋IO＋DO的句型？

　　(A) Our school provides students with the opportunity to study abroad.

　　(B) Diamond cuts Diamond.

　　(C) She told the children a boring story.

　　(D) I'll buy a drink for the lady.

解答：1. (B) 2. (B)

解析：① (A) S+V+O　(C) S+V+O+OC　(D) S+V+時間副詞
　　　　② (B) S+V+O

主題五 | 句型：S＋V＋O＋OC

　　此為**主詞＋（及物）動詞＋受詞＋受詞補語**的結構，用來補充説明受詞狀態者，稱為受詞補語（OC），形式有名詞、形容詞、分詞、片語、子句……等。此句型的動詞有其特殊性質，類型如下：

❶帶有**認為受格具有某種狀態或某種性質**的動詞，包括：think（想）、believe（相信）、find（發現）、consider（認為）等。

* **I find his jokes so boring.**
  我發現他的笑話很無聊。

❷帶有**使受格進入某種狀態或某種性質**的動詞，包括：make（使）、want（想要）、cut（切斷）、keep（守住）、leave（遺留）等。

* **Can you keep it a secret?**
  你可以守住這個祕密嗎？

* **Just leave me alone, will you?**
  別打擾我，好嗎？

* **I want my coffee black.**
  我想要黑咖啡。

❸表示**命名、稱作**的動詞，後面出現的補語通常是名詞，包括：name（命名）、call（稱呼）、nickname（為……取小名）。

* **Don't call me a liar!**
  別叫我騙子！

* **They named/called their baby Max.**
  他們將他們的小寶寶命名為麥克斯。

* **People nicknamed me Fatty when I was little.**
  我小時候都被人叫胖子。

❹表示**認為……是**的動詞，這些動詞後面的補語之前要先加**as**，包括：
regard（把……看作）、treat（看待）、think of（認為）、look upon
（視為）、 refer to（認為）等。

- **Don't treat my warning as a joke.**
  別把我的警告當笑話。

- **I regard money as a means to an end, not an end in itself.**
  我把金錢看作一種達到目的的手段，而不是目的本身。

- **These people refer to him as their hero.**
  這些人認為他是他們的英雄。

例句講解

- <u>**My father**</u> <u>**makes**</u> <u>**it**</u> <u>**a rule**</u> to jog before going to bed.
    S   V   O   OC （→OC 為名詞）

  我爸習慣睡前先慢跑。

- <u>**He**</u> <u>**tried to make**</u> <u>**himself**</u> <u>**understood**</u>.
   S   V   O   OC（→OC 為過去分詞）

  他設法使他自己能被理解。

- <u>**His devotion to world peace**</u> <u>**has made**</u> <u>**him**</u> <u>**famous**</u> worldwide.
              S   V   O   OC（→OC 為形容詞）

  他對世界和平的貢獻使得他全世界聞名。

- <u>**They**</u> <u>**beat**</u> <u>**the boy**</u> <u>**black and blue**</u>.
    S   V   O   OC（→OC 為形容詞）

  他們把這男孩打得遍體鱗傷。

- <u>**They**</u> <u>**consider**</u> <u>**the car**</u> <u>**to be too expensive**</u>.
    S   V   O   OC（→OC 為不定詞片語）

  他們認為這輛車太貴了。

- <u>**We**</u> <u>**should leave**</u> <u>**the angry words**</u> <u>**unsaid**</u>.
   S   V   O   OC（→OC 為過去分詞）

  我們不該口出惡言。

- **Rain makes the grass green** and **helps the plants grow**.
    S   V1   O1   OC1   V2   O2   OC2

  （→OC green為形容詞，grow為原形動詞）

  雨水使草地翠綠並幫助植物成長。

- **Once in a while I hear her sing** that Japanese song in her lovely voice.
    頻率副詞   S V   O   OC（→OC 為原形動詞）

  我偶爾會聽到她用美妙的嗓音唱那首日文歌。

- **Light blue can make people feel** more patient and loving.
      S   V   O   OC（→OC 為原形動詞）

  根據這些研究顯示，舉例來說，淡藍色使人覺得較有耐心和親切。

 **隨堂測驗**

(　　) 1. 下列何者為S＋V＋O＋OC的句型？

    (A) A cat has nine lives.

    (B) The total jackpot in yesterday's draw was NT$252 million.

    (C) Still water runs deep.

    (D) I had my money stolen.

(　　) 2. 下列何者不是S＋V＋O＋OC的句型？

    (A) Charles called the game Monopoly.

    (B) Both parents make the hole comfortable for their babies by making a nest inside it out of grass, leaves and twigs.

    (C) International signs have become increasingly important around the world.

    (D) The tragedy nearly drove him mad.

解答： 1. (D) 2. (C)

解析：

① (A) S+V+O

    (B) S+ SC+V+O

    (C) S+V+O

② (C) S+V+O+地方副詞

主題六　名詞子句

一、子句的定義

　　子句是由一組包含主詞及述詞的字群所組成的。述詞包括動詞及和此動詞有關之受詞或補語。

二、子句的概念

　　子句構成句子的一部份：

❶主要子句：能表達完整意思。

❷從屬子句：不能表達完整意思，需用從屬連接詞或關係代名詞將其和主要子句連接在一起。

　　名詞子句的文法意義等同於**名詞**，與名詞片語相同，都具有：**主詞、受詞、補語、同位語**的功能。其結構皆為連接詞＋完整句子，可置於句首、句中或句尾。

★名詞子句的種類

	(1) that子句
名詞子句→**當名詞用**	(2) 表是否（whether/if）的名詞子句
	(3) 複合關代的名詞子句
	(4) 意志動詞的名詞子句
	(5) 疑問詞引導的間接問句

★名詞子句在主要子句內的不同功能

❶作為主詞：

• **That the sun rises in the east** is true.　太陽從東邊升起是個事實。

• **That smoking is a danger to the health** is a fact.
抽菸對身體不好，這是個事實。

❷作為受詞：

- I hope **that James will give me a call**.
  我希望詹姆士會打電話給我。

- This story teaches us **that we must help one another**.
  這個故事告訴我們要幫助別人

- My parents have made **what I am today**.
  我的父母成就了今日的我。

❸作為補語：

- I am not **what I used to be**.
  我已經不是從前的我了。

- The reason why he was late for class is **that he overslept**.
  他上課遲到的原因是他睡過頭了。

❹作為同位語：

- The fact **that the earth is round** is true.
  地球是圓的這個事實是真的。

- He gave us the impression **that he was indifferent to fame**.
  他給我們的印象是他不在乎名望。

★ POINT 1-A that/whether/if 引導之名詞子句

❶以that為引導的名詞子句

　　一般以that＋子句=名詞子句的形式最常見，通常可省略，但置於句首時則不行。而that引導的名詞子句做「主詞」時，可換為"It is＋adj.＋that＋S＋V"

• It is wonderful that we will have a party on Christmas.
　我們將在聖誕節舉辦派對，這真是太棒了。

例句講解

• My mother says that **I shouldn't worry** and that **I'm just a late developer, but I am worried.**（→名詞子句做受詞）
　我的母親說我不必擔心，我只是大器晚成而已，不過我還是很擔心。

• Another good reason for using e-mail is that **there are no problems with time zones.**（→名詞子句做補語）
　另一個使用電子郵件的好理由是沒有時差的問題。

• That **we will have a party on Christmas** is wonderful.（→名詞子句做主詞）
　我們將在聖誕節舉辦派對，這真是太棒了。

• Mary told me the good news that **her brother won the first prize in the contest.**（→名詞子句做同位語）
　瑪麗跟我說了一個好消息，她哥哥在那場比賽裡得了第一名。

❷以whether/if（是否……）引導的名詞子句

　　whether和if都可當做「是否」解釋，並引導名詞子句做受詞。但「if＋子句」做受詞時，後面不可接 or not。

- I don't know **whether** he will come or not.（→名詞子句做受詞）
= I don't know if <u>he will come</u>.
  我不知道他是否會來。

- Tell me **whether** <u>Tom is a good student or not</u>.（→名詞子句做受詞）
= Tell me if <u>Tom is a good student</u>.
  告訴我Tom是不是個好學生。

★ 注意要點

whether 引導的名詞子句可當主詞，但if則不可。

- Whether he will show up is still a question. (○)
  If he will show up is still a question. (X)

❸What與複合關代，通常用來引導做主詞或受詞的名詞子句。

- <u>What you say</u> is wrong.（→名詞子句做主詞）
  你所說的話是錯誤的。

- You may invite <u>whoever wants to come</u>.（→名詞子句做受詞）
  你可以邀請任何想來的人。

❹疑問詞除了構成直接疑問句外，由疑問詞所引導的子句也可接在主要子句後面構成間接問句，這種子句為名詞子句，可做主詞、受詞或補語。

- <u>Who did it</u> is still unknown.（→名詞子句做主詞）
  是誰做的仍未知。

- I asked him <u>what he was doing</u>.（→名詞子句做受詞）
  我問他在做什麼。

- The question was <u>when we could get there</u>.（→名詞子句做主詞補語）
  問題是我們何時能到達那邊。

⏰ 隨堂測驗

( ) 1. _____ he is living in Paris. 【南一中】

(A) People generally believe that
(B) That is generally believed that
(C) It generally believes that
(D) People are generally believed that

( ) 2. Your success depends on _____ you work hard or not. 【附中】

(A) how　　　　　　　　(B) whether
(C) when　　　　　　　　(D) if

( ) 3. We don't know _____ his hand sign means "money." 【彰中】

(A) what　　　　　　　　(B) which
(C) where　　　　　　　 (D) that

( ) 4. "Are you hungry?" Frank asked me. = Frank asked _____.

【屏中】

(A) I was hungry　　　　 (B) you were hungry
(C) if I was hungry　　　 (D) what if I was hungry

解答： 1. (A) 2. (B) 3. (D) 4. (C)

解析：

①大家普遍都相信他現居巴黎。

②whether和if都可當做「是否」解釋，並引導名詞子句做受詞。但「if＋子句」做受詞時，後面不可接 or not，故選 (B)。

③我們不知道他的手勢代表著「錢」。

④If意為「是否」。

★ POINT 1-B 「疑問副詞」引導之名詞子句

疑問副詞是用來詢問訊息的副詞，包括how（如何、怎麼樣）、when（何時）、where（何地）、why（為什麼）。這一類名詞子句的結構為**疑問副詞＋直述句**，或稱為間接問句。

例句講解

• **My friends ask me when <u>my mother makes cookies</u>.**
（→名詞子句做直接受詞）

我的朋友問我我媽媽何時會做餅乾。

• **Let's take a close look at how <u>children learn a language</u>.**
（→名詞子句做受詞）

讓我們近一點看孩子們如何學習語言。

隨堂測驗

( ) 1. A: Could you tell me _____?

　　B: Go straight ahead for two blocks. It's on the corner.

(A) if you will go to the bank
(B) where the post office is
(C) how to get the ticket
(D) which bus goes to the zoo

( ) 2. Choose the correct sentence.

(A) He asked me what my name was and where I lived.
(B) He asked me what is my name and where do I live.
(C) He asked me what my name is and where live.
(D) He asked me what my name was and where did I live.

( ) 3. I know exactly _____, dear.

(A) how to feel　　　　　　　(B) how you feel
(C) what to feel　　　　　　　(D) what you feel

( ) 4. Don't worry; I'll show you _____.

　　(A) how should you do it
　　(B) how you should do it
　　(C) what are you going to do
　　(D) that you should do

( ) 5. He had no idea _____.

　　(A) how satisfied I was with the grades
　　(B) whom she wanted to talk
　　(C) where does he live
　　(D) what is happening

解答： 1. (B) 2. (A) 3. (B) 4. (B) 5. (A)

解析：

①譯：

A：你可以告訴我郵局在哪裡嗎？

B：繼續往前走兩個街區，就在轉角。

其他選項均文意不符。

②譯：他問了我的名字和住處。

③譯：我完全理解你的感覺，親愛的。

談論感受所以用「how」，又因為是和對方說話而不是自顧自地談論自己該「如何感受」所以不用how to feel。

④how引導名詞子句。

⑤譯：他完全不知道我對於成績有多滿意。

★ POINT 1-C 「疑問代名詞」引導之名詞子句

疑問代名詞為疑問詞＋代名詞，包括who（誰—主詞）、whom（誰—受詞）、what（什麼）、which（哪一個）、whose（誰的—所有格）。在這一種名詞子句裡，因為疑問代名詞代替了子句裡的主詞或受詞，所以結構為疑問代名詞＋不完整子句（缺S或O）。

例句講解

- **No one can tell us what <u>will come next</u>.**（→名詞子句做直接受詞）
  沒有人能告訴我們接下來會發生什麼。

- **We are not sure whom <u>Mary likes best</u>.**（→名詞子句做同位語）
  我們沒辦法確定瑪麗最喜歡誰。

- **No language is necessary to know what <u>these symbols mean</u>.**
  （→名詞子句做直接受詞）
  不需要靠語言就可以明白這些標誌的意思。

- **To prove their point, they told a story about what <u>might happen to a person who becomes too greedy</u>.**（→名詞子句做補語）
  為了證明他們的論點，他們說了一個故事，內容關於一個人如果過於貪婪就有可能遇到的事。

隨堂測驗

( ) 1. In fact, he didn't realize _____ was going on.

    (A) what   (B) which

    (C) that   (D) how

( ) 2. _____ I will never forget is how you have tried your best to help me.

    (A) That   (B) How

    (C) What   (D) It

( ) 3. No one knows _____ life will be like without watches and clocks.

(A) when　　　　　　　(B) where

(C) how　　　　　　　(D) what

( ) 4. The manager showed the newcomers _____ they should handle the problems.

(A) what　　　　　　　(B) which

(C) how　　　　　　　(D) where

( ) 5. If each of the blind men could feel a real elephant, they would all know _____.

(A) how was this huge animal like

(B) what the huge animal was like

(C) how the huge animal likes

(D) what was the huge animal like

解答： 1. (A) 2. (C) 3. (D) 4. (C) 5. (B)

解析：

①沒有意識到「什麼事」正在發生，故用what。

②表達絕對不會忘記的「事情」，用what。

③表達少了手錶和時鐘的生活不知道會變成「什麼樣子」，用what。

④該「如何」處理問題，故用how。

⑤就會知道巨大的動物像「什麼」樣子，用what。

★ POINT 1-D 名詞子句與不定詞片語之轉換

當主要子句的**主詞**和疑問副詞／疑問代名詞引導的子句**主詞相同**時，常用**不定詞片語**來替換。原本的名詞子句為疑問詞＋子句，替換後則變成疑問詞＋to＋原形動詞。

例句講解

• **I don't know** what I should do. = **I don't know** what to do.
（→去掉名詞子句內的I should，保留主要動詞do）

我不知道（我）該怎麼做。

• **You'll know** how you should solve **the problem as long as you listen carefully.**

= **You'll know** how to solve **the problem as long as you listen carefully.**
（→去掉名詞子句內的I should，保留主要動詞do）

只要你仔細地聽，（你）就可以知道該怎麼解決問題。

隨堂測驗

(   ) 1. He showed me _____ the faucets in the bathtub.

    (A) how operating
    (B) how to operate
    (C) what to operate
    (D) operate

(   ) 2. She told me _____ in my composition.

    (A) what could I write
    (B) what to write
    (C) what to write it
    (D) how should I write

( ) 3. She will tell you _____ to talk and _____ to say.

(A) who, how
(B) how, how
(C) how, what
(D) who, what

( ) 4. The little girl didn't know_____ to put her clothes after the shower.

(A) what
(B) who
(C) where
(D) how

解答： 1. (B) 2. (B) 3. (C) 4. (C)

解析：

① 「如何」操作，故用how。

② 該寫「什麼」，用what。

③ 「如何」說話，用how；該說「什麼」，用what。

④ 該把她的衣服放在「哪裡」，用where。

主題七 | 副詞子句

從屬連接詞所引導的子句，稱為副詞子句。其文法作用與副詞相同，副詞子句最常修飾主要子句中的**時間與因果**，可置於句首、句中、句尾。

副詞子句的種類

不同連接詞所形成的**副詞子句**	(1) 表時間的副詞連接詞 (2) 表原因／結果的副詞連接詞 (3) 表讓步的副詞連接詞 (4) 表條件的副詞連接詞 (5) 表目的的副詞連接詞 (6) 表對比／相反的副詞連接詞

功用	副詞連接詞	連接詞片語
表時間	before, after, by the time, as, while, when, whenever, until, since, during	as soon as
表條件	if, unless	in case of/that, as long as, in case that
表原因	because, since, as	because of, now that, due to, owing to
表目的	lest	in order to/that, so that
表結果	so/such...that	
表讓步	although, though, despite	in spite of, even if, even though

各種副詞子句

❶表「時間」之副詞子句：

　　表「時間」之副詞子句，是指以when（當）、while（當）、whenever（每當）、since（自從）、after（在……之後）、before（在……之前）、during（在……期間）、until（直到）、as（當）、by the time（在……的時候）、as soon as（一……就）等詞所引導的完整子句。

• **What did your parents do to celebrate when <u>you were born</u>?**
　當你出生的時候，你的父母親是怎麼慶祝的？

• **But remember that when <u>little sisters grow up</u>, they can become good friends to their older sisters.**
　但是要記住，當妹妹們長大後，她們會成為姊姊的好朋友。

❷表「條件」之副詞子句

　　表「條件」之副詞子句，是以if（如果）、as long as（只要）、unless（除非）、in case of（萬一）等詞所引導的完整子句。

• **It is all right to make mistakes as long as <u>we don't give up</u>.**
　只要我們不放棄，犯錯是沒關係的。

• **You won't get much out of a painting unless <u>you experience it in your own way</u>.**
　你沒辦法從一幅畫裡得到什麼，除非你親身經歷過。

❸表「原因」之副詞子句

　　表「原因」之副詞子句，是以because（因為）、since（由於、既然）、as（因為）、because of（因為）、now that（既然）、due to（由於）、owing to（由於）等詞所引導的完整子句。

• **Because <u>I was sick yesterday</u>, I didn't go to work.**
　因為我昨天生病了，我沒有去上班。

• **Since <u>you don't feel well</u>, you'd better stay at home and take a rest.**
　既然你覺得不舒服，你最好待在家裡好好休息。

❹表「目的」之副詞子句：

　　表「目的」之副詞子句，是以in order to（為了）、so that（為了⋯⋯而）、lest（以免）等詞所引導的完整子句。

- **Tom has behaved badly in class** so that **the teacher will punish him and make him sit on the girls' side of the classroom.**

湯姆在上課的時候搗蛋，為了懲罰他，老師安排他坐到教室裡的女生區去。

- **Candy and other things that children like are on lower shelves** so that **children can see them easily.**

糖果和其他小朋友喜歡的東西都放在比較低的架子上，如此一來小朋友們就可以輕易的看見。

★注意要點

　　目的若為完整的句子，則用in order that或so that連接兩個動作，但此時in order不可省略；so that不可置於句首！

❺表「結果」之副詞子句：

　　表「結果」之副詞子句，是以so (such) ... that（太⋯⋯所以）等詞所引導的完整子句。

- **Yvonne is** so beautiful that **every boy in my class likes her.**

伊芳長得很漂亮，所以我班上的每個男生都喜歡她。

- **Mr. Lin is** such **a wise person that** everybody respects him.

林先生是個如此有智慧的人，所以每個人都很尊敬他。

❻表「讓步」之副詞子句：

　　表「讓步」之副詞子句，是以although、though、despite、in spite of、even if、even though（皆為儘管、即使之意）等詞所引導的完整子句。

- **Although** we are far away from each other, **we are always in close contact.**

儘管我們彼此相隔遙遠，我們一直保持密切聯絡。

• Even though **you do these things**, marketing specialists at the supermarket make some of your buying decisions for you.

即使你做了這些事，在超市裡的銷售專家已經替你的購買行動作了決定。

 隨堂測驗

(　　) 1. 下列劃線部分，哪一個是副詞子句？

(A) <u>Whether he will come</u> is not known to anyone.

(B) The goods <u>which we ordered</u> have not arrived yet.

(C) He ran so fast <u>that I couldn't catch him</u>.

(D) She wonders <u>where to put the piano</u>.

(　　) 2. _____ you go to the MRT station over there, you can take a rapid transit train and get off right in front of the zoo.

(A) When　　　　　　　　(B) Although

(C) If　　　　　　　　　(D) Whether

(　　) 3. Sportsmen often do better _____ the weather is nice and cool.

(A) when　　　　　　　　(B) with

(C) because　　　　　　　(D) before

解答：1. (C) 2. (C) 3. (A)

解析：

①that I couldn't catch him用以修飾fast。

②If代表如果。

③「當」天氣很好、很涼爽的前提下，運動員會表現很好，故用when。

滿分追擊模擬試題

一、判斷以下例句為何種句型：

例：The children play.
　　　S　　　 V

1. The excited little boy waited happily by the door.

2. James will have to wake up early in the morning every day next week for work.

3. The old man lay dying on the stretcher.

4. He stood motionless for a few moments.

5. The new movie about the robots sounds interesting and funny.

二、選擇題：

(　　) 6. The problem ＿＿＿＿ overworking all day long impairs his health.
　　　(A) is　　　　　(B) that　　　　　(C) which　　　　　(D) is that

(　　) 7. Sean drove to the farm in the afternoon and spent the night there, ＿＿＿＿ he could start out early the next morning.
　　　(A) so that　　　　　　　　　(B) therefore
　　　(C) so long as　　　　　　　　(D) provided that

(　　) 8. It is not safe to get off a car ＿＿＿＿.
　　　(A) unless it is in motion
　　　(B) until it has come to a stop
　　　(C) after you have opened the window
　　　(D) before the traffic light turns red

(　) 9. The rain is over. You must not stay any longer.

　　= You must not stay any longer ＿＿＿＿ the rain is over.

　　(A) when　　　(B) that　　　　(C) now that　　　(D) as for

(　) 10. Mia had to work several years ＿＿＿＿ she could continue her studies in the USA.

　　(A) as　　　　(B) while　　　　(C) before　　　　(D) then

三、中翻英：

11. James直到清晨兩點才就寢。

_____

12. 既然我們沒咖啡，就用茶代替。

_____

13. 雖然他辛勞的工作，但仍無法使父母高興。

_____

解答

一、判斷以下例句為何種句型：

1. The excited little boy waited happily by the door.
           S   V   MOD

2. James will have to wake up early in the morning every day next week for work.
     S   V   MOD

3. The old man lay dying on the stretcher.
         S   V   SC   MOD

4. He stood motionless for a few moments.
     S   V   SC   MOD

5. The new movie about the robots sounds interesting and funny.
           S   V   SC

二、選擇題：

6. (D)   7. (A)   8. (B)   9. (C)   10. (C)

三、中翻英：

11. James didn't go to bed until two o'clock in the morning.

12. Now that we don't have coffee, we substitute tea for it.

13. In spite of his hard work, he could not make his parents happy.

解析：

6. 此句缺乏動詞以及連接後面子句之連接詞，故選(D)。

7. so that 可以用以表示目的。

8. 只有(B)選項在車子「完全停止後」再下車否則不安全符合文意。

9. 原句的因果關係為因為雨停，所以你不能繼續久留，故選(C)「既然」。

10. 在她可以繼續在美國的學業「以前」。

Part 2

動詞時態

英文跟中文最大的差異之一即在時態。中文敘述中，只要時間闡明即可，但是英文卻不只要有時間副詞，還需要有動詞變化。動詞的變化中，會受時間基點跟動作形式影響，所以總共會有12種變化。我們會在以下的章節一一說明。

要想清楚知道時態的用法，就要清楚每個時態所代表的時間動作意義。這樣一來，在寫作或考試時，就能做出正確的判斷。

★ 時態的基本觀念

依時間基點	現在、過去、未來
依動作形式	簡單式、進行式、完成式、完成進行式

時間 動作形式	現在	過去	未來
簡單式	現在簡單式 I write.	過去簡單式 I wrote.	未來簡單式 I shall write.
進行式	現在進行式 I am writing.	過去進行式 I was writing.	未來進行式 I will be writing.
完成式	現在完成式 I have written.	過去完成式 I had written.	未來完成式 I shall have written.
完成進行式	現在完成進行式 I have been writing.	過去完成進行式 I had been writing.	未來完成進行式 I shall have been writing.

★ POINT 1-A 現在簡單式及現在進行式

一、現在簡單式的使用時機：

❶表示永恆事實、不變真理

- **Water freezes at 32 Fahrenheit.**
  水的冰點是在華氏32度。

- **The sun rises in the east and sets in the west.**
  太陽在東邊升起，西邊落下。

❷格言諺語

- **Where there is a will, there is a way.**
  有志者，事竟成。

- **There is no royal road to learning.**
  學習是沒有捷徑的。

❸表示習慣或反覆的動作，常與以下頻率副詞連用

  (1) always/often/usually/sometimes/seldom/frequently
  (2) every＋時間
  (3) 次數＋時間

- **Both my parents work, so I often go home to an empty house after school.**
  我的爸媽都在工作，所以我常常在放學後回到空無一人的家。

- **He writes to his parents once a week.**
  他每個禮拜都會寫信給他父母。

- **My grandma goes to the market every Friday morning.**
  我奶奶每個星期五早上都去市場。

❹表示時間或條件的副詞子句，用現在式代替未來式。

（「來去」動詞：come/go/fly/return/arrive/leave代替未來）

- **If it rains tomorrow, I will stay at home.**

  如果明天下雨，我就會待在家。

- **John will leave for New York tomorrow afternoon.**
- = **John leaves for New York tomorrow afternoon.**

  約翰明天下午會去紐約。

二、現在進行式（am/is/are＋V-ing）的使用時機：

❶表示目前或說話時正在進行的動作常與以下副詞連用：

(1) now/right now

(2) at this time/at present

(3) at the moment/for the time being

- **Peter is talking to Jimmy now.**

  彼德現在正在跟吉米講話。

- **Look! The cat is chasing the mouse.**

  你看！那隻貓正在追那隻老鼠。

❷表示「反覆發生」或「老是……」之意。搭配的副詞列表：

(1) always（總是）

(2) constantly （不斷地）

(3) continually （不停地）

(4) forever （不斷地）

(5) perpetually （不斷地）

(6) repeatedly （再三地）

- **Kevin is always coming late, so the teacher is angry with him.**

  凱文老是遲到，所以老師對他很生氣。

- **Why are you constantly forgetting to bring your books?**

  為何你老是忘了帶你的書？

例句講解

• **Why are you wearing the pearl necklace?** （→正在發生的事）

你為什麼現在戴著珍珠項鍊？

• **Why do you wear the pearl necklace?** （→個人習慣）

你為什麼習慣戴珍珠項鍊？

• **I live in Kuala Lumpur.** （→表達事實）

我家住吉隆坡。→可能是指我的老家，不是我現在人所居住的地方。

• **I am living in Kuala Lumpur.** （→正在發生的事）

我現在住在吉隆坡。→我的現居地，可能是在外地工作居住的地方。

隨堂測驗

( ) 1. She never _____ up early.

(A) wakes   (B) woke   (C) wake   (D) waken

( ) 2. The professor is very forgetful. He always _____ his glasses.

(A) lost   (B) losses   (C) loses   (D) loss

( ) 3. If silver _____ scarcer（稀有的）than gold, it will no doubt（毫無疑問）have a greater value.

(A) became   (B) will become

(C) becomes   (D) had become

( ) 4. For the time being（目前）, the students _____ their exercise.

(A) write   (B) wrote

(C) are writing   (D) will write

( ) 5. The largest whales _____ between 200 and 250 metric tons（公噸）.

(A) have weighed   (B) weigh

(C) weighed   (D) are weighing

(　) 6. The number of（許多的） Asian students in American universities
　　　_____ grown rapidly（快速的） since 1980.

　　(A) are　　　　　(B) is　　　　　(C) has　　　　　(D) have

※請填入正確時態的動詞變化

7. Right now Mia is in the science building. The chemistry experiment she
　　(do) _____ is dangerous, so she (be) _____ very careful
　　when she does a chemistry experiment.

8. Look. It (begin) _____ to rain. Unfortunately
　　（不巧地）, I (have, not) _____ my umbrella with me.
　　James is lucky. He (wear) _____ a raincoat. I (own, not)
　　_____ an umbrella. I (wear) _____ a waterproof（防
　　水的）hat on rainy days.

解答： 1. (A) 2. (C) 3. (C) 4. (C) 5. (B) 6. (C)
7. is doing; is being
8. is beginning; don't have; is wearing; don't own; wear

解析：
①表示一件常態性發生的事實，用現在式。
②表示一件反覆發生的事實，用現在式。
③表示時間或條件的副詞子句，用現在式代替未來式。
④從提示for the time being中可以判斷此句要用現在式。
⑤表示客觀事實，用現在式。
⑥從「自從1980年以來」和grown可以判斷這邊要使用完成
式；因為主詞是the number而不是強調有多少亞洲學生，故
使用has，不用have。

★ POINT 1-B 現在完成式

現在完成式用以表示從之前到現在為止的經驗或做過某個動作的次數，或表過去到現在的動作、性質、狀態，或表過去的努力，今天的成果。是英文獨有的時間觀念，中文沒有。現在完成式的使用時機：

❶表示動作的完成：常與already/just/yet等副詞連用。

• **Has Sam done his homework yet?**

山姆完成他的作業了嗎？

• **I have already bought Mayday's latest album.**

我已經買了五月天的最新專輯。

❷表示經驗或次數常與以下副詞連用：

(1) ever/never

• **Have you ever said "OK" by holding your hand up with the thumb and index finger forming a circle?**

你有過在邊講「ok」的時候，邊把中指和食指擺成一個圓圈的姿勢嗎？

(2) once/twice/數字＋times

• **I have watched _Back to the Future_ thirty times, so I can almost recite every line in the movie.**

我看「回到未來」三十次了，所以我幾乎可以背出裡面所有的台詞。

(3) How long...?/How many times...?

• **How long have you lived in Taipei?**

你在住台北多久了？

❸「have been to...」和「have gone to...」的區別

　　(1) 表經驗：**My father has been to America.** 我爸爸有去過美國。

　　(2) 表現在狀況：**My father has gone to America.** 我爸爸去美國了。（人正在美國）

★**注意要點**

表示「由過去延續到現在」的動作、狀態，常與以下副詞（片語）連用：S＋have/has＋V-p.p.表：**發生經驗、持續狀態、完成事件、最後結果**

(1) 次數：once/two times

(2) 點/段：since＋時間點；for＋時間段

(3) 最近：recently/lately/of late

(4) 介系詞：in/for/over/during/throughout the last/past＋時間N

(5) 到目前：so far/thus for/as yet/up to now/up to the present time

★**句型要點**：

現在完成式：S＋ have＋V-p.p.

＋現在進行式：S＋ be＋V-ing

＝現在完成進行式：S＋have been＋V-ing

例句講解

- **James has taught in cram school for 16 years.**（→現在可能結束）
  James has been teaching in cram school for 16 years.（→未來仍會進行）
  詹姆士已經在補習班教16年書了。

- **My grandparents have lived in the countryside all their lives.**（→仍然活著）
  My grandparents lived in the countryside all their lives.（→已經過世）
  我的祖父母在鄉下住了一輩子。

- **Cockroaches have existed**（生存）**on the earth for more than two hundred million years.**（→for＋一段時間＝從何時開始）
  蟑螂已經在地球上生存了超過兩億年了。

- **People's passion**（熱情）**for doughnuts has decreased**（減少）**in the past two years.**（→in＋一段時間＝某段時間內）
  人們對甜甜圈的熱情在這兩年內已經減少了。

⏰ 隨堂測驗

( ) 1. The Great Wall in China _____ to the body of a dragon.

   (A) has compared   (B) is like

   (C) in comparison with   (D) has been compared

( ) 2. For years he _____ against us, but now he seems to be friendly enough.

   (A) has been   (B) were

   (C) being   (D) to be

( ) 3. I _____ English since I was six but I cannot speak it.

   (A) was studying   (B) had studied

   (C) studied   (D) have been studying

( ) 4. He has been studying in the library every night _____ the last three months.

   (A) since   (B) until

   (C) before   (D) for

( ) 5. What have you been doing _____ I last saw you?

   (A) from   (B) since

   (C) after   (D) before

解答： 1. (D) 2. (A) 3. (D) 4. (D) 5. (B)

解析：

①「被」和龍的軀體「比較」，故選(D)。

②表示已經持續多年，故用現在完成式。

③表示「自從6歲以來」並且「持續至今」，故用完成式。

④for+一段時間；since+一個明確時間點。

⑤「自從」我上一次看到你，用since。

主題二 | 過去式

★ POINT 2-A 過去簡單式及過去進行式

一、過去簡單式的使用時機：

　　過去簡單式用以表示過去某個時間所發生的事，通常與明確的過去時間連用。

　　而**現在完成式**用以表示從過去某一個時間點開始，一直到現在為止，動作的完成，通常與不明確的時間連用或沒有時間規定。

❶常與表示「過去時間」的副詞或片語連用：

　　(1) yesterday/the day before yesterday/one day/formerly/previously/this morning/in the past

　　(2) 時間＋ago

　　(3) last＋時間

- **This morning, I woke up finding I was home alone.**
  今天早上，我一醒來發現自己一人在家。

- **Mr. Li just left for Japan on business several hours ago.**
  李先生幾小時前才動身前往日本洽公。

- **My parents had a serious fight last night, so I couldn't sleep well.**
  我父母昨晚大吵一架，所以我睡不好。

❷表示過去的習慣：used to＋原形動詞

- **She used to take a walk in the evening.**
  她以前習慣在晚上散步。

- **My father used to be a heavy smoker, but he has quit smoking.**
  我父親曾是個老菸槍，但他已經戒菸了。

❸表示過去的動作、史實、或狀態：

• **Human ancestors**（祖先）**first appeared in African plains**（平原）**four million years ago**。
  四百萬年以前，人類的祖先第一次出現在非洲平原上。

二、過去進行式（was/were＋V-ing）的使用時機：

❶表示「過去某時正在進行」的動作。

• **He was watching TV at eight o'clock last night.**
  他昨天晚上八點時正在看電視。

• **George and Mary were talking with each other one hour ago.**
  喬治和瑪莉一個小時前正在和對方談話。

❷表示「過去正在同時進行」的兩個動作。

• **It was raining while she was waiting for the bus.**
  當她正在等公車的時候，雨下了下來。

• **While Helen was writing a letter, John was reading the newspaper.**
  當海倫正在寫信的時候，約翰正在看報紙。

❸過去發生的兩個動作→時間長的用過去進行式→時間短的用過去簡單式。

• **I was taking a shower when the phone rang.**
  當我正在洗澡時，電話響了。

• **Dogs were barking and barking when the earthquake struck last night.**
  昨晚當狗狗正在吠個不停時，地震發生了。

 隨堂測驗

( ) 1. Ron _____ hard, but now he doesn't study very hard any more.

    (A) used to studying   (B) used to study

    (C) is used to study   (D) is used to studying

( ) 2. The umbrella is not a new invention. The Chinese _____ umbrellas in the 11th century.

    (A) have   (B) having   (C) had   (D) had have

( ) 3. I _____ English when you called me last night.

    (A) had studied   (B) was studying

    (C) am studying   (D) studied

( ) 4. We all know that the World War II _____ in 1945.

    (A) ends   (B) have ended

    (C) ended   (D) will end

( ) 5. The Great Depression（經濟大蕭條）was a period of worldwide business slump（蕭條）in history that _____ from 1929 to 1938.

    (A) is lasting   (B) has lasted

    (C) lasted   (D) was lasting

( ) 6. Throughout the United States, city residents now suffer from far more juvenile delinquency（青少年犯罪）than they (do) _____ a decade ago.

    (A) have done   (B) did

    (C) was doing   (D) had done

( ) 7. In the past, the rulers of the country _____ selfish, but the present king has great respect and concern（關心）for his people.

    (A) has been   (B) had been

    (C) were   (D) are

※請填入正確時態的動詞變化

8. While James (read) _____ his daughter a story, she (fall) _____ asleep, so he (close) _____ the book and quietly (tiptoe) _____ out of the room.

9. It was my first day of class. I (find, finally) _____ the right room. The room (be, already) _____ full of students. On one side of the room, students (talk, busily) _____ to each other in Spanish. Other students (speak) _____ Japanese, and some (converse) _____ in Arabic. It sounded like the United Nations. Some of the students, however, (sit, just) _____ quietly by themselves. I (choose) _____ an empty seat in the last row and (sit) _____ down. In a few minutes, the teacher (walk) _____ into the room and all the multilingual conversation (stop) _____.

解答： 1. (B) 2. (C) 3. (B) 4. (C) 5. (C) 6. (B) 7. (C)
8. was reading; fell; closed; tiptoed
9. finally found; was already; were talking busily; were speaking; were conversing; were just sitting; chose; sat; walked; stopped

解析：
①句中想表達「曾經……但現在再也不……」的概念，故用 use to+原形動詞。
②在11世紀就已經有，故用過去式即可。
③強調在對方打過來的時間點「正在」讀書，故用was搭配 studying。
④講述二戰結束的「時間點」，故用過去式。
⑤講述過去發生的一件事，用過去式，last在此表示「持續」。
⑥跟過去的一個明確時間點做比較（十年前），故用過去式。
⑦「以前」的國家統治者很自私，用過去式描述即可。

★ POINT 2-B 過去完成式及過去完成進行式

❶過去完成式及過去完成進行式要點：

	Before/when	
S＋have V-p.p.	by the time	S＋V-p.t.
（先發生）	by＋過去時間	（後發生）

過去完成式：	S＋had＋V-p.p.
＋過去進行式：	S＋　　　was/were＋V-ing
＝**過去完成進行式**	S＋had＋been＋V-ing

❷過去完成式（had＋V-p.p.）的使用時機：

(1) 表示「過去某一點時間之前」的動作或狀況。

* **By 1930, the American economy had collapsed.**
  在1930年之前，美國的經濟已經崩塌了。

* **By the time I entered the primary school, I had learned to spell "pnu emonoultramicroscopicsilicoconiosis."**
  在我進小學之前，我就已經學會拼「火山矽肺症」了。

(2) 過去的兩個動作，→先發生用**過去完成式**→後發生用**過去簡單式**（兩個動作皆發生在過去，一先一後，先發生的動作若早已完成，用過去完成式。）

* **Finally, Christine understood how lonely her life had been.**
  最後，克麗絲汀明白了她的人生是多麼的孤獨。

* **They couldn't imagine where he had been on such a dreadful night.**
  他們不能想像在這麼可怕的夜晚他去了哪裡。

❸過去完成進行式使用時機：

過去完成進行式與過去完成式的異同：

同：皆表示**動作的發生早於過去式的動作**。

異：強調**動作的連續性**。過去完成式表示完成，過去完成進行式表示動作極可能會繼續進行下去。

　　所搭配的時間副詞與過去完成式相同，皆代表動作早於過去，但過去完成進行式只是強調動作的連續性而已。所以過去完成進行式也一樣不能單獨使用，需要過去式與之搭配。

• **I had been smoking three packs of cigarettes a day** before I decided **to quit.**
在我決定戒菸前，我一天抽三包菸。

• **Lisa had been working for Tom** before she graduated **from college.**
莉莎在大學畢業之前，就已經為湯姆工作了。

• **James had been driving all day** before he had **the crucial accident.**
在那場意外之前，詹姆士已經開了一整天的車了。

隨堂測驗

(　) 1. Mary was caught in a traffic jam and by the time she got to the airport, her father's plane _____.

(A) took off　　　　　　　(B) had taken off
(C) was taken off　　　　　(D) had been taken off

(　) 2. He _____ her for a long time before he finally got married to her.

(A) has known　　　　　　(B) knew
(C) had known　　　　　　(D) knows

(　) 3. We were surprised to hear that she _____ the examination at the age of 17.

(A) passes　　　　　　　　(B) passed
(C) has passed　　　　　　(D) had passed

(　) 4. I _____ the work by the end of last week.

(A) finished　　　　　　　(B) have finished
(C) had finished　　　　　(D) will had finished

( ) 5. He _____ lunch by the time his guests arrived.

(A) eats   (B) has eaten

(C) had eaten   (D) will have eaten

6. Yesterday at a restaurant, I (see) _____ Neglus Cage, an old friend of mine. I (see, not) _____ him in years. At first, I (recognize, not) _____ him because he (lose) _____ a great deal of weight.

解答: 1. (B) 2. (C) 3. (D) 4. (C) 5. (C)
6. saw; hadn't seen; didn't recognize; had lost

解析:

①在Mary抵達機場前,父親的飛機就起飛了,表示「過去某一點時間之前」的動作或狀況,故選B。

②在他娶她前已經認識她一段時間,表示「過去某一點時間之前」的動作或狀況,故選C。

③聽到對方在17歲就已經通過考試時很驚訝,表示「過去某一點時間之前」的動作或狀況。

④兩個過去的時間點,要使用比過去式更早的「過去完成式」。

⑤兩個過去的時間點,要使用比過去式更早的「過去完成式」。

主題三 | 未來式

★ POINT 3-A 未來簡單式及未來進行式

一、未來簡單式

表達發生在未來的事情，需注意條件句型的用法（請見POINT 1-A 第4點）。

❶形成方式

(1) 第一人稱＋shall/will

- **I always carry a dictionary and look up any words I don't know. Then I will test myself the next time I see those words.**

  我總是帶著字典並查詢不懂的字，然後在下一次看到這些字時做自我測驗。

(2) 第二、三人稱＋will

- **The boy will be very upset if he knows the game will be cancelled.**

  如果男孩知道比賽取消，他一定會很沮喪。

(3) be going to＋VR

- **Who are you going to dress up as in the costume party this year?**

  你今年的化裝舞會想要扮成誰？

(4) be to＋VR

- **I am to meet you at five o'clock this afternoon.**

  我將於下午五點與你會面。

❷表示未來的動作或狀態：與表示「未來時間」的副詞或片語連用

(1) tomorrow/the day after tomorrow/soon/some day

(2) next＋時間

二、未來進行式（will be＋V-ing）的使用時機：

❶表示「未來某時正在進行」的動作。

- **We will be having dinner when you come back.**
  你回來的時候，我們應正在吃晚餐。

- **My mother will be cooking dinner when I arrive.**
  我到的時候，我媽媽正在煮晚餐。

❷未來發生的兩個動作，⇨**時間長的用未來進行式**⇨**時間短的用簡單式**

- **I will be grading students' papers when you come tomorrow.**
  你明天過來的時候，我正在打學生的成績。

- **When you come visiting next summer, I will be preparing my wedding.**
  當你明年夏天來訪時，我將在籌備我的婚禮。

★ POINT 3-B 未來完成式及未來完成進行式

❶未來完成式及未來完成進行式要點

> 句型要點：
> 未來：S＋will＋VR
> 完成：S＋have＋V-p.p.
> ┌before/when
> ├by the time ─┐ S＋V（過去／現在式）
> └By＋未來時間 ┘
>
> 未來完成式： S＋will have   V-p.p.
> ＋進行式： S＋   be   V-ing
> **未來完成進行式**： S＋ will have been V-ing

❷未來完成式（will have＋V-p.p.）的使用時機：

(1) 表示「未來某點時間將已完成」的動作。

• **Next April, I will have worked here for 20 years.**
到下個四月，我就在這裡工作20年了。

• **Come back at 5:00. Your car will have been fixed by then.**
五點過來這裡。你的車那時候就會修好了。

(2) 未來發生的兩個動作，➪較早完成的用**未來完成式**
➪較晚完成的，在副詞子句中，用**現在式**代替未來式

• **By the time I graduate from college, I will have saved thirty thousand dollars.** 當我大學畢業時，我就會已經存了三萬塊了。

• **When I receive the next letter from Jane, we will have been pen pals for ten years.** 當我收到下一封來自珍的信時，我們就已經當了十年的筆友了。

❸未來完成進行式的使用時間，大致與未來完成式相同，但強調動作的連續及延續性。

• **In two more minutes, she will have been talking on the phone for 7 hours.**
再兩分鐘，她就講了7個小時的電話。

 隨堂測驗

(　) 1. In two days he'll _____ Mia.

(A) marry to (B) be married to

(C) be married (D) be marry to

(　) 2. By the time we meet again, summer _____.

(A) has arrived   (B) had arrived
(C) is arriving   (D) will have arrived

(　) 3. By the time you graduate, I shall have been _____ here for five years.

(A) work   (B) worked   (C) working   (D) to be working

(　) 4. By the end of next June all of us _____ from this school.

(A) will be graduated   (B) will be graduating
(C) shall be graduating   (D) will have been graduated

(　) 5. By next Sunday you _____ with us for three months.

(A) will have stayed   (B) will stay
(C) shall stay   (D) have stayed

(　) 6. I _____ here for 10 years by the end of this month.

(A) will work   (B) have been working
(C) will have worked   (D) was working

解答： 1. (C) 2. (D) 3. (C) 4. (D) 5. (A) 6. (C)

解析：
①譯：兩天後，他就會和Mia結婚。
②表示未來當我們再見面的一個時機，故用D。
③譯：當你畢業時，我就已經在這工作五年了。
④表示「未來某點時間將已完成」的動作，用未來完成式。
⑤表示「未來某點時間將已完成」的動作，用未來完成式。
⑥表示「未來某點時間將已完成」的動作，用未來完成式。

★ POINT 4-A When/While 當……的時候

❶此句型用來表達「兩件事同時發生」的情況。句型為：

When S1＋V-p.t. , S2＋was/were＋V-ing ⇨瞬間動作→時間點

= While S2＋was/were＋V-ing, S1＋V-p.t. ⇨持續動作→時間段

❷when 主要強調事件發生的時間點，其子句常用簡單式；while 和 as 主要用於某事持續進行時所發生的狀況，其子句常用進行式，但所引導子句為持續性動詞時（如：last、live、sit、sleep），亦可用簡單式。

例句講解

• **When <u>I arrived</u> home, <u>my parents</u> <u>were watching</u> TV.**
    S1 V-p.t.   S2   were V-ing （→瞬間動作）

  當我到家時，我的父母正在看電視。

• **While <u>she</u> <u>was cooking</u> supper, <u>she</u> <u>burned</u> her hand.**
      S1   was V-ing   S1   V-p.t. （→持續動作）

  當她在煮晚餐時，她的手燙到了。

★ 注意要點

    兩件事發生時，以發生時間的**先後**或**同時**來決定時式。

• **When/While Mom was preparing dinner, I was setting the table.**
  媽媽在準備晚餐時，我則準備餐桌。

• **When he informed me of the news, I had already known.**
  當他告知我這個消息時，我已經知道了。

★ 延伸學習

❶一般情況下，when、while、as 引導時間副詞子句，動詞要用現在式表達未來。

• **When you grow up, you will know how great your parents are.**
當你長大，你就會知道父母有多偉大。

❷指年齡或人生某個階段時，會用 when 來表示。

• **When I was a high school student, we went to Japan on vacation.**
我高中的時候，我們去了日本度假。

隨堂測驗

( ) 1. When I saw the man steal a book, I _____ a police officer right away.

   (A) am telling
   (B) was telling
   (C) had told
   (D) told

( ) 2. As I _____ to eat breakfast, my neighbor _____ on my door.

   (A) sat down; knocked
   (B) was sitting down; knocked
   (C) sat down; was knocking
   (D) was sitting down; was knocking

( ) 3. I saw the lady with a briefcase while I _____ into the building.

   (A) walked
   (B) was walking
   (C) had walked
   (D) had been walking

( ) 4. _____ Peter was fifteen years old, he broke his arm playing soccer.

(A) While
(B) When
(C) As
(D) Whenever

( ) 5. We _____ television when the lights went out.

(A) are watching
(B) were watching
(C) was watching
(D) watched

解答：1. (D) 2. (B) 3. (B) 4. (B) 5. (B)

解析：
①when 主要強調事件發生的時間點，其子句常用簡單式。
②強調「當」鄰居來敲門時，我「正準備要」坐下吃早餐，故前用進行式，後用簡單式即可。
③while 和主要用於某事持續進行時所發生的狀況，其子句常用進行式。
④講述一件當Peter15歲時發生的事，用when即可。
⑤強調停電的當下正在進行的活動，故用進行式。

★ POINT 4-B since的用法

❶since的句型用來表示「自從……」，句型如下：

作為介系詞＋N/V-ing

作為連接詞＋S＋V

ever since ＋（加強語氣）

❷since＋時間點 = for＋時間段

例句講解

• **I have stayed in Tainan** for six years.

我已經待在台南六年了。

I have stayed in Tainan since I flew here six years ago.

自從我六年前飛到這裡，就一直待在台南。

• **I have lived in Kaohsiung** since **1990/moving here in 1990.**

（→介系詞＋N）

= **I have lived here** since **I moved to Kaohsiung in 1990.**

（→連接詞＋S＋V）

= **I moved to Kaohsiung in 1990 and I have lived here** ever since.

（→ever since作加強語氣）

我從1990年起就住在高雄（一直至今）。

隨堂測驗

(　　) 1. The idea of space travel has begun _____ two decades ago.

(A) since (B) for

(C) if (D) where

(　　) 2. Yesterday I was told that John had gone to the U.S. It was three weeks since John _____.

(A) went abroad (B) were abroad

(C) had gone abroad (D) had been abroad

( ) 3. Shanghai has been one of the largest cities in the world in terms of
（就……而言）population _____ the 1960's.

(A) about   (B) since

(C) as   (D) from

( ) 4. The Lin family _____ in Kaohsiung ever since they came to
Taiwan.

(A) has lived   (B) is living

(C) lived   (D) will live

( ) 5. It has been two years _____ my family moved to America.

(A) for   (B) when

(C) on   (D) since

( ) 6. My sister has studied in Hong Kong _____ 2000.

(A) for   (B) in

(C) from   (D) since

解答： 1. (A) 2. (C) 3. (B) 4. (A) 5. (D) 6. (D)

解析：

①「自從」過去某個時間點，故用 since。

②自從他出國以來已經三個禮拜，要用完成式表達比過去式更早的時間點。

③搭配現在完成式，講述自從 1960 年代以來上海的狀況，故選 (B)。

④自從來台灣以後就一直住在高雄（至今仍是）。

⑤「自從」……「已經」兩年，故要用 since。

⑥since+特定過去時間點表示「自從」。

★ POINT 4-C 在……之前

句子中若出現by＋一個時間或by the time所引導子句，是用以表示「到了……時候，……已經……」。時態之使用以發生的時間為準。若為過去的時間，主要子句用**過去完成式**，若為未來的時間，主要子句用**未來完成式**。句型為：

(1) ┌ By the time＋S＋過去簡單式
    └ By＋一個過去的時間 ＋，S+had+V-p.p

(2) ┌ By the time＋S＋現在簡單式
    └ By＋一個未來的時間 ＋，S+will+have+V-p.p.

- **By the time I arrived at the airport, the plane had taken off.**
  到我抵達機場時，飛機已經起飛了。

- **By 1930, the American economy had fallen apart.**
  到1930年時，美國的經濟已經崩潰。

- **By next July, he will have gotten a doctor's degree.**
  到明年七月時，他將已獲得博士學位了。

隨堂測驗

( ) 1. I _____ my work by the time you come.

    (A) had been finished

    (B) would have finished

    (C) had finished

    (D) would have been finished

( ) 2. By the time you travel to Italy, you _____ ten countries in Europe.

    (A) will visit

    (B) are going to visit

    (C) will have visited

    (D) are visiting

( ) 3. Mia will have lost ten pounds by the time she _____ married.

    (A) will be

    (B) gets

    (C) is getting

    (D) got

( ) 4. Helen had finished her third novels by the time her daughter

    _____.

    (A) was born

    (B) is born

    (C) will be born

    (D) had been born

解答： 1. (C) 2. (C) 3. (B) 4. (A)

解析：

①譯：當你來時，我已經完成工作了。

②表示「未來某點時間將已完成」的動作，用未來完成式。

③表示「未來某點時間將已完成」的動作，用未來完成式搭配現在簡單式。

④表示「過去某點時間將已完成」的動作，用過去完成式搭配過去式。

滿分追擊模擬試題

( ) 1. By next May they _____ the bridge for nine months.
   (A) will build
   (B) will have been building
   (C) will have been built
   (D) will be built

( ) 2. When you come at midnight, I _____.
   (A) will sleep
   (B) might sleep
   (C) shall have been sleeping
   (D) could be sleeping

( ) 3. By the end of the week, I _____ for a month.
   (A) will travel
   (B) will be traveling
   (C) will have traveled
   (D) have traveled

( ) 4. By the time you come back, I _____ writing my report.
   (A) finish
   (B) will have finished
   (C) have finished
   (D) had finished

( ) 5. Next year they _____ married for 20 years.
   (A) have been
   (B) will have
   (C) will have been
   (D) will be

( ) 6. The whole area was flooded because it _____ for weeks.
   (A) rains
   (B) has rained
   (C) had been raining
   (D) was raining

( ) 7. Since Darwin's' time, the theory of natural selection _____.
   (A) was debated and tested
   (B) has debated and was tested
   (C) has been debated and tested
   (D) has been debated and being tested

( ) 8. Tom's salaryis still only NT$15,000 per month, even though he _____ for this company since 1986.

(A) have worked   (B) have been worked

(C) has worked   (D) has been worked

( ) 9. For the past centuries, there _____ various（不同的）theories（理論）presented（呈述）to account for（說明）the origin（起源）of the universe.

(A) has been   (B) have been

(C) was   (D) were

( ) 10. Last night we met the Smiths, who _____ to these concerts（音樂會）lately.

(A) comes   (B) is coming

(C) has coming   (D) have come

( ) 11. Space expedition（探險）is a landmark（里程碑）of technology that _____ great progress（進步）during the past decades.

(A) has made   (B) have made

(C) has been made   (D) have been made

( ) 12. About 200 million years ago this super-continent（大陸）broke up into two continents: Laurasia and Gondwana. About 60 million years ago Gondwana broke up into what later became South America, Africa, Antarctica, India and Australia. Since then Australia _____ from the rest（剩餘部份）of the world by vast oceans.

(A) is isolated   (B) had isolated

(C) has isolated   (D) has been isolated

( ) 13. When I got home, I found that someone _____ into my house and _____ my expensive fur coat.

(A) has broken; has stolen   (B) broken; stolen

(C) broke; stole   (D) had broken; had stolen

解答

1. (B) 表示「未來某點時間將已完成」的動作，用未來完成式。

2. (C) 表示「未來某點時間將已完成」的動作，用未來完成式。

3. (C) by＋過去時間，主要子句時態用過去完成式；by＋未來時間，主要子句用未來完成式。雖然是the end of the week看不出是過去時間或未來時間，但是從選項中判斷，只有未來完成式符合文法規則，故選(C)。

4. (B) 表示「未來某點時間將已完成」的動作，用未來完成式。

5. (C) 結婚的用法是 sb.＋be/get married，又從next year可知道是未來時間，故選(C)。

6. (C) 主句為過去式，且講述從過去時間點持續至今的一件事，故用過去完成進行式。

7. (C) 自從達爾文的時代，天擇論就不斷被辯論和測試。

8. (C) 自從1986年並持續至今日，用現在完成式。

9. (B) for＋一段時間（過去幾世紀），搭配完成式。此處主詞為theories，故用複數完成式，選(B)。

10. (D) 譯：昨晚我們遇見史密斯一家人，他們最近會來這些音樂會。

11. (A) 從過去的數十年「至今」，故使用現在完成式。

12. (D) 解題關鍵在空格前的since then，then表過去時間，而澳洲(Australia)與世界各洲隔海相對，被隔絕在外，從過去到現在都還是這樣的狀況，所以選(D)。

13. (D) 依照文意，我到家時，發現（用過去式）有人闖進我家，偷了我的皮草大衣，所以闖入跟偷東西應該是在發現之前，故用過去完成式。

Part 3

分詞

Part3
分詞

分詞（V-ing/V-p.p.）一直是英文學習者在學習過程中最大的障礙，不論是大考命題比例，或寫作的正確使用，都占有舉足輕重的地位，所以務必掌握好本章節的各個重點。

★ POINT 1-A 前位修飾的分詞：V-ing/V-p.p.＋N

分詞基本概念說明

現在分詞（V-ing）表**主動、進行**	過去分詞（V-p.p.）表**被動、完成**
主動	被動
1. a winding path（起風的小徑） 2. leading actors（主要的演員）	1. written English （書寫的英文） 2. an estimated 1.25 billion smokers（估計約12.5億的吸菸者）
進行	完成或已發生的狀態
1. boiling water（正在煮沸的水） 2. falling leaves （正在掉落的樹葉） 3. a developing country （開發中國家）	1. boiled water （煮開的水） 2. fallen leaves （已經掉落的樹葉） 3. a developed country （已開發國家）
現在分詞與動名詞容易搞混，請比較下列兩者	
現在分詞表**動作進行的狀態**	動名詞表**名詞的用途與功能**
1. a sleeping baby （正在睡覺的嬰兒） 2. a walking man（正在走路的人）	1. a sleeping bag（睡袋） 2. a walking stick（拐杖）

主題一 | 分詞的類別

　　分詞可以簡單粗略的分為現在分詞和過去分詞。

　　現在分詞（V-ing）代表的是主動、或正在進行的動作，而過去分詞（V-p.p）則相反，代表的是相較之下比較被動、或已經完成的動作。為了讓大家能夠更清楚分辨兩者之間的差異，接下來請好好的比較例句的用法。

例句講解

- **Look at those dazzling waves; they are so beautiful.**
  看看那些閃爍的波浪；真是漂亮。（→波浪使人眩目，為現在分詞）

- **Because of my decayed tooth, I need to see the dentist.**
  因為我的蛀牙，我需要去看牙醫。（→牙齒是被蛀的，為過去分詞）

- **The exciting news cheered up the losing team.**
  這令人興奮的消息使落後的球隊大為振作。（→消息令人興奮，為現在分詞）

- **The determined boy made up his mind to get through the job.**
  那堅決的孩子下定決心完成那份工作。（→心意已決的，為過去分詞）

- **Tourists are reminded to watch out for falling rocks on the path.**
  遊客被提醒在小徑上要當心落石。（→正在掉落的石頭，為現在分詞）

- **Every morning students sweep fallen leaves on campus to keep the environment clean.**
  每天早上學生們在校園內清掃落葉，以維護環境清潔。
  （→已經掉落的葉子，為過去分詞）

 隨堂測驗

( ) 1. Lastly, the hare carries the tortoise again on its back. Thus they reach the _____ line together. 【學測】

(A) ending
(B) finished
(C) finishing
(D) ended

( ) 2. This service is available seven days a week during normal _____ hours. 【學測】

(A) operating
(B) open
(C) operated
(D) opened

( ) 3. So if you ask a _____ adolescent boy to tell what his feelings are, he often cannot say much. 【學測】

(A) tortured
(B) troubled
(C) torturing
(D) troubling

解答：1. (C) 2. (A) 3. (B)

解析：①finishing line為「終點線」之意。
②operating hours表「營業時間」。
③troubled表「心煩意亂的」。

★ POINT 1-B 後位修飾的分詞：N＋V-ing/N＋V-p.p.

❶ 定義：動詞後接分詞，當主詞補語，表示主詞的性質或狀態。

❷ 分詞當形容詞使用時，可放在所修飾名詞之前或之後，通常短如一個字的分詞放在名詞之前，多字組成的分詞片語則接在名詞之後。

❸ 分詞後位修飾可視為由關代所引導的形容詞子句簡化而來，簡化步驟：

(1)**省略關代**：關係代名詞who/which/that是形容子句中的主詞時，將關係代名詞省略。

(2)**動詞改分詞**：將動詞部份改成現在分詞（表主動）或過去分詞（表被動）。

例句講解

• It's an appointment **(which is) made** twenty years ago. 【遠東】
= It's an appointment made twenty years ago.

　那是二十年前所訂的約會。（→省略關代＋beV，保留表被動的過去分詞）

• She threw away a broken vase.
= She threw away a vase **which is broken**.

　她把破花瓶丟了。

→ She threw away the vase **(which is) broken by those naughty kids at play**.

　她把那些頑皮的小孩玩耍時所打破的花瓶丟了。
　（→省略關代＋beV，保留分詞及分詞後的補語）

• There are white clouds **floating/drifting** above the green fields.

　朵朵白雲飄過綠油油的田野。（→省略which are）

• Many celebrities attended the charity concert **held** to raise funds for the orphans.

　許多名人出席那場為孤兒籌募基金而舉行的慈善音樂會。

　（→省略which was）

 隨堂測驗

( ) 1. He felt sad when he saw her eyes _____ with tears.

    (A) filling   (B) falling

    (C) filled   (D) fell

( ) 2. I always dream of living in a house _____ a beautiful lake.

    (A) facing   (B) locating

    (C) faced   (D) located

( ) 3. The number of athletes _____ in the Summer Paralympics Games has increased from 400 athletes from 23 countries in 1960 to 3,806 athletes from 136 countries in 2004. 【學測】

    (A) participate   (B) participated

    (C) participating   (D) to participate

( ) 4. Here all the dogs are given a bath _____ professional shampoo and conditioners in a massaging tub. 【學測】

    (A) use   (B) used

    (C) using   (D) to use

( ) 5. Most parents dread（害怕） a note or call from school _____ that their child's behavior is "not normal". 【指考】

    (A) say   (B) said

    (C) saying   (D) to say

( ) 6. A common mistake _____ in parenthood（父母身份）is that parents often set unrealistic（不切實際的）goals for their children. 【學測】

    (A) find   (B) found

    (C) finding   (D) founded

( ) 7. At the moment EU tobacco manufacturers only have to put written health warnings on cigarette packets _____ the dangers of smoking. 【學測】

(A) highlight
(B) highlights
(C) highlighting
(D) highlighted

解答： 1. (C) 2. (A) 3. (C) 4. (C) 5. (C) 6. (B) 7. (C)

解析：
①be filled with表「充滿⋯⋯的」。
②facing表「面、朝向」。
③動詞後接分詞，當主詞補語，表示主詞的性質或狀態。
④此處為將動詞部份改成現在分詞（表主動）。
⑤同第4題。
⑥在父母身上「被」找到的一個常見錯誤，因為為被動，故用分詞。
⑦此處為將動詞部份改成現在分詞（表主動）。

★ POINT 1-C 複合形容詞I：N/adj./adv.＋V-ing

❶ 分詞可和**副詞**、**形容詞**、**名詞**或**介系詞**搭配，以連字號連接，形成複合形容詞，做形容詞用。

❷ 複合形容詞可視為**形容詞子句的簡化**，形容詞子句中的動詞與所修飾名詞（即先行詞）之間，若為主動關係則用現在分詞，若為被動關係則用過去分詞。

• **The radar detected a rapidly-moving unknown object.**

（→ an unknown object which moved rapidly）

雷達偵測到一個**快速移動**的不明物體。

• **For centuries, Confucianism has had a far-reaching influence on Chinese society.**

（→influence which reaches far）

好幾世紀以來，儒家思想對中國社會產生**深遠的**影響。

• **The kids enjoyed playing in the white-painted tree house.**

（→ the tree house that was painted white）

孩子們喜歡在**漆成白色的**樹屋裡玩。

• **Many people are waiting in line for the freshly-baked egg tarts.**

（→the egg tarts that are baked freshly）

很多人排隊買**剛出爐的**蛋塔。

❸ N與V-ing/V-p.p. 搭配的用法，說明如下：

N＋V-ing	定義 相當於形容詞子句中，**及物動詞**與**受詞**的關係。(S＋V＋O) →吃人的怪物 man-eating beast（beast eats man）
	範例解說 1. an energy-saving machine = a machine which saves energy 一台節能的機器 2. a peace-loving people = a people that loves peace 愛好和平的人 3. a law-abiding citizen = a citizen who abides by the law 遵守法律的公民 4. flag-raising ceremony = a ceremony that raises flags 升旗典禮 5. a time-wasting hobby 浪費時間的嗜好 a body-building food 有助身體成長的食物 a heart-breaking story 令人心碎的故事

❹ adv. 與V-ing/V-p.p. 搭配的用法，說明如下：

adv.＋V-ing	定義 等於形容詞子句中，**不及物動詞**與**副詞**的關係。(S＋V＋adv.) →深遠的影響 far-reaching influence（influence reaches far）
	範例解說 1. a hard-working man = a man who works hard 認真工作的男人 2. a slowly-flowing river = a river that flows slowly 流速緩慢的河 3. a never-ending quarrel = a quarrel which never ends 永不停止的爭吵

❺ adj. 與V-ing/V-p.p. 搭配的用法，説明如下：

adj.+ V-ing	定義 相當於形容詞子句中，**動詞**與**形容詞**（當主詞補語用）的關係，此類動詞常為連綴動詞，如look, taste, smell。(S＋V＋adj.) →難聽的語言 harsh-sounding language（language sounds harsh）
	範例解説 1. stinky-smelling tofu = tofu that smells stinky 聞起來很臭的豆腐 2. a good-looking guy = a guy who looks good 很好看的男生 3. a lovely-looking girl = a girl who looks lovely 很好看的女生 4. a sweet-smelling flower = a flower which smells sweet 聞起來很香的花 5. an ill-fitting clothes = a clothes that fits ill 不合身的衣服

例句講解

• **Under the trend of environmental movements, energy-saving appliances are getting more and more popular.**
（→appliances that save energy，為N＋V-ing）

在環保運動的趨勢下，**節能家電愈來愈受歡迎**。

• **We are all living in this ever-changing world.**
（→world ever changes，為adv.＋V-ing）

我們都生活在這個**不斷改變的**世界裡。

• **My father prefers bitter-tasting coffee.**
（→coffee that tastes bitter，為adj.＋V-ing）

我父親偏愛**苦味的**咖啡。

★ POINT 1-D 複合形容詞II：N/adj./adv.＋V-p.p.

❶ N與V-p.p. 搭配的用法，説明如下：

N＋V-p.p.	定義 相當於形容詞子句中，被動語態裡S＋V-p.p.或O＋V-p.p.的關係。 (S＋be動詞＋V-p.p.＋by/with/like/to＋O) →因飢餓而瘦弱的男孩 hunger-weakened boy (a boy is weakened by hunger)
	範例解説 1. a heart-broken girl = a girl whose heart is broken 心碎的女孩 2. smoking-related death=death which is related to smoking 和吸菸有關的死亡 3. a drought-stricken area = an area that is stricken by drought 被乾旱侵襲的國家 4. a poverty-stricken family = a family which is stricken by poverty 被貧窮侵襲的家庭

❷ adj.與V-p.p.搭配的用法，説明如下：

adj.＋V-p.p.	定義 相當於形容詞子句中，**及物動詞**與**形容詞**（當受詞補語用）的 關係。(S＋V＋O＋adj.或S＋be動詞＋V-p.p.＋adj.) →染成金色的頭髮 blond-dyed hair (hair is dyed blond)
	範例解説 1. ready-made clothes = clothes that are made ready 現成的衣服 2. a ready-made dress = a dress which is made ready 現成的洋裝 3. a green-painted wall = a wall which is painted green 漆成綠色的牆壁

❸ adv.與V-p.p.搭配的用法，說明如下：

adv.＋V-p.p.	定義 相當於形容詞子句中，**及物動詞**與**副詞**的關係。(S＋V＋O＋ adv.或S＋be動詞＋V-p.p.＋adv.) →精雕細琢的句子 carefully-crafted sentence (a sentence is crafted carefully)
	範例解說 1. a carefully-designed machine = a machine which is carefully designed 精心設計的機器 2. a never-taken path = a path that is never taken 沒有走過的路 3.a well-dressed man = a man who is dressed well 打扮得很好看的男人

❹ 其他用法

V-p.p.＋prep.	定義 相當於形容詞子句中，**動詞**與**介系詞／介副詞**的關係。(S＋V＋O＋prep.)
	範例解說 1. a computer with a built-in microphone = a microphone which is build in the computer 內建麥克風的電腦 2. a built-up area = an area that is built up 建築物密集的地區 3. a burnt-out house = a house that is burnt out 被燒光的房子

	定義 「擬分詞」由Number/adj.＋N-ed組成，這類的名詞大多與**人體器官**或**物品構造的名稱**有關。
adj.＋N-ed	範例解説 1. a kind-hearted girl = a girl with a kind heart 好心的女孩 2. a grey-haired man = a man with grey hair 灰髮的男子 3. a three-legged stool = a stool with three legs 三隻腳的凳子 4. a long-sleeved shirt = a shirt with long sleeves 長袖的襯衫 5. a good-tempered man 好脾氣的男人 6. an iron-hearted man/stone-hearted man 鐵石心腸的男人 7. narrow-minded man 心胸狹窄的男人 8. king-sized bed 特大號的床 9. high-heeled shoes 高跟鞋

例句講解

- **She sent her grandma a hand-written greeting card to wish her well.**
  （→a greeting card which is written by hand，為N＋V-p.p.）

  她寄給祖母一張**手寫的**問候卡祝她身體健康。

- **The green-painted house is going to be sold at auction.**
  （→the house which is painted green，為adj.＋V-p.p.）

  那棟**漆成綠色的**房子將會在拍賣會上賣掉。

- **There is a beautifully-decorated room in this villa**
  （→a room which is decorated beautifully，為adv.＋V-p.p.）

這棟別墅裡面有一間**裝飾得很美的**房間。

• **He has been working hard day and night for days and he looks worn-out now.**
（→he has worn himself out，為V-p.p.＋prep）

他日以繼夜的辛勤工作了好幾天，現在他看起來**精疲力竭**。

• **Being a hot-tempered man, he is hard to get along with.**
（→a man with hot temper，為adj.＋N-ed）

他是個**脾氣暴躁的**人，很難跟人相處得很好。

 隨堂測驗

(　　) 1. We fantasize（想像） about what it will be like when we reach the
_____ goal. 【學測】

  (A) long-awaited   (B) long-awaiting
  (C) long-waiting   (D) long-waited

(　　) 2. Nowadays people have to pass various tests for professional
certificates so that they can be qualified for a _____ job. 【指考】

  (A) well-gaining   (B) well-gained
  (C) well-pay   (D) well-paid

(　　) 3. The major theme in the forthcoming issue of the _____ monthly
magazine will be "Love and Peace." 【學測】

  (A) best-promoted   (B) best-sold
  (C) best-promoting   (D) best-selling

(　　) 4. By providing _____ space in a world crowded with people,
tall buildings have solved a great problem of the city and have
completely changed our way of life. 【學測】

  (A) much-needing   (B) much-needed

(C) needed-much   (D) needing-much

(   ) 5. It is a world that avoids heavy _____ language in favor of words that are simple, fresh and playful. 【學測】

(A) scientifically-sounding   (B) scientifically-sounded
(C) scientific-sounding   (D) scientific-sounded

(   ) 6. A new analysis of _____ data has given precisely the rate at which the country is losing size as it pushes northward against the Himalayas. 【學測】

(A) satellite-based   (B) satellite-basing
(C) based-satellite   (D) basing-satellite

(   ) 7. In 1848 the Carnegies arrived in Pittsburgh, then the _____ center of the country. 【指考】

(A) manufactured-iron   (B) manufacturing-iron
(C) iron-manufacturing   (D) iron-manufactured

(   ) 8. Diamonds mined in some _____ areas, such as Liberia, are being smuggled into neighboring countries and exported as conflict-free diamond. 【指考】

(A) rebel-holding   (B) rebel-held
(C) holding-rebel   (D) held-rebel

(   ) 9. The elevation gain（海拔）from the subtropical plains（亞熱帶平原）to the _____ Himalayan heights exceeds 7,000 m. 【指考】

(A) glacier-covered   (B) glacier-covering
(C) covered-glacier   (D) covering-glacier

10. 一座新的橋搭建在湍急的河流上，這村落恢復了與外界的交通往來。

（請判斷並做適當變化）

A new bridge built over the fast-_____ (flow) river, the village restored its communication with the outside world.

解答：1. (A) 2. (D) 3. (D) 4. (B) 5. (C) 6. (A) 7. (C) 8. (B) 9. (A) 10. flowing

解析：

①「被」等待實現很久的，被動用分詞。

②待遇良好的工作，用分詞。

③best-selling表示「暢銷的」。

④很被需要的空間，被動故使用分詞。

⑤此處為主動，故用動名詞。

⑥「衛星作為基礎的」。

⑦製鐵為一主動動作，故用動名詞，且manufacture是用以講述「鐵」的製造，故置於iron後。

⑧rebel-held用以表示「被」反抗軍佔據處（被動），故要用分詞。

⑨glacier-covered用以表示「被」冰河所覆蓋住的（被動），故要使用分詞。

⑩河水流動使用主動態。

★ POINT 1-E 情緒形容詞

❶

表自身的身心感受，如：驚訝、高興、滿意、失望、疲倦等的動詞概念，通常用**過去分詞**V-p.p.。	外界事物令人產生之各種身心感受，如令人驚訝、令人高興、令人滿意表意、令人厭倦、令人疲倦等的動詞概念，通常用**現在分詞**V-ing。
某人「感到……的」、某物「顯露出 內心……感到……的」 1. a surprised expression 一個吃驚的表情 2. an interested audience 一個有興趣的聽眾	某事物或某人「令人覺得……的」、「使人感到……的」 1. a surprising result 令人吃驚的結果 2. an interesting lecture 一場有趣的演說
(be) obliged 感激的 (be) perplexed 困惑的 (be) confused 感到疑惑的 (be) puzzled 困惑的 (be) embarrassed 感到困窘的 (be) annoyed 惱怒的 (be) disgusted 作嘔的 (be) discouraged 洩氣的 (be) disappointed 失望的 (be) amused 被逗樂的 (be) delighted 感到開心的 (be) astonished 吃驚的 (be) horrified 恐懼的 (be) terrified 害怕的 (be) exhausted 筋疲力竭的 (be) satisfied 滿意的 (be) tired 疲累的 (be) pleased 歡喜的 (be) amazed 驚奇的 (be) excited 興奮的 (be) irritated 被惹惱的	(be) obliging 樂於助人的 (be) perplexing 令人費解的 (be) confusing 令人困惑的 (be) puzzling 令人不解的 (be) embarrassing 令人尷尬的 (be) annoying 惱人的 (be) disgusting 令人作嘔的 (be) discouraging 令人沮喪的 (be) disappointing 令人失望的 (be) amusing 引人發笑的 (be) delighting 令人開心的 (be) astonishing 令人驚訝的 (be) horrifying 令人驚駭的 (be) terrifying 恐怖的 (be) exhausting 使人筋疲力盡的 (be) satisfying 令人滿意的 (be) tiring 累人的 (be) pleasing 令人愉快的 (be) amazing 令人吃驚的 (be) exciting 令人激動的 (be) irritating 引人惱怒的

❷ 英文中有些動詞常以被動形式出現，但並未帶有被動的意思，也特別注意其後所接的介系詞。

(be) related to 與……相關的	(be) divided (into) 被分成……
(be) associated with 與……有關聯的	(be) connected with 與……相連結的
(be) suited for 與……相稱的	(be) obliged to 對……感激的
(be) experienced in 在……方面有經驗的	(be) involved in 牽涉……其中
(be) shaped with 被劃分……	(be) inclined to 傾向於……
(be) seated in 坐在……	(be) dressed in 著裝
(be) wounded 受傷的	(be) mistaken for 被誤認為……
(be) bounded for 注定要……	(be) addicted to 沉溺在……
(be) qualified for 合乎標準	(be) destined to 注定要……
(be) acquainted with 熟習……	(be) concerned about 關於……
(be) prepared for 為……作準備	(be) determined to 決心要……
(be) absorbed in 全神貫注於……	(be) made (up) of 由……製成
(be) engaged in 投入於……	(be) composed of 由……所組成
(be) dedicated to 致力於……	(be) well-known for/as 以……聞名
(be) devoted to 致力於……	(be) noted for/as 以……著名
(be) accustomed to 習慣於……	(be) celebrated for/as 慶祝……
(be) used to 習慣於……	(be) based on 以……為基礎
(be) situated in/at 座落於……	(be) married to 嫁娶……
(be) opposed to 反對……	(be) convinced of 為……所信服
(be) supposed to 應該……	(be) located in/at 座落於……
	(be) exposed to 暴露在……

- **The school kids are excited about going camping this weekend.**
學童們對週末的露營**感到非常興奮**。

- **You would never believe that Mary was married to John last year.**
你不會相信瑪麗去年已經**嫁給**了約翰。

- **I was exhausted from a long trip to New York; therefore, I went straight to bed when I got home.**
從紐約長途旅行回來我**感到筋疲力盡**；因此，我回到家倒頭就睡。

- **Monica's parents are quite satisfied with her performance at school.**
莫妮卡的父母對於她在學校的表現**感到滿意**。

- **Betty turned off the TV now because she was tired of watching the same program.** 貝蒂關掉電視，因為她對於看一樣的節目**感到厭倦**。

主題二 | 分詞構句

★ POINT 2-A 一般分詞構句簡化（前後子句主詞相同時）

❶ 副詞子句改為分詞構句，首先必須先將引導副詞子句的**連接詞去掉**。再者，若副詞子句的主詞與主要子句的**主詞相同**時，則將**副詞子句的主詞去掉**；如不相同則保留。最後，將動詞（包括be動詞）改為**現在分詞**，其餘照抄。

• After the sun had set, we arrived at the station.

= ~~After~~ the sun ~~had~~ → **having set**, we arrived at the station.

= The sun having set, we arrived at the station.

　太陽下山後，我們抵達了車站。（→主詞不同予以保留）

❷ 副詞子句中如是**進行式**，則須把be動詞去掉才行。

• When he was buying the book, he met an old friend.

= ~~When he was~~ buying the book, he met an old friend.

= Buying the book, he met an old friend.

　他買書的時候，遇見一位老朋友。

❸ 從屬子句中的動詞若是be動詞則須變為being並判斷是否省略。

• As James was exhausted after work, he went to bed early.

= Being exhausted after work, James went to bed early.

= Exhausted after work, James went to bed early.

　詹姆士因為工作後疲累不堪，很早就去睡了。

❹ 分詞為being和having been時，可省略。

• As he has been praised too much, he becomes too proud.

= (Having been) praised too much, he becomes too proud.

　他因為受到過份的誇獎，而變得驕傲。

❺ 原副詞子句中有**否定詞**，則將否定詞放在分詞**前**形成分詞構句。

• Because his didn't know what to do, he went home.
= Not knowing what to do, he went home.
因為不知道要做什麼，他就回家了。

• Because Joyce was not happy about my performance, she asked me to try again.
= Not being happy about my performance, Joyce asked me to try again.
因為喬伊斯對我的表現不滿意，便叫我再試一次。

❻ 分詞構句所顯示的連接詞意思，從句子的前後關係來判斷，但為了使其意義明確，方有將連接詞置於分詞之前面。

• While fighting in Korea, he was taken prisoner.
在韓國作戰時，他被俘了。

❼ 分詞構句依其意義可分為：

(1) 表**時間**（由when, while, as soon as, as, after等引導的副詞子句）

• When he swam in the sea, he saw a shark.
= Swimming in the sea, he saw a shark.
當他在海裡游泳時，他看到一條鯊魚。

(2) 表**原因、理由**（由as, because, since等引導的副詞子句）

• Because I was sick, I was absent from school yesterday.
= Being sick, I was absent from school yesterday.
因為生病，我昨天沒去上學。

(3) 表**條件**：（由if引導的副詞子句）

• If you speak of the wolf, you will see his tail
= Speaking of the wolf, you will see his tail.
【諺】説曹操，曹操到。

(4) 表**讓步**：（though等為引導的副詞子句）

• **Though she is not living very close to my house, she visits me every day.**

= **Not living very close to my house, she visits me every day.**

　雖然她住得離我家不近，她天天來看我。

　　(5) 表**附帶狀況**：（由and引導的子句）

• **His father died, and left nothing but a lot of debts.**

= **His father died, leaving nothing but a lot of debts.**

　他的父親去世了，除了許多債務外，什麼也沒留下。

　　❽ 分詞構句的位置，可置於句首、句中（主詞之後）、句尾，但都要用逗點隔開。

• **Crying for milk, the baby woke everyone up.**

= **The baby, crying for milk, woke everyone up.**

= **The baby woke everyone up, crying for milk.**

　寶寶哭著要喝牛奶，把大家都吵醒了。

 例句講解

• **Tom sat beside the girl he loved and he felt embarrassed.**

= **Sitting beside the girl he loved, Tom felt embarrassed.**

　坐在他喜歡的女生旁邊，湯姆覺得很不好意思。

• **When Jane saw the boy she admired, she felt her heart beating very fast.**

= **Seeing the boy she admired, Jane felt her heart beating very fast.**

　當珍看到她很崇拜的男孩時，她的心跳得很快。

• **As it was fine, I went in-line skating with my brother.**

= **The weather being fine, I went in-line skating with my brother.**

　因為天氣好，所以我和弟弟去溜直排輪。

- After they walked in the mountains for two days, the hikers were exhausted.
= Walking in the mountains for two days, the hikers were exhausted.
  在山裡走了兩天，登山者都累垮了。

- I was doing my homework, and my sister was playing with her dolls.
= I was doing my homework, my sister playing with her dolls.
  我在做功課，我妹妹在玩她的洋娃娃。

★延伸學習

❶ 若分詞構句由being或having been引導時，常常會省略being或having been，而形成**形容詞或名詞引導的句子**。

- The old woman was penniless, and kept body and soul together by collecting scraps.
= Penniless, the old woman kept body and soul together by collecting scraps.
  一貧如洗，這老婦人靠著拾荒勉強糊口。

- He is a world-famous star, and he is on full alert against any invasion of privacy by the paparazzi.
= A world-famous star, he is on full alert against any invasion of privacy by the paparazzi.
  身為國際知名巨星，他高度戒備提防狗仔隊對私生活的侵犯。

❷ 以分詞構句描述過去事件時，若兩個動作的發生有先後之分，先發生的動作用Having＋V-p.p.表示，亦可保留**表時間之連接詞**，以釐清兩動詞的相對先後關係。

- Having finished his homework, he played on-line games with friends.（○）

  After finishing his homework, he played on-line games with his friends.（○）

  Finishing his homework, he played on-line games with his friends.（✗）

  做完功課後，他和朋友玩線上遊戲。

🕐 **隨堂測驗**

( ) 1. _____ how to study effectively, Lisa got frustrated with her poor academic performance.

  (A) Not knowing
  (B) Don't know
  (C) Not to know
  (D) Doesn't know

( ) 2. The little boy ran out of his room, _____ for Mom.

  (A) and cry   (B) cried
  (C) crying   (D) to cry

( ) 3. Once _____ the environment where the purchasing occurred, the feeling of a personal reward would be gone. 【指考】

  (A) aware
  (B) bewaring
  (C) left
  (D) leaving

( ) 4. The number of athletes _____ in the Summer Paralympics Games has increased from 400 athletes from 23 countries in 1960 to 3,806 athletes from 136 countries in 2004. 【學測】

  (A) participate
  (B) participated
  (C) participating
  (D) to participate

( ) 5. When he found her, he said, "I know how valuable this stone is, but I'm giving it back to you, _____ that you can give me something even more precious. 【學測】

  (A) hope   (B) hoping
  (C) hoped   (D) to hope

( ) 6. Although located close to the equator, Rwanda's "thousand hills," _____ from 1,500 m to 2,500 m in height, ensure that the temperature is pleasant all year round. 【學測】

(A) differing   (B) wandering

(C) ranging   (D) climbing

解答： 1. (A) 2. (C) 3. (D) 4. (C) 5. (B) 6. (C)

解析：

①原副詞子句中有否定詞，則將否定詞放在分詞前形成分詞構句。

②此為由and引導之子句改寫的分詞構句。

③此為分詞構句。

④此為分詞構句。

⑤And I hope在此處被改為hoping

⑥分詞構句

★ POINT 2-B 獨立分詞構句 S1＋V-ing/V-p.p., S2＋V...

❶ 分詞構句的主詞與主要句子的**主詞不同時**，**必須將主詞保留**，形成**獨立分詞構句**。此外，在簡化的步驟與用法上均與分詞構句相同。簡化步驟如下：

(1) **先判斷主詞**：前後兩子句的主詞不同，將主詞保留。

(2) **刪去連接詞**：需要時可將連接詞保留，使語意明確。

(3) **動詞改分詞**：將連接詞所引導的子句中的動詞改成分詞，主動關係用現在分詞，被動關係用過去分詞。

• If time permits, we will stop at 7-11 to do some shopping.

= If time permits→permmting, we will stop at 7-11 to do some shopping.

= Time permitting, we will stop at 7-11 to do some shopping.

　如果時間許可，我們將在7-11停留一下買些東西。

❷ 分詞構句中的意思上的主詞必須和主要句子中的**主詞一致**，及分詞結構應與主詞有關，否則務必在分詞前加上其意思上的主詞，亦即要使用「獨立分詞構句」，以免寫出如下列例句般錯誤而可笑的句子來。

• 獅子被關在籠子裡，孩子們不怕牠。

Kept in the cage, the children are not frightened of the lion.（X）
（→此句意為孩子們在籠子裡）

The lion kept in the cage, the children are not frightened of it.（○）

例句講解

• **There is no bus at night, so we decided to take a taxi home.**

 =There being no bus at night, we decided to take a taxi home.
　夜裡沒有公車行駛，我們決定搭計程車回家。

• **Because John have grown up overseas, many girls ask him about the life of living abroad.**

= **John having grown up overseas, many girls ask him about the life of living abroad.**
　因為約翰在國外長大，所以很多女生去問他在國外生活的事。

- When the clock stroke six, we then had our dinner.
= The clock striking six, we then had our dinner.

當時鐘敲六下時,我們就吃晚餐了。

- They were trembling, and their mouths were watering at the thought of the beer.
= They were trembling, their mouths watering at the thought of the beer.

他們顫抖著,一想到啤酒,口水就流出來。

★延伸學習

表「連續或附帶狀態」的獨立分構,可與with+O+OC的句型互換。

- She smiled and tears glistened in her eyes.
= She smiled, tears glistening in her eyes.
= She smiled with tears glistening in her eyes.

她笑中帶淚,眼裡淚光晶瑩。

 隨堂測驗

( ) 1. James got lost in thought, his eyes _____ over the desk.

(A) drifts
(B) to drift
(C) drifting
(D) drifted

( ) 2. "There it is," he _____, his eyes _____ with sudden tears.

(A) whispering; shimmering
(B) whispering; shimmered
(C) whispered; shimmering
(D) whispered; shimmered

( ) 3. _____ the chocolate cake, her mouth began to water. 【英檢初級】
   (A) Seen
   (B) Seeing
   (C) The little girl saw
   (D) The little girl seeing

4. If weather permits, we will have a barbeque on the riverbank tomorrow.

（以分詞構句改寫）

5. He was sitting next to Mrs. Smith, and his eyes rested on her daughter.

（以分詞構句改寫）

解答： 1. (C) 2. (C) 3. (B)
4. Weather permitting, we will have a barbeque on the riverbank tomorrow.
5. He was sitting next to Mrs. Smith, his eyes resting on her daughter.

解析：
①眼神會「主動飄移」，故選C。
②講述一句過去他說過的話，故前面要使用過去式，後面子句主詞為his eyes，故使用ing的理由同上一題。
③前後兩句主詞相同且主詞為可以使用「see」的人，故使用代表主動的進行式。

★ POINT 2-C with＋O＋OC

❶ with表伴隨主要動作所發生的動作、狀態或提供細節的描述。

❷ 此句型**以分詞作為受詞補語，補充說明受詞的狀態**，用現在分詞表示動詞與受詞間的主動關係，過去分詞則表示被動關係。

❸ 如果從屬子句和主要子句主詞**不同**而兩動作發生於**同時**，可用(S＋V..., with ＋O＋OC)的附帶狀態句型，with有時亦可省略。

例句講解

- **The mother walked ahead and her three children followed her closely.**
= **The mother walked ahead, with her three children following her closely.**
  那母親走在前頭，她的三個小孩緊跟在後。

- **Sally enjoys riding a bicycle and her hair blows in the wind.**
= **Sally enjoys riding a bicycle with her hair blowing in the wind.**
  莎莉很愛騎著腳踏車，讓頭髮在空中飄揚。

- **Jason sent me an e-mail and a file is attached to it.**
= **Jason sent me an e-mail with a file attached to it.**
  傑森寄了一封夾帶附加檔案的電子郵件給我。

- **Mr. Li sat reading newspapers on the sofa and his legs were crossed.**
  Mr. Li sat reading newspapers on the sofa with his legs crossed.
  李先生翹著二郎腿，坐在沙發上看報紙。

★延伸學習

此句型的OC是現在分詞或過去分詞之外，也可以是形容詞片語、介系詞片語或介副詞、不定詞片語。

- **Don't speak with your mouth full.**（→OC為adj.）
  嘴裡塞滿食物時不要說話。

- **Her friends stepped into the room with a cake and gifts in their hands.**
  （→OC為介系詞片語）

  她的朋友們走進房間，手裡拿著蛋糕和禮物。

- **The cake dropped to the floor with the upside down.** （→OC為介系詞／副詞）

  蛋糕正面朝下掉到地板上。

- **He was stressed out with so many deadlines to meet.** （→OC為不定詞片語）

  他有多項得在規定日期之前完成的工作，為此備感壓力。

隨堂測驗

( ) 1. The children gave a gasp of surprise with their eyes _____ at the magician.

    (A) stare   (B) staring

    (C) stared   (D) to stare

( ) 2. The contestants anxiously awaited the announcement of the result with their hearts _____ violently.

    (A) beats   (B) to beat

    (C) beating   (D) beaten

( ) 3. With a DJ playing various kinds of music rather than just rap, and a mix of clothing labels designed more for taste and fashion than for a precise age, department stores have managed to appeal to successful middle-aged women _____ losing their younger customers.

【學測】

    (A) in   (B) while   (C) after   (D) without

( ) 4. After the 1960s, and especially since the 1980s, the high school prom in many areas has become a serious exercise in excessive consumption, with boys _____ expensive tuxedos and girls _____ designer gowns.

【學測】

    (A) rented; wore   (B) put on; dressed

    (C) renting; wearing   (D) putting on; dressing

( ) 5. You'll see the old men in navy berets; ultra-thin, bronzed women with hair _____ bright orange; and schoolchildren sharing an afternoon chocolate with their mothers. 【指考】

(A) colored   (B) coloring   (C) dyed   (D) dyeing

( ) 6. Andy listened to his mom talking with her eyes _____ on the newspaper headlines.

(A) rested   (B) rests   (C) rest   (D) resting

( ) 7. With one out of every two American marriages _____ in divorce, custody of children has become an issue in the Americans society. 【指考】

(A) end   (B) ended   (C) ending   (D) ends

( ) 8. The organic food products are made of natural ingredients, with no artificial flavors _____. 【學測】

(A) to add   (B) add   (C) adding   (D) added

解答：1. (B) 2. (C) 3. (D) 4. (C) 5. (A) 6. (D) 7. (C) 8. (D)

解析：
①眼睛可以「主動」盯著魔術師，故用B。
②心臟跳動為主動，故用C。
③在顧好兩邊的條件下，百貨公司可以成功的「不失去」年輕客群，故使用without。
④這裡說的是高中男女生花費大筆金錢「租」西裝、「穿」禮服的現象，主詞是人，用ving。
⑤頭髮是「被」弄成亮橘色的，用被動式。
⑥這邊修飾的是媽媽的視線放的地方，故用ving。
⑦這邊講的是每兩段婚姻就有一段會走到離婚這步，要使用主動用法。
⑧「被」添加，故使用ed。

★ POINT 2-D 分詞慣用語

此類分詞慣用語又稱為「**無人稱獨立分詞片語**」。因其意思上的主詞為一般人，如we、you、one、they等，故通常將該主詞省略無須寫出，具獨立分詞構句的結構。常見的分詞慣用語有：

(1) 由於 owing to＋N

(2) 依據…… based on/upon＋N

(3) 關於…… concerning/regarding/respecting＋N

(4) 從……來判斷 judging from＋N

(5) 和……相較之下 compared with＋N

(6) 談到、提到 speaking of＋N

(7) 因為、鑑於 seeing that＋S＋V

(8) 倘若、假設 provided/providing/supposing that＋S＋V

(9) 考慮到 considering＋N/that＋S＋V

(10) 如果考慮到 given＋N/that＋S＋V

(11) 根據……所説／而定 according to＋N

(12) 説來……ly speaking,

（大致説來） roughly speaking,

（廣泛説來） broadly speaking,

（法律上説來） legally speaking,

（坦白説來） frankly speaking,

（正確説來） correctly speaking,

（嚴格説來） strictly speaking,

（一般説來） generally speaking,

（比較上説來） comparatively speaking,

例句講解

- Judging from **her cold attitude, we felt we were not wanted at all.**
  從她冷淡的態度來看，我們感覺根本不受歡迎。

- Speaking of **GM food, more and more scientists warn the public of its possible health effects.**
  說到基因改造食物，愈來愈多的科學家警告大眾它對健康可能的影響。

- Considering that **your best friend were to find out you lied to her, what would you do?**
  要是你最好的朋友發現你騙她，你怎麼辦？

- Given that **they got only one week to work on the project, they've done a marvelous job.**
  考慮到他們只有一星期的時間做這個作業的話，他們已經做得很好了。

- Roughly speaking**, women are better able to handle their emotions than men.**
  大致上來說，女人比男人更會控制自己的情緒。

隨堂測驗

(   ) 1. _____, he is more of a novelist than of a journalist.

    (A) Strictly speaking   (B) Strict speak

    (C) Strictly speak   (D) Strict speaking

(   ) 2. Each year, tens of millions of animals, _____ dogs and cats, needlessly suffer and die to fuel the fur industry. 【學測】

    (A) include   (B) included

    (C) including   (D) inclusive

(   ) 3. Westerner, the Japanese are more connected with packaging as a symbol _____ of appreciation, love and care. 【指考】

    (A) Comparing with   (B) Compared with

    (C) Compare with   (D) To compare with

※請填入適當的分詞慣用語

4. 一般來説，如果我們僅僅移動到下一個時區，我們的生理時鐘只會受到些微的影響，但是一旦我們穿越三或四個時區，時差就會成為一個問題。
【學測】 _____, our biological clock is slightly disturbed if we just move into the next time zone, but jet lag becomes a problem once we have passed through three or four time zones.

5. 根據普遍的民間傳説，許多動物比他們看起來的樣子更聰明。【學測】
_____ popular folklore, many animals are smarter than they appear.

6. 從他的言行來判斷，他是個值得信賴的工作夥伴。
_____ his words and actions, he is a trustworthy partner to work with.

7. 這歌手的許多朋友認為就她的名氣與豐厚的收入來説，放棄演藝生涯步入婚姻是不值得的。【TOEFL】Many of the singer's friends thought giving up her career for marriage was not worth it, _____ her fame and handsome income.

解答：1. (A) 2. (C) 3. (B)
4.Generally speaking
5.According to
6.Judging from
7.considering

解析：
①「嚴格來説」，此為固定用法。
②此處為分詞構句。
③和……比較。

滿分追擊模擬試題

( ) 1. He began his career as a zoologist, _____ mollusks（軟體動物） and their adaptations（適應度） to their environment. 【指考】
(A) study
(B) studied
(C) studying
(D) being studied

( ) 2. The earth is made up of oceans and continents（洲）, and is _____ into two hemispheres（半球）.
(A) divided
(B) dividing
(C) dividend
(D) division

( ) 3. Every year tens of thousands of tourists admire at the beauty of the _____ sun at Mt. Ali.
(A) rose
(B) rising
(C) rises
(D) rise

( ) 4. Besides their sharing traditional male roles, women also play roles entirely different from those _____ by men.
(A) playing
(B) preyed
(C) prayed
(D) played

( ) 5. The largest salt mine（礦） in the world _____ in a lake in Sinkiang, China.
(A) is located
(B) locating
(C) local
(D) location

( ) 6. The sun _____, we arrived at the station.
(A) have being set
(B) having set
(C) have set
(D) setting

( ) 7. After a spa treatment at Happy Puppy, dogs come home _____ pampered and relaxed. 【學測】

(A) will feel   (B) to feel

(C) have felt   (D) feeling

( ) 8. As he had expected, a policeman came _____ around the corner. 【指考】

(A) run   (B) running

(C) ran   (D) to run

( ) 9. With the help of modern technology, some supermarkets are now able to keep customers _____ about what others are buying. 【指考】

(A) inform   (B) informed

(C) informing   (D) to inform

( ) 10. _____ his words and actions, he is a trustworthy partner to work with.

(A) Judging from   (B) Judged from

(C) Judging by   (D) Judged by

( ) 11. The reader must interpret the _____ words depending on the context in which it is used, as there are many examples of words or phrases which use the same abbreviations. 【指考】

(A) minimizing   (B) criticized

(C) shortening   (D) abbreviated

( ) 12. _____ to this campaign and save three lives for only $5, send your donation to: American Assistance for Cambodia, P.O. Box 2716, GPO, New York, NY 10116. Credit Card donations are also accepted. 【學測】

(A) Contributing   (B) Contribute

(C) To contribute   (D) For contributing

(   ) 13. He wandered through the zoo with his face _____ in a strange cloth. 【指考】

(A) covering   (B) covered

(C) cover   (D) to cover

(   ) 14. At the moment EU tobacco manufacturers only have to put written health warnings on cigarette packets _____ the dangers of smoking. 【學測】

(A) highlight   (B) highlights

(C) highlighting   (D) highlighted

(   ) 15. The University of Virginia was planned and _____ by Thomas Jefferson, the third president of the United State.

(A) fund   (B) founded

(C) funded   (D) find

(   ) 16. Oniomania is the technical term for the compulsive desire to shop, more commonly _____ as compulsive shopping or shopping addiction. 【指考】

(A) referring to   (B) referred to

(C) serving   (D) served

17. There are two kinds of heroes: heroes who shine in the face of great danger, who perform an __(1)__ act in a difficult situation, and heroes who live an ordinary life like us, who do their work __(2)__ by many of us, but who __(3)__ a difference in the lives of others. 【學測】

(   ) (1) (A) annoying (B) interfering (C) amazing (D) inviting

(   ) (2) (A) noticing (B) noticeable (C) noticed (D) unnoticed

(   ) (3) (A) make (B) do (C) tell (D) count

解答

1. (C) 為分詞構句，前後主詞同一，用主動用法。

2. (A) 「被」劃分為兩個半球，用ed。

3. (B) 正在上升的太陽，故用rising。

4. (D) 「被」男人們所扮演的，故用played。

5. (A) be+located表示「位於」。

6. (B) 此處表示太陽已經西沈。

7. (D) 狗「感到」，故可以使用主動形式。

8. (B)

9. (B)

10. (A) 此為分詞慣用語。

11. (D) （句意：讀者必須根據縮寫的文字所使用的上下文來解釋，因為有許多的單字或片語使用相同的縮寫。）

12. (C)

13. (B) with＋O＋OC的用法，接過去分詞表被動關係。

14. (C)

15. (B)

16. (B)

17. (1) (C) (2) (D) (3) (A) 解析：英雄有兩種：一種在危險的處境下發光發熱，面對困境卻有驚人的表現；也有像我們一樣活在一般生活中的英雄，默默做著不被人注意的事情，但是卻為別人的生活中帶來重大的改變或影響。

Part 4

關係詞與形容詞子句

—— Part4 ——
關係詞與形容詞子句

學習關係詞就如同學習各類法則，最重要的是架構清楚，概念完整，再加上適當的練習即可。在閱讀上，關代如果現身，要能夠明確的知道是用來代替其前方的哪一個名詞（即所謂的先行詞）；如果省略，則要看出其後的形容詞子句是用來修飾哪一個名詞。

一、何為關係詞

關係詞分成**關係代名詞**、**關係副詞**、**複合關係代名詞**。此處請記得，關係代名詞與關係副詞都是用來**引導形容詞子句**的文法用字。

二、關係詞的口訣

(1) 關係代名詞→**連接詞＋代名詞**→引導**不完整子句**→作**受詞**時可省略

(2) 關係副詞→**連接詞＋副詞**→引導**完整子句**

(3) 關代三缺一：（主詞／受詞／補語）→大家看前（**先行詞**）後（**缺項**）

(4) 關代之前有**逗點**→非限定用法→**唯一** →**補述**

(5) that 之前無**逗點／介系詞**

三、關係子句

由關代所引導的子句為關係子句，又稱為形容詞子句，其作用為修飾先行詞。應注意其簡化之後所形成的分詞。

• The man who is standing on the platform is my teacher.

→The man standing on the platform is my teacher.

　站在月台上的男人是我的老師。

• Language which is spoken in Taiwan is called Taiwanese.

→ Language spoken in Taiwan is called Taiwanese.

　在台灣說的語言被稱為台語。

關係子句係由關係代名詞(who, whom, whose, which, that)或關係副詞(when, where, why)所引導的形容詞子句。

有三種型式：

　　一、關係代名詞+主詞+動詞

　　二、關係副詞+主詞+動詞

　　三、關係代名詞+動詞

主題一 | 關係代名詞的用法

★ POINT 1-A 關係代名詞及關係子句

❶ 關係代名詞的種類

格 先行詞	主格	受格	所有格	子句內含介系詞時	
人	who	whom	whose	by from of about	whom
人以外的事物 （含動物）	which	which	whose (=...of which)	by in on of	which
人、事物通用	that	that	that無所有格	that前不加介系詞	

關代的「格」小公式
1. **主格＋V**
2. **受格＋S＋V**
3. **受格＋S＋V＋prep.**
4. **prep.＋受格＋S＋V**
5. **所有格＋N＋V**

❷ 關代的定義：**連接詞＋代名詞**

❸ 先行詞定義：**被形容詞子句修飾的名詞，常在關代正前方**

❹ 關代的出現：**缺什麼補什麼**

例句講解

• **Last summer I went to Hawaii, which <u>was called the heaven for Americans</u>.**

（→先行詞為Hawaii，關代為which作主詞，關係子句為which was called the heaven for Americans）

　去年夏天我去了一趟夏威夷，那裡被稱為美國人的天堂。

• **A man who <u>has no knowledge of himself</u> can't rule others.**

（→先行詞為a man，關代為who作主詞，關係子句為who has no knowledge of himself）

　一個不了解自己的人，是沒辦法支配別人的。

• **Kevin bought the designer watch which/that <u>his girlfriend liked</u>.**

（→先行詞為the designer watch，關代為which/that作受詞，關係子句為 which/that his girlfriend liked.）

　凱文買了那支他女朋友很喜歡的設計師手錶。

★注意要點

　❶ 關代若為**主格**時，後面的beV或V的單複數由**先行詞**決定。

• **The animals which/that are abandoned will be adopted by the rich man.**

　被棄養的動物們將會被那個有錢人領養。

　❷ 關代作為**受格**時，可被省略。

• **There comes a man whom/that we never met before.**

= **There comes a man we never met before.**

　來了一個我們從來沒見過的男人。

 **隨堂測驗**

(　) 1. The Egyptians were the first people _____ measured their land.

(A) when　　(B) whom　　(C) which　　(D) that

(　) 2. Those _____ are honest are deserving of respect.

(A) who　　(B) whom　　(C) which　　(D) that

(　) 3. That is the man _____ I met in London last year.

(A) who　　(B) whom　　(C) which　　(D) that

(　) 4. He was a man _____ conduct was beyond reproach（責備）.

(A) who　　(B) whom　　(C) whose　　(D) that

(　) 5. "A mature person" usually refers to a person _____ character（個性）is firmly（堅定地）established.

(A) of which　(B) whose　　(C) in which　　(D) whom

解答： 1. (D) 2. (A) 3. (B) 4. (C) 5. (B)

解析：

①此處並非受格，不能使用whom。

②主格，使用who表示「那些誠實的人」。

③此處為受格位置，故用whom。

④Whose表示「誰的」。

⑤Whose表示「誰的」，用來修飾character。

★ POINT 1-B 修飾人的形容詞子句

❶ 句型結構

先行詞（人）	關代	動詞
he/she/it		
the person		
people	who	視先行詞決定**單複數**及**時態**
those		
(any)one		

❷ he/the (a) man/one who＋V... 表達同樣的意義，who引導的形容詞子句及主要子句的動詞用**單數**型。

❸ 若who引導形容詞子句修飾先行詞為those/people/they時，形容詞子句及主要子句的動詞用**複數**型，用在先行詞為特別指稱特定人物時使用。

❹ 此句型的關係代名詞，**固定用**who，**不用**that。

❺ 此句型除了放在主要子句的**主詞**位置外，也可以放在**受詞**位置。

例句講解

• **God helps those who help themselves.**
（→**先行詞為受詞**those，**關代動詞為複數型**）

天助自助者。

• **Those (who live in glass houses) should not throw stones.**
（→**先行詞為主詞**those，**主句動詞及關代動詞為複數型**）

住在玻璃屋的人不該丟石頭。

• **One who violates the rules is sure to be fined.**
= **Those who violate the rules are sure to be fined.**
（→**先行詞為主詞**one，主句動詞及關代動詞為單數型；先行詞為主詞 those，主句動詞及關代動詞為複數型）

違反規則的人會被罰錢。

 隨堂測驗

( ) 1. Prom night can be a dreadful experience for socially awkward teens or for _____ do not secure dates. 【學測】

(A) he who　　(B) those who　　(C) one who　　(D) the person who

( ) 2. _____ learned a second language as children used the same region in Broca's area for both languages. 【學測】

(A) People who　　　　　　(B) Those
(C) A man whom　　　　　　(D) They which

( ) 3. Balad was _____ changed him into a gentleman. 【學測】

(A) one who　　(B) a man whom　　(C) who　　(D) the person who

( ) 4. _____ exercises regularly is more likely to look young. 【學測】

(A) Those　　(B) A person who　　(C) Who　　(D) Those who

( ) 5. _____ practice folk medicine need lots of formal education on herbs. 【學測】

(A) Anyone that　　　　　　(B) He who
(C) People who　　　　　　(D) Those which

解答： 1. (B) 2. (A) 3. (D) 4. (B) 5. (C)

解析：
①those who用代指「那群人」。
②People who用來表示「那群人」。
③The person who表示把他變成一個紳士的「那個人」。
④由此句的動詞excercises判斷主詞應為單數，故選B。
⑤People who代指「那群人」。

★ POINT 1-C 介系詞＋which

❶ 句型結構

先行詞	介系詞＋關代		關係子句
事物／人	in by with	which	完整子句
人	to by with	whom	完整子句

❷ 此句型中，which為關係代名詞，做介系詞in/by/with……等的受詞。

❸ 此句型中，which因為前面有介系詞，**所以不可以替換為**that。

❹ 此句型中，「介系詞＋which」之後須接完整的形容詞子句（子句中不缺主詞或受詞）。

❺ 此句型中，介系詞也可以放在關係子句的**最後面**。

❻ 此句型中，which若替換成whom也有類似的用法，但先行詞必須為「人」。

例句講解

• **My father gave me a laptop with which I can deal with data wherever I go.**

（→先行詞為物laptop，介系詞with，關代which）

我父親送給我一部無論我在哪裡都可以處理資訊的筆記型電腦。

• **The police urged that people keep away from the dangerous streets in which the robbery often happened.**

= **The police urged that people keep away from the dangerous streets which the robbery often happened in.**

（→先行詞為物street，介系詞in，關代which，介系詞可置於關係子句的最後面）

警方力勸民眾遠離搶案常發生的危險街道。

• Going further, we may see the ferry with which <u>the villagers crossed the river</u>.

= Going further, we may see the ferry which <u>the villagers crossed the river</u> with.

（→先行詞為物ferry，介系詞with，關代which，介系詞可置於關係子句的最後面）

往前走，我們可以看到村民們用來渡河的船。

• In our class, she is the girl with/to <u>whom everyone likes to talk</u>.

（→先行詞為人the girl，介系詞to或with，關代whom）

在我們班上，她是大家都喜歡和她聊天的女孩。

★延伸學習

in that（因為）是連接詞，後面接表原因的子句。

• To tell the truth, I don't like her in that she is a girl putting too much emphasis on her appearance.

說實話，我不喜歡她，因為她太注重她的外表。

🕐 隨堂測驗

（　　）1. The reader must interpret（解讀）the abbreviated（縮寫的）words depending on the context _____ it is used, as there are many examples of words or phrases which use the same abbreviations.

【指考】

(A) in which

(B) on which

(C) at which

(D) during which

（　　）2. The presidential US $1 coins have a special design. For the first time since the 1930s, there are words (which are) carved into the edge of each coin, including the year _____ the coin was issued and traditional mottos.

【指考】

(A) in which

(B) on which

(C) at which

(D) during which

(   ) 3. French readers, young and old, already have plenty of free options
_____ to choose, including newspaper websites and the free
papers (which are) handed out daily in many city centers. 【指考】

(A) in which
(B) on which
(C) at which
(D) from which

(   ) 4. A new analysis of satellite-based data has given precisely the rate
_____ the country is losing size as it pushes northward against
the Himalayas. 【學測】

(A) in which
(B) on which
(C) at which
(D) from which

(   ) 5. Joshua gave his girlfriend a diamond ring _____ he proposed
to her. 【學測】

(A) that
(B) with that
(C) which
(D) with which

解答：1. (A) 2. (A) 3. (D) 4. (C) 5. (D)

解析：

①Used "in" the context
②"in" the year
③To choose "from"
④"at" the rate
⑤He proposed to her "with" a diamond ring

★ POINT 1-D 數量形容詞片語＋關代

❶ 句型結構

先行詞	數量形容詞片語＋關代	關係子句
人， 物，	some of　　which 　　　　　　whom	以which或whom為主詞的補述句

❷ 此句型中，whom/which為關係代名詞，引導一**補述用法**的形容詞子句，whom/which做子句中的**主詞**。

❸ 此句型中，whom/which也是**連接詞**，連接前後兩個句子，whom代替前面句子提過的人，which代替前面句子提過事或物。

❹ 表示數量的片語如: some of, many of, most of, none of, two of, half of, both of, neither of, each of, all of, several of, a few of, little of, a number of置於**代名詞**之前，只能使用whom或it。

❺ 此句型中，whom/which除了是兩個句子的連接詞外，也是為其引導的形容詞子句之**受詞**。

❻ 以數量形容詞片語引導的形容詞子句之前要加**逗號**。

例句講解

- With the development of economy, lots of plants are built up in the mountain areas, and the fish usually live in some of these areas.

= With the development of economy, lots of plants are built up in the mountain areas, some of which the fish usually live in.

（→which為**連接詞**，也是受詞these areas）

隨著經濟的發展，許多工廠蓋在山區，其中有些地方通常是魚的棲息地。

- Those students are often made fun of, and their classmates like to bully some of them.

= Those students are often made fun of, some of whom <u>their classmates like to bully</u>.

（→whom為**連接詞**，也是受詞those students）

那些學生常被取笑，其中有些人甚至是同學喜歡欺負的對象。

 隨堂測驗

( ) 1. The Penghu archipelago consists of nearly one hundred islands, _____ are famous for their pure white-sand beaches. 【指考】

(A) many of them
(B) of which many
(C) of much which
(D) and very of which

( ) 2. There are many legends about the painting, _____ are very different from the others. 【指考】

(A) and some of which
(B) some of them
(C) some
(D) some of which

( ) 3. Macarthur controls thousands of soldiers, _____ must obey his orders in both war and peace. 【TOEFL】

(A) all of whom (B) all of who (C) all of them (D) whoever

4. The village has around 200 people, the majority of（大多數）_____ are farmers. 【TOEFL】

5. Last night the orchestra（管絃樂團）played three symphonies（交響曲）, one of _____ was Beethoven's Seventh. 【英檢初級】

6. After the riot（暴動）, over one hundred people were taken to the hospital, many of _____ had been innocent bystanders. 【英檢初級】

解答：1. (B) 2. (D) 3. (A) 4.whom 5.which 6.whom

解析：①consist "of"；many則是代表許多的小島。
　　　②some of which代表著some of the paintings。
　　　③all of whom代表著thousands of soldiers。

主題二 | 含先行詞的關代：what

★ **POINT 2-A 複合關係代名詞what**

❶ 定義：what本身是**先行詞**，也是**關係代名詞**，引導名詞子句，故what之前不可再有先行詞。

❷ what引導的子句為名詞子句，做主要句的主詞、受詞或補語，作主詞時，其後動詞用**單數**。

例句講解

- **Taipei is quite different from** what it was/used to be **twenty years ago.**
  （→先行詞和關代應為the city which，由what取代，作主詞）
  台北和二十年前大不相同。

- **No one knows** what it will happen next.
  （→先行詞和關代應為the thing which，由what取代，作受詞）
  沒有人知道下一步會發生什麼事。

- **What** I am worried about **is her health condition.**
  （→先行詞和關代應為the thing which，由what取代，作受詞）
  我所擔心的是她的健康狀況。

- **Do what** you think **is right.**
  （→先行詞和關代應為anything that，由what取代，作主詞）
  照你認為對的去做。

★注意要點

　　此句型也常合併起來在同一個句子中做比較。

- **We should not judge a man by what he has but by what he is.**
  我們不應該以一個人的財富來判斷這個人，而是要以他的為人來判斷。
  （what one is：一個人的為人；what one has：一個人的財富）

 隨堂測驗

( ) 1. _____ should be done should be done.

    (A) why   (B) which   (C) what   (D) whatever

( ) 2. It is not exactly _____ a child eats that truly matters, but how much time it stays in his mouth. 【學測】

    (A) why   (B) which   (C) what   (D) whatever

( ) 3. The telephone has changed beyond recognition in recent years. In both form and function, it has become totally different from _____ before. 【指考】

    (A) what was   (B) what it had   (C) which it was   (D) what it was

( ) 4. The world's largest collection of Khmer sculpture resides at Angkor, the former royal capital of Cambodia. The 7,000 pieces-full statues, heads and carved inscriptions－are breathtaking not only for their individual beauty, but also for _____ they represent: a road map to the origins of much of Southeast Asian culture. 【指考】

    (A) what   (B) which   (C) that   (D) when

解答： 1. (C) 2. (C) 3. (D) 4. (A)

解析：
①what代表的是「該被做的事」。
②重要的不是一個孩子吃了「什麼」，故用what。
③這邊是要說現在的電話與過去的做比較，用what it was最適合。
④代表著「什麼」樣的意義，故此處用what。

★ POINT 2-B what有關的慣用語與句型

❶ what is better → 更好的是

❶ what is worse → 更糟的是

❶ what we call/what is called = (the) so-called = and that is → 所謂的

❶ what I am today → 今天的我

❶ A is to B what C is to D → A之於B猶如C之於D

❶ what with A and (what with) B → 半因⋯⋯半因⋯⋯

❼ what by A and what by B → 半藉⋯⋯半藉⋯⋯

 例句講解

• **The store is well-decorated; what's more, the food the chef cooked is delicious.**

這家店的裝潢不錯,此外,廚師煮的菜也很好吃。

• **What with sickness and what with laziness, his homework has been delayed.**

一半因為生病,一半因為懶惰,所以他的作業遲交了。

隨堂測驗

( ) 1. Books are to mankind ＿＿＿＿＿ memory is to the individual.

     (A) what   (B) that   (C) whose   (D) whom

( ) 2. Can you tell me ＿＿＿＿＿ prevented him from coming last night?

     (A) why   (B) for which   (C) what   (D) the reason

( ) 3. He is a wise boy, and ＿＿＿＿ is more, he is diligent and obedient.

     (A) as   (B) that   (C) which   (D) what

( ) 4. A man is usually judged by ＿＿＿＿＿ he does.

     (A) whomever   (B) what   (C) that   (D) which

5. 半因戰爭，半因饑荒，這個國家幾乎滅亡了。

What _____ war and what _____ famine, the nation was almost terminated.

6. 半用賄賂，半用威脅，媽媽把她女兒的頭髮剪掉了。

What by _____ and what by _____, the mother had her daughter's hair cut.

7. 在這本小說裡，不懂魔法的人就是所謂的「麻瓜」。

In this novel, people who don't know magic are _____ "muggles."

解答： 1. (A) 2. (C) 3. (D) 4. (B)
5. with; with
6. bribe; threat
7. what we call/what is called/so-called

解析：
①譯：書對於人類的意義就如同記憶對於一個人的意義。
②使他昨晚不能來的是「什麼」。
③what表示更進一步要說明的事。
④what he does表示他做的事。

★ POINT 2-C ······必須要做的事就是······

❶ 句型架構

All(that)				
what	＋S＋	have(has)	to do is	＋(to)＋V...
The only thing		had	was	

❷ 此句型中的what為複合關係代名詞，引導名詞子句作主要子句的主詞，用**單數動詞**（is/was），不定詞（to V）作主詞補語。

❸ 動詞is/was之後也可以接原形動詞（VR）。

❹ what可用all that來替換，that為關代可省略。

例句講解

- In my opinion, what we students have to do is do our best to pass the exam.

  依我之見，我們學生必須要做的事就是盡力通過考試。

- To know the meanings and usages of the new English words, all you have to do is to consult the dictionary.

  為了瞭解英文單字的意義和用法，你必須要做的事就是查字典。

★延伸學習

have/has/had to的意思是「必須」，視句子意義可用其他動詞片語替換。

- What I can do is give Max a hug to make him feel better.

  我**所能做**的就是給我兒子一個擁抱讓他覺得好過些。

- All you need to do is press the button and the machine will be activated.

  你**所需要做的**就是壓下按鈕，機器就會啟動了。

⏰ 隨堂測驗

(　　) 1. No matter what other people say, _____ I want to know _____ the truth coming from you.　　　　　　　　　　　【英檢初級】

(A) that; is　　(B) what; are　　(C) all; is　　(D) all; are

(　　) 2. _____ a gardener in my house should do _____ water flowers every day and trim branches of trees once in a while. 【英檢初級】

(A) All; are　　(B) What that; are　　(C) If; is　　(D) What; is

(　　) 3. Now _____ he needs to do is _____ for what he has done.

(A) that; apologizing　　　　(B) things which; apologizing
(C) all; to apologize　　　　(D) what; apologized

(　　) 4. The whole construction scheme is not hard at all. _____ is more time.

(A) That we need　　　　(B) Which is needed
(C) What we need　　　　(D) What do we need

(　　) 5. Rice is to the Chinese _____ potatoes are to many Europeans.

(A) whose　　(B) that　　(C) what　　(D) which

解答：1. (C) 2. (D) 3. (C) 4. (C) 5. (C)

解析：
①all代指所有我想知道的事，視為單數，故be動詞使用is。
②what代指園丁在我家該做的事，視為單數，故後面使用is。
③all用來代指所有他需要做的事。
④what we need表示我們所需要的。
⑤譯：對華人來說米飯的地位就跟馬鈴薯在許多歐洲人心中一樣。

主題三 | 關係副詞及關係子句

★ **POINT 3-A** 關係副詞

❶ 關係副詞的定義

(1) 關係副詞為**連接詞＋副詞 = 連接詞＋介系詞＋名詞（代名詞）**

　　　　　　　= 介系詞＋關係代名詞

(2) 關係副詞連接**完整子句**就會是**名詞子句**

❷ 關係副詞的種類

功能 先行詞	副詞兼連接詞	（相等語）介詞＋關代
地點(place)	where	in/on at/from which
時間(time)	when	in/on at/during which
理由(reason)	why	=(for) which
方式(way, manner)	how	=(in) which

❸ 關係副詞的範例

介係詞+先行詞	先行詞	介系詞+關代+關係子句
at the speed	the speed	(at which)+S+V
at the rate	the rate	(at which)+S+V
by the method	the method	(by which)+S+V
by the process	the process	(by which)+S+V
to the extent	the extent	(to which)+S+V

against the standard	the standard	(against which)+S+V
in the 1990's	the 1990's	(in which)+S+V
during the 1990's	the 1990's	(during which)+S+V
in Tainan	Tainan	(in which)+S+V

例句講解

• **This is the city and I live in the city.**

→**This is the city and in the city I live.**（→連接詞＋介詞＋名詞）

→**This is the city in which I live.**（→介詞＋關代）

→**This is the city where I live.**（→關副）

　我就住在這城市。

• **Peddling is the way and he makes living by peddling.**

→ **Peddling is the way and by peddling he makes his living.**

　（→連接詞＋介詞＋名詞）

→ **Peddling is the way by which he makes his living.**（→介詞＋關代）

→ **Peddling is the way how he makes his living.**（→關副）

　沿街叫賣就是他謀生的方式。

• **The Stone Age is the period in which our primitive ancestors learned to use stone tools and weapons.**（→介詞＋關代）

= **The Stone Age is the period when our primitive ancestors learned to use stone tools and weapons.**（→關副）

　石器時代就是我們原始祖先學會使用石頭作為工具及武器的時代。

• **I lost my iPhone,** ⎧**and the cover of it is black.**
　　　　　　　　　　⎨**the cover of which is black.**
　　　　　　　　　　⎩**whose cover is black.**

我弄丟了我的iPhone，它的外殼是黑色的。

- **Give this prize to anyone whose composition is thought excellent.**

（→根據句意，應用表所有格的whose表示composition屬於anyone。）

只要有人覺得他的作文寫得絕佳，就把這獎金給他。

- **The workers are repairing the house whose windows are all broken.**

（→根據句意，應用所有格的 whose或是of which來表示windows屬於the house。）

那些工人在整修的那棟房子，所有窗戶玻璃都破了。

- **The sick man for whose sake you are doing all this work ought to be very grateful to you.**

（→for one's sake「為了某人的緣故」，形容詞子句中應用whose來取代 one's。）

你為了那病人的緣故而做了這些工作，他應該對你會很感激。

隨堂測驗

( ) 1. A supermarket is a large grocery（雜貨）＿＿＿＿ customers can select their purchases from open shelves and pay in cash for them at the exit. 【英檢初級】

(A) why   (B) how   (C) where   (D) when

( ) 2. The reason ＿＿＿＿ the Amazon rain forest is important is that nearly forty percent of the oxygen of the earth is producedthere. 【英檢初級】

(A) why   (B) how   (C) where   (D) when

( ) 3. Democracy has another merit. It allows criticism, and if there is no public criticism, there are bound to（注定）be hushed-up（秘密的）scandals. That is ＿＿＿＿ I believe in the Press, despite all its lies and vulgarity（粗俗）. 【英檢初級】

(A) why   (B) how   (C) where   (D) when

4. The pineapple was __(1)__ found in Paraguay and in the southern part of Brazil. Natives（當地人）planted the fruit across South and Central America and in the Caribbean region, __(2)__ Christopher Columbus first found it. 【學測】

(　) (1) (A) nearly　　　(B) recently　　(C) originally　　(D) shortly

(　) (2) (A) that　　　　(B) what　　　　(C) which　　　　(D) where

(　) 5. That is _____ green tea is so good for health. The only reported negativeeffect of drinking green tea is a possible allergicreaction and insomnia（失眠）due to the caffeine it contains. 【學測】

　　(A) whether　　(B) whenever　　(C) what　　　　(D) why

(　) 6. One of his books, the title of _____ caught my attention at the first sight, deals with the author's childhood. 【英檢初級】

　　(A) which　　　(B) what　　　　(C) where　　　　(D) who

(　) 7. They own an original Picasso painting, the value of _____ is more than a million dollars. 【TOEFL】

　　(A) where　　　(B) when　　　　(C) which　　　　(D) whose

8. 我買了一本雜誌，名字叫做《當代建築風格》。（中翻英）

I bought a magazine, _____ title（書名）is Contemporary Architectural Style（當代建築風格）. 【TOEFL】

解答：1. (C) 2. (A) 3. (A) 4. (1) C (2) D　5. (D) 6. (A) 7. (C) 8. whose

解析：

①where用來修飾前面的a large grocery。

②the reason why還可以把why改成that替換。

③why代表「我之所以信任媒體的原因」。

④(1)originally found表示一開始被發現。

(2)where用來代指前句所提到的地區。

⑤why用來表示綠茶有益身體健康的「原因」。

⑥which代指的是書。

⑦which代表的是原版的畢卡索畫作。

⑧whose用來表示那本「我買的雜誌」。

★ POINT 3-B 表達「這就是為何……」的句型

❶ 這是簡化的「解釋」句型，使句子更簡潔。句型為：

That's why/how/...＋S＋V... 那就是為何／如何的……（原因／方法）

❷ 關係副詞why/how/when/where語意上省略前面的先行詞the reason/ the way/the time/the place，後面則接名詞子句。

❸ 此句型也常保留先行詞而省略關係副詞，也就是That's the reason/ the way...。惟需注意the way與how不可連用。

例句講解

1. **She studies at least six hours a day. That's <u>how/the way that/the way in which she can make great progress in such a short time</u>.**
她每天唸書至少六個小時。那就是她能在這麼短時間內大幅進步的方法。

2. **He always laughs at me. That's (the reason) why <u>I don't like him</u>.**
他總是嘲笑我。那就是為什麼我不喜歡他的原因。

3. **That's how the newly-opened restaurant attracts customers. (○)**
   That's the way how the newly-opened restaurant attracts customers. (╳)
那就是這家新開的餐廳吸引客人的方法。

隨堂測驗

1. 他總是在我覺得挫折的時候鼓勵我。那就是我愛上他的原因。（中翻英）
He always encouraged me when I felt frustrated. That's _____ I fell in love with him.

(   ) 2. That's _____ I get along with people.（選錯）

(A) how   (B) the way how
(C) the way that   (D) the way in which

(　) 3. She does not see the reason _____ he would like to join them.

(A) why

(B) when

(C) how

(D) which

(　) 4. Could you please tell me the reason _____ made her feel so offended?

(A) why

(B) which

(C) what

(D) which is

(　) 5. Comprehensive reading of religious documents has changed _____ he thinks.

(A) the way

(B) when

(C) why

(D) in which

解答：1. why 2. (B) 3. (A) 4. (B) 5. (A)

解析：

①why表示「原因」。

②譯：那就是我和人們相處的方式。

③The reason why表示「……的原因」。

④Which用來表示reason。

⑤此處的the way也可以改成how。

主題四 | 複合關係副詞

❶ 定義：

複合關係副詞，顧名思義就是在原有的關係詞上加上ever。使文意增加了「無論」或「任何」。

❷ 引導副詞子句時，複合關係副詞對等列表

whatever	=no matter what	無論什麼
whoever	=no matter who(m)	無論是誰
whichever	=no matter which	無論哪一個
whenever	=no matter when	無論何時
wherever	=no matter where	無論何處
however	=no matter how	無論如何

例句講解

- **Whoever <u>comes</u> will be welcomed.**

  任何人來都是被歡迎的。

- **Whichever <u>wins</u>, it will make no difference to me.**

  無論哪個獲勝，對我來說都是一樣的。

- **However <u>clever you may be</u>, you will not make out the meaning of this sentence.**

  無論你有多聰明，你都猜不出這句話的意思。

- **You may come whenever <u>it is convenient to you</u>.**

  你可以在任何你覺得方便的時候過來。

★注意要點

whatever/who(m)ever/whichever 當句子中的**主格**或**受格**。

- <u>Whoever</u> says so is wrong. 無論誰這麼說都是錯的。

　　主詞

- <u>Whatever</u> I have is yours. 無論我有什麼都是你的。

　　主詞

- You may give it to <u>whoever</u> likes it. 你可以把它給任何喜歡它的人。

　　　　　　　受詞

- You may give it to <u>whomever</u> you like. 你可以把它給任何你喜歡的人。

　　　　　　　受詞

- You can choose the pink handbag or the red backpack. Whichever is five hundred dollars. （→whichever 用做主詞）

  你可以選購粉紅色的手提包或是紅色的背包。價錢都一樣。

- The President is determined to resist whatever he regards as blackmail by the terrorists. （→用whatever接後面缺受詞的子句。）

  總統決心要反抗所有他認為是恐怖份子的勒索。

- I dislike his personality, so I refuse all his proposals, for whatever reason. （→用whatever修飾後面的名詞。）

  我不喜歡他的個性，因此我拒絕了他所有的提案，無論是為了什麼理由。

★ POINT 4-A ...whatever＋S＋V... 任何……

❶ whatever為複合關係代名詞，等於anything that，引導**名詞子句**，指事或物，但不能指人，為what的強調用法。

❷ 此句型中，主要子句為不完整子句（即子句缺主詞、受詞或補語），而 whatever引導的名詞子句可作為主要子句的**主詞**、**受詞**或**補語**。

例句講解

* **Whatever <u>you choose</u> is best choice for me.**
（→whatever you choose**為整句主詞**）

你所做的任何選擇對我而言都是最好的選擇。

* **When the patient was recovered, he could eat whatever <u>he liked</u>.**
（→whatever he liked**為整句受詞**）

當病人康復了，他可以吃任何他喜歡吃的東西。

* **The best gift for him is whatever <u>his girlfriend bought</u>.**
（→whatever his girlfriend bought**為整句補語**）

對他來說，任何他女朋友買的禮物就是最棒的禮物。

★延伸學習

whatever後面若引導副詞子句，則意義為「無論什麼……」，相當於「no matter what...」。

* **Whatever <u>the result may be</u>, he has done his best to express his opinions.**
= **No matter what <u>the result may be</u>, he has done his best to express his opinions.**

無論結果是什麼，他已經盡力表達他的意見了。

* **Whatever <u>the president will eat</u> should be carefully checked.**
（→名詞子句）

總統要吃的任何東西都應該仔細檢查過。

【學測】

⏰ 隨堂測驗

( ) 1. _____ you go, there are buildings in Romanic, Baroque, and Rococo styles that were popular hundreds of years ago.　【學測】

(A) Since　　　(B) Before　　　(C) Whatever　　(D) Wherever

( ) 2. The disciple said he would do _____ his guru asked him to do.
　　　　　　　　　　　　　　　　　　　　　　　　　　　　　　　　　　　　【學測】

(A) whatever　　　　　　　　　(B) no matter where

(C) whichever　　　　　　　　　(D) whenever

( ) 3. _____ I set foot on the soil of Rwanda, a country in eastcentral Africa, I feel as if I have entered paradise.　　　【學測】

(A) Wherever　　　　　　　　　(B) Whenever

(C) Whatever　　　　　　　　　(D) No matter how

( ) 4. But _____ a child eats, brushing after each meal is still the best way to fight cavities.　　　　　　　　　　　　　　【學測】

(A) however　　　　　　　　　(B) no matter what

(C) whenever　　　　　　　　　(D) no matter which

解答： 1. (D) 2. (A) 3. (B) 4. (B)

解析：

①「無論去哪裡」用wherever。

②whatever表示無論guru要他做什麼，他都會照做。

③whenever表示每當我踏上盧安達的時候。

④譯：無論小孩吃什麼，要預防蛀牙最好的方法還是飯後刷牙。

★ POINT 4-B ...whoever＋V... 任何……的人

❶ 此句型中，whoever為複合關係代名詞，等於anyone who、he who、one who、the (a) man who，是**主格**用法，後面接**單數動詞**。

❷ 複合關係代名詞是當主格或受格，與前面的介系詞或動詞無關，而是以其在所引導的名詞子句的地位而定。

❸ whoever為後面引導的**名詞子句**的主詞，同時此名詞子句也是主要的主詞。

❹ whoever本身為後面引導的名詞子句的主詞，但其所引導的名詞子句則為主要句的受詞，不因介系詞with之故而用whomever。

例句講解

• Whoever <u>wants to participate in the activity</u> can sign his name here.
（→whoever為名詞子句的主詞，整個名詞子句為主句的主詞）

凡想參加此活動的人都可以在此簽名。

• Whoever <u>was infected the contagious disease</u> should avoid going to the public places.
（→whoever為名詞子句的主詞，整個名詞子句為主句的主詞）

任何染上傳染性疾病的人都應該避免到公共場所去。

• Please share this good news with whoever <u>wants to know about it</u>.
（→whoever為名詞子句的主詞，整個名詞子句為主句的主詞）

請將這些好消息分享給任何想知道的人。

★延伸學習

whoever除了當複合關係代名詞外，也可以當複合關係副詞，相當於no matter who，後面引導**副詞子句**，解釋為「不論誰」。以下例句中，whoever引導**表讓步的副詞子句**，whoever為子句中的主詞，同時也是整個句子的**連接詞**。

- Whoever <u>is invited to the party</u>, the host will welcome him very much.

= No matter who <u>is invited to the party</u>, the host will welcome him very much.

不論是誰受邀參加派對，主辦者都非常歡迎。

- Whoever <u>finds this notebook</u>, please send it to the address written on the cover of the notebook.

= No matter who <u>finds this notebook</u>, please send it to the address written on the cover of the notebook.

不論是誰找到了這本筆記，請把它寄到筆記本封面上寫的地址。

隨堂測驗

( ) 1. _____ still has problems about this chapter can ask your teacher in private. 【英檢初級】

(A) Those (B) Whatever

(C) Whoever (D) People

( ) 2. The teacher will give a special gift to _____ can answer this difficult question. 【英檢初級】

(A) people (B) these

(C) whomever (D) whoever

( ) 3. _____ told you this story must be full of imagination.

(A) Anyone (B) Whoever

(C) The people (D) Whenever

( ) 4. Mother Teresa offered a helping hand to _____ was in need of help.

(A) those (B) people

(C) whoever (D) whichever

( ) 5. _____ she may marry, she won't be happy.

(A) whoever (B) however

(C) whenever (D) wherever

6. 任何收到請柬的人都可以來參加我們的婚禮。 【英檢初級】

_____ has received the invitation can come to our wedding.

7. 這份精美的禮品只送給任何申辦這家銀行信用卡的人。 【英檢初級】

This _____ present is only given to _____ applies for the credit card of this bank.

解答： 1. (C) 2. (D) 3. (B) 4. (C) 5. (A)
6. Whoever 7. exquisite; whoever

解析：
①whoever代表「任何還有問題的人」。
②whoveer代表「任何可以回答這個難題的人」。
③whoever代表「任何告訴你這個故事的人」。
④whoever代表「任何需要幫助的人」。
⑤whoever代表「任何她可能嫁的人」

★ POINT 4-C ...whenever＋S＋V 無論何時、每次

...wherever＋S＋V 無論何處

...however＋adj./adv.＋S＋V 無論如何

whenever為複合關係代名詞，等於every time以及no matter when，引導表時間的**副詞子句**。

wherever則等於no matter where引導表地方的副詞子句。

however 後面則一定要接 adj./adv.，表示無論……的狀態。

 例句講解

- Every time <u>I travel abroad</u>, I always carry the charm my mother gave me.

= Whenever <u>I travel abroad</u>, I always carry the charm my mother gave me.

= No matter when <u>I travel abroad</u>, I always carry the charm my mother gave me.

  每次我出國旅行，我總是帶著我母親給我的護身符。

- Every time <u>she was in a bad mood</u>, she ate a lot of fast food.

= Whenever <u>she was in a bad mood</u>, she ate a lot of fast food.

= No matter when <u>she was in a bad mood</u>, she ate a lot of fast food.

  每次她心情不好時，她就會吃很多速食。

- Wherever <u>Tom traveled</u>, he couldn't stop thinking of his country, Taiwan.

= No matter where <u>Tom traveled</u>, he couldn't stop thinking of his country, Taiwan.

  不管湯姆旅行到何處，他都無法停止不想他的家鄉，台灣。

- However strong <u>their child is</u>, parents still think it's their responsibility to protect him.

= No matter how strong <u>their child is</u>, parents still think it's their responsibility to protect him.

  不論孩子有多強壯，父母親仍認為保護他是他們的責任。

- However carefully **you checked the paper,** there were still some mistakes found by the professor.
= No matter how carefully **you checked the paper,** there were still some mistakes found by the professor.

不管你有多仔細檢查過你的論文，還是會有錯誤被教授挑出。

隨堂測驗

( ) 1. Mia was on the verge of nervous breakdown. She insisted that _____ she went, her English teacher, James, stalked her.

   (A) wherever (B) whichever   (C) whatever   (D) whoever

( ) 2. Jeremy Lin is the perfect example that we should never lose hope, _____ disappointed and helpless we are.

   (A) whenever (B) whatever   (C) however   (D) whichever

( ) 3. _____ I call my boyfriend, he always tells me that he is busy.

   (A) When   (B) Whenever   (C) Why   (D) Wherever

( ) 4. I will discuss it with you _____ you like.

   (A) where   (B) when   (C) whenever   (D) wherever

( ) 5. Whenever he was bored, he turned on the radio and listened to _____ program was on.

   (A) however (B) whatever   (C) any   (D) which

解答：1. (A) 2. (C) 3. (B) 4. (C) 5. (B)

解析：
①wherever表示「無論哪裡」。
②however=no matter how
③whenever表示「每當我打給男朋友的時候」
④whenever表示「任何時間」
⑤whatever表示「任何節目」

主題五 | 關係代名詞that的限定用法

在以下情況時，所有的關係代名詞都只能用that表示。

❶ **最高級**形容詞，如：the greatest/the smallest

❷ **序數**，如：the first/the last

❸ **限定意義**較強的形容詞，如：the only/the main/the chief/the very

❹ 先行詞為：no/any/all/both/much/each/every/anything

❺ 先行詞為：**人與非人**並列時

❻ 先行詞為：who/which為首的問句為避免重覆

❼ that 之前無**逗點**及**介系詞**

例句講解

- **Try to figure out the main idea that <u>is between the lines</u>.**
  （→先行詞限定意義強）

  試著去找出字裡行間的主旨。

- **He is one of the best teacher that <u>our school has ever had</u>.**
  （→先行詞為最高級形容詞）

  他是我們學校從以前到現在最好的老師。

- **Was it you or the wind that <u>shut the door</u>?**
  （→先行詞為人與非人並列）

  是你還是風把門關上的？

★注意要點

分裂強調句It is/was＋**強調部分**＋that（關代）＋**剩餘結構**

sb.→**who /whom**

sth.　→**which**

　　　　　　地方副詞　→**where**

　　　　　　時間副詞　→**when**

- **James** broke <u>a vase in the living room yesterday</u>.
  詹姆士昨天在客廳打破了花瓶。

→It was James <u>that broke a vase</u> in the living room yesterday.
  是詹姆士昨天在客廳打破花瓶的。

→It was a vase <u>that James broke</u> in the living room yesterday.
  昨天詹姆士在客廳打破的是花瓶。

→It was in the living room <u>that James broke a vase</u> yesterday.
  詹姆士是在客廳打破花瓶的。

→It was yesterday <u>that James broke a vase</u> in the living room.
  詹姆士是昨天在客廳打破花瓶的。

隨堂測驗

(　　) 1. This is the poem _____ he has written up to the present.

(A) whoever　　　　　　　(B) that

(C) what　　　　　　　　(D) where

(　　) 2. Much _____ had been said about her proved true.

(A) which　　　　　　　(B) who

(C) what　　　　　　　　(D) that

(　　) 3. Every student _____ attended the class was deeply impressed.

(A) those　　　　　　　(B) them

(C) this　　　　　　　　(D) that

( ) 4. All (the things) _____ glitter are not gold. = All _____ glitters is not gold.

(A) those
(B) that
(C) who
(D) what

( ) 5. Is there anything in this book _____ is worth reading?

(A) which
(B) who
(C) that
(D) whom

( ) 6. Look at the man and his donkey _____ are walking up the street.

(A) which
(B) who
(C) that
(D) whom

( ) 7. Who _____ saw the accident will not feel sorry?

(A) where
(B) which
(D) those
(D) that

解答： 1. (B) 2. (D) 3. (D) 4. (B) 5. (C) 6. (C) 7. (D)

解析：
①譯：這是他到現在為止所寫的詩。
②譯：很多關於她的謠傳都被證實是真的。
③譯：每個參加這個課程的學生都非常印象深刻。
④譯：所有那些亮亮的東西都不是金子。
⑤譯：在這本書裡有任何值得閱讀的東西嗎？
⑥譯：看看那個在街上走的男人還有他的驢子。
⑦譯：有誰目睹了意外不會替對方感到抱歉？

主題六 關係子句的限定及非限定用法

	限定用法	非限定用法
定義	修飾並限定先行詞	補充、說明、唯一或專指之先行詞
形式	關代之前沒逗點	關代之前有逗點
特性	1. 可使用關代that 2. 關代為受格可省略	1. 不可使用關代that 2. 關代為受格不可省

例句講解

• **I met Jay's girlfriend who <u>lived in Taipei</u>.**（→Jay's girlfriend≧2）
  我遇到傑住在台北的女朋友。

• **I met Jay's girlfriend, who <u>lived in Taipei</u>.**（→Jay's girlfriend=1）
  我遇到傑的女朋友，而她住在台北。

• **The convict, whom <u>many people are afraid of</u>, just escaped from the prison.**（→The convict =1）
  那個令人聞風喪膽的罪犯，剛剛越獄了。

★注意要點

　　關代之前有逗點→非限定用法→後翻譯

　　關代之前無逗點→限定用法→先翻譯

• **I live in a town (X) which <u>is situated in a valley</u>.**
  我住的小鎮位於山谷裡。

• **Vivi (,) who <u>speaks Japanese</u>, should apply for the job.**
  會說日文的薇薇，應該要應徵那份工作。

- **Rice (,) which <u>is grown in many countries,</u> is a staple food**（主食）
throughout much of the world.

在許多國家都有生長的稻米，在世界各地都被當作主食。

隨堂測驗

( ) 1. He was trapped in a traffic jam, _____ made him late for his appointment.

(A) that　　　　　　　　(B) which
(C) what　　　　　　　　(D) and

( ) 2. I gave him a warning, _____ he turned a deaf ear.

(A) of what　　　　　　　(B) for which
(C) to that　　　　　　　(D) to which

解答：1. (B) 2. (D)

解析：
①which代指前面主要子句的那件事。
②he turn a deaf ear to...他假裝沒聽見，而which則是代指前面子句説的事。

滿分追擊模擬試題

1. For instance, many satellites in space are equipped with large panels __(1)__ solar cells transform sunlight directly __(2)__ electric power.

【指考】

( ) (1) (A) what   (B) which   (C) whose   (D) when

( ) (2) (A) with   (B) for   (C) to   (D) into

( ) 2. Whether simple or lavish, proms have always been more or less traumatic events for adolescents _____ worry about selfimage and fitting in with their peers. 【學測】

(A) what   (B) who   (C) that   (D) when

( ) 3. Gateway drugs are substances (which) people take that _____ them to take more drugs. 【指考】

(A) lead   (B) leads   (C) leading   (D) led

( ) 4. The retiring teacher made a speech _____ she thanked the class for the gift.

(A) in which   (B) which   (C) that   (D) what

( ) 5. This is exactly the house _____.

(A) where he lives in   (B) which he lives

(C) where he lives   (D) in that he lives

( ) 6. She does not see the reason _____ he would like to join them.

(A) why   (B) when   (C) how   (D) which

( ) 7. The day will soon come _____ humankind will set foot on another planet.

(A) which   (B) when   (C) why   (D) where

(   ) 8. You cannot succeed without perseverance, _____ you may go.

(A) whenever (B) whatever   (C) however   (D) wherever

(   ) 9. Give this to _____ you think can do the work well.

(A) that   (B) whom   (C) whomever   (D) whoever

(   ) 10. Thank you very much for _____ you have done for my sister.

(A) whenever (B) whichever   (C) whomever   (D) whatever

(   ) 11. Joe believed without question _____ in his daily newspaper.

(A) about what he read   (B) of what he read

(C) whatever he read   (D) whichever he read

(   ) 12. John was the only person _____ I had invited to the wedding.

(A)which   (B) that   (C) whom   (D) who

(   ) 13. She is the very _____ we have been seeking for years.

(A)that   (B) one   (C) who   (D) one who

(   ) 14. Coronavirus may be the most frightening disease _____ we have met with so far.

(A) which   (B) because   (C) whichever   (D) that

解答

1. (1) (C) whose代指的是large panels。

　(2) (D) 先行詞是large panels（大型面板）依文意可知，上面的太陽能電池可以把太陽光直接轉成（turn into）電能。所以，此處用所有格，表示面板的太陽能電池。

2. (B) who用以代指adolescents。

3. (A) 會讓吸食的人吸食更多毒品的就是前面所述的入門毒品這種物質(substances)。此處空格正前方的that是代指前面的substances，是複數名詞，故選(A)的複數動詞。※注意，這裡不用C，因為關代that並無省略。

4. (A) 從空格中可知，我們需要一個字代替前面的a speech，而後面的形容詞子句應為she thanked the class for the gift in the speech，speech不當受格，而是指在這個演講中，選(A)。

5. (C) 譯：這間房子就是他住的地方。

6. (A) 譯：她看不出他要加入他們的原因。

7. (B) when表示人類踏上另一顆星球的時機。

8. (D) wherever表示無論哪裡。

9. (D) whoever代表任何你覺得可以把工作做好的人。

10. (D) whatever代表任何你為我妹妹所做的事。

11. (C) Joe毫無疑問的相信他在報上所讀到的東西。Without question（無疑地）是副詞，所以此處所需要的是believed後的受格。believe是及物動詞，又因為文意中沒有指定所相信的範圍，不能選whichever，故選(C)。

12. (B) John是唯一一個我邀請到婚禮的人。

13. (B) 空格前的the very是形容詞，不能當代名詞，所以此空格一定需要一個前面可接形容詞的代名詞（所以(A)/(C)不行）。而(D)選項的錯誤點，是因為先行詞用the very 修飾，不能用who，要用that。

14. (D) 冠狀病毒大概是截至目前為止我們碰過最可怕的疾病。

Part 5

so(such)...that/enough to/
too...to 等用法及感嘆句

Part5

so (such)...that/enough to/ too...to 等用法及感嘆句

　　so/such都是常見的易混淆的修飾語，要搞懂enough到底該放在要修飾的字的前面還是後面更有難度。但其實這些句型都具有文意類似可替換的特性，所以學了可以用在作文中當代換句型喔！

　　so...that.../ such...that...兩者都是用來表達「如此……以致於……」，但兩者用法不太一樣。So是副詞，後面要接形容詞或副詞，而such後面則要接名詞。另外，當such後面為有形容詞的名詞片語時，並且為可數單數名詞，則可以和so...that...句型互換。

例句講解

- **Mom has <u>such a big kitchen</u> that it's hard for her to clean it.**
= **Mom has <u>so big a kitchen</u> that it's hard for her to clean it.**
　媽媽的廚房很大，所以很難清理。

主題一 | 表「如此……以至於……」的句型

★ **POINT 1-A** so/such...that... 如此……以至於及相關用法

❶ 句型要點：

so（adj.＋**冠詞**＋N）that＋子句

such（**冠詞**＋adj.＋N）that＋子句

＝ so...as to＋VR（原形動詞）

＝ such...as to＋VR（原形動詞）

＝ adj.＋enough＋to VR（原形動詞）

❷ 若出現名詞為**單數可數名詞**時，要注意冠詞a/an的位置，判斷使用 so/such。

❸ 若出現**複數名詞**或**不可數名詞**，要使用such。

❹ 若名詞前面出現many/much/few/little修飾的話，要使用so。

例句講解

• **James is such a hard-working student that all the teachers like him.**
（→such＋冠詞＋adj.＋N＋that＋子句）

= **James is so hard-working a student that all the teachers like him.**
（→so＋adj.＋冠詞＋N＋that ＋子句）

　詹姆士是如此用功的學生，以至於所有的老師都喜歡他。

• **These are such delicate antique vases that they cost a fortune.**
（→such＋複數N＋that＋子句）

　這些是如此精緻的古董花瓶，價值一大筆錢。

• **We were in such confusion that we didn't know what to do.**
（→such＋不可數N＋that＋子句）

　我們是如此迷惑，以至於不知道該怎麼辦。

- **He ate so** much delicious food **that he was putting on weight.**
（→so＋much＋不可數N＋that＋子句）

　他吃了這麼多美食，以至於變胖了。

- **He spent so** little time **on his schoolwork that he fell way behind his classmates.**
（→so＋little＋不可數N＋that＋子句）

　他花在課業上的時間如此少，以至於比同學落後許多。

★延伸學習

　　❶ such與so的分別頗為類似感嘆句中what與how。

- **It was such pleasant weather that we all enjoyed our holidays there.**
　天氣如此宜人，以至於我們在那裡渡過了愉快的假期。

- **She is such a lovely child that we all adore her.**
- **= She is so lovely a child that we all adore her.**
　她是如此可愛的孩子，以至於我們都愛她。

　　❷ so和such 都可以放在句首，但主要子句**要倒裝**。

- **James is so kind that everyone is his friend.**
- **= Such a kind person is James that everyone is his friend.**
- **= So kind is James that everyone is his friend.**
　詹姆士是那麼仁慈以至於每個人都是他的朋友。

- **I was so stunned that I could hardly speak.**
- **= So stunned was I that I could hardly speak.**
　我是如此目瞪口呆，以至於說不出話來。

　　❸ such也可以用來**替代某名詞**，如果放在句首，後面主要子句要**倒裝**。

- **Such was my amazement that I forgot what to say.**
　我是如此的驚訝，以至於忘了該說什麼。

- **Such was the amazing sight that they couldn't take their eyes off it.**
　那個景象如此驚人，以至於他們無法把眼光移開。

 隨堂測驗

( ) 1. They are _____ clever geniuses that they always come up with innovative ideas.

(A) so   (B) such

(C) how   (D) what

( ) 2. He ate _____ delicious food at the restaurant that he felt quite contented.

(A) so   (B) such

(C) how   (D) much

( ) 3. She has _____ friends that she hardly knows how to get along with others.

(A) such few   (B) so little

(C) such little   (D) so few

( ) 4. He is _____ man that many women fall in love with him at first sight.

(A) such handsome a

(B) such a handsome

(C) so a handsome

(D) so handsome

( ) 5. I am studying so hard for the forthcoming entrance exam _____ I do have the luxury of a free weekend to rest. 【學測】

(A) which   (B) that

(C) what   (D) thus

6. 他口才這麼好，以至於我們很快就接受他的想法。

He talked _____ eloquently _____ we were soon convinced of his ideas.

7. 那些是如此昂貴的進口車，以至於普通人是買不起的。

Those are _____ expensive imported cars _____ ordinary people cannot afford them.

8. 他是如此興奮所以到處宣布這個消息。

_____ was _____ that he went around telling people about the good news.

解答： 1. (B) 2. (B) 3. (D) 4. (B) 5. (B)
6. so; that 7. such; that 8. So excited; he

解析：
①such後接adj.＋N。
②同第一題。
③Few friends為要修飾的字，故搭配so。
④such後接冠詞＋adj.＋N。
⑤so...that

★ POINT 1-B so...as to的用法

　　so...as to＋V的句型和so...that... 的句型相同，主要子句和從屬子句的主詞相同時，就可以改成so...as to＋V的句型。so...as to表「如此……以至於……」，so as not to＋V表「為了不要……」。

 例句講解

• James is so **tall** that he can touch the ceiling.
= James is such **a tall boy** that he can touch the ceiling.
= James is so **tall** as to touch the ceiling.
= James is **tall** so as to touch the ceiling.
　　詹姆士高得可以摸到天花板。

• At the party, she looked so **charming** that she catches everybody's eye.
= At the party, she looked so **charming** as to catch everybody's eye.
　　在舞會上，她看起來如此迷人，以至於吸引了每個人的目光。

• He studied so **hard** that he will not fall behind in his schoolwork.
= He studied so **hard** as not to fall behind in his schoolwork.
　　他用功讀書是為了不要在課業上落後。

★延伸學習

　　比較so as to的用法

　　so as to＋V = in order to＋V = so that＋cl. 表「為了」

• I study hard in order to get into my ideal university.
= I study hard so as to get into my ideal university.
= I study hard so that I can get into my ideal university.
　　我很用功讀書，為了能進入我理想的大學。

(　　) 1. He worked part-time _____ his way through college.

　　(A) in order that　(B) so that　　　(C) such as to　　(D) so as to

(　　) 2. She walked on tiptoe _____ awake the sleeping baby.

　　(A) so as not　　(B) so that not　(C) so as not to　(D) so as to

(　　) 3. He was _____ rude _____ say that.

　　(A) so; as to　　　(B) so; as not to　(C) such; as to　　(D) such; as no to

(　　) 4. She dressed herself up _____ elegantly _____ get everyone's admiration at the class reunion.

　　(A) so; and to　　(B) such a; to　　(C) so; as to　　(D) such; as to

(　　) 5. The boy made _____ much noise _____ attract everybody's attention.

　　(A) so; as not to　(B) so; as to　　　(C) such; as to　　(D) such; as no to

6. 她輕易地相信他的話。（中翻英）

She was _____ credulous that she believed him.

= She was so credulous _____ believe him.

解答：1. (D)　2. (C)　3. (A)　4. (C)　5. (B)　6. so; as to

解析：

① so as to表示「為了」。

② so as not to表示「為了不要」。

③ 譯：他這樣說話真的很失禮。

④so修飾elegantly，as to表示為了。

⑤so修飾much noises，as to用來表示目的。

⑥so; as to

★ POINT 1-C 容易混淆的so that用法

so that視其在句中的不同位置，會有不同的意義及用法

(1) 置於句**中**其前**無**逗點，表**目的**，中譯：**為了** = in order that＋子句

(2) 置於句**中**其前**有**逗點，表**結果**，中譯：**如此一來** = ; as a result, 子句

(3) 置於句**首**其前**無**逗點，表**條件**，中譯：**只要** = as long as＋子句

例句講解

• **Tom behaves badly in class so that his teacher will punish him and make him sit on the girl's side of the classroom.** 【龍騰】
（→so that **置於句中其前無逗點，表目的**）

湯姆在課堂上表現很差，為了懲罰他，老師安排他坐在教室裡的女生區中。

• **Climb higher, so that you can get a better view.**
（→so that **置於句中其前有逗點，表結果**）

爬高一點，這樣你才能得到更好的視野。

• **So that I grow up, you don't have to worry about our family.**
（→so that **置於句首其前無逗點，表條件**）

只要我長大，你就不用為家裡擔心。

隨堂測驗

( ) 1. Animals are able to feel pain _____ they can use it for self-protection.

　　(A) although　　(B) because　　(C) when　　(D) so that

( ) 2. To gain more publicity, some legislators（立法委員）would get into violent physical fights _____ they may appear in TV news reports. 【學測】

　　(A) so that　　(B) for fear that　　(C) lest　　(D) which

( ) 3. Mrs. Lee put on her reading glasses _____ she could read the fine print at the bottom of the contract.

(A) as long as (B) such that
(C) as a result (D) in order that

( ) 4. Julie wants to buy a portable computer _____ she can carry it around when she travels. 【學測】

(A) so that (B) for fear that
(C) lest (D) which

( ) 5. Give him humanity, _____ he may always remember the simplicity of true greatness, the open mind of true wisdom, and the meekness of true strength.

(A) as long as (B) such that
(C) so that (D) in order that

解答： 1. (D) 2. (A) 3. (D) 4. (A) 5. (C)

解析：
①譯：動物可以感覺到痛，如此一來才能自保。
②So that可以用來表示目的。
③In order that可以用來表示目的，that後面要接子句，若是in order to，則後面要接原形動詞。
④So that用來表示目的。
⑤同上一題。

主題二 | 感嘆句

❶ 感嘆句基本上有兩種，包括以What和How開頭的句子。

(1) 感嘆句：How＋adv./adj./cl.（子句）句意：……是多麼地／如此地

(2) 感嘆句：What＋a/an＋adj.＋N

❷ 感嘆句中what與how的分別

(1) How後面可以加上形容詞、副詞或子句，但是要搭配後面主要子句的句型，不可胡亂使用。

(2) 以What開始的句子，後面一定要加上名詞，可以是單數名詞、複數名詞、不可數名詞等。如果是不可數或複數名詞，一律用What...!

例句講解

• **How gracefully they danced in the ballroom!**
（→主要子句的動詞是一般動詞，所以前面要用副詞修飾）
  他們在舞池裡的舞姿多麼優雅呀！

• **How insanely she behaved in front of others!**
（→主要子句的動詞是一般動詞，所以前面要用副詞修飾）
  她在人前表現得多麼瘋狂呀！

• **How beautiful she looks on stage!**
（→主要子句的動詞是連綴動詞，所以前面要用形容詞修飾）
  她在舞臺上看起來多麼美麗呀！

• **How insane she has become!**
（→主要子句的動詞是連綴動詞，所以前面要用形容詞修飾）
  她變得多麼瘋狂呀！

- **How he wishes he were a rich man who could afford such a luxurious trip!**

（→主要子句中，沒有形容詞或副詞，所以直接接子句）

他多麼希望自己是個有錢人，可以負擔得起這麼奢華的旅程！

- **What charming eyes she has!**

（→what後接複數名詞）

她所擁有的，是多麼迷人的眼睛呀！

★注意要點

　　要讚嘆的是**單數可數名詞**時，須要注意不定冠詞 a/an 的位置，來決定該以 What或How開頭。以下的例句，請注意 a/an的位置，因為位置的不同，就要用不同的感嘆詞。

- **What a precious experience it is to go abroad for further studies!**
- **= How precious an experience it is to go abroad for further studies!**

可以出國留學是多麼珍貴的經驗呀！

隨堂測驗

(　　) 1. _____ difficult math problems we have to solve!

    (A) What　　　　　　　　　　(B) What a

    (C) How　　　　　　　　　　　(D) How much

(　　) 2. _____ she has changed over the years!

    (A) How　　　　　　　　　　　(B) What

    (C) That　　　　　　　　　　　(D) Which

(　　) 3. Boll's wife fails to understand _____ her husband feels after the destruction of Hiroshima.　　　　　　　　　　【指考】

    (A) how troubled

    (B) how troubling

    (C) what trouble

    (D) what troubled

( ) 4. Rap's rise and sustained global popularity is a good illustration of
_____ youth culture is on youth attitudes and behavior.　【學測】

(A) how influence (B) what influence
(C) how influential (D) how influentially

( ) 5. _____ the sunrise looks!

(A) What magnificent (B) How magnificent
(C) What magnificently (D) How magnificently

解答： 1. (A) 2. (A) 3. (A) 4. (C) 5. (B)

解析：
① what修飾的是difficult math problems。
② 此處感嘆這些年來她變了多少，用how最適合。
③ 這邊要講的是「有多困擾」，因此用how最適合。
④「多有影響力」，因此用C。
⑤日落看起來有多壯觀，用how+形容詞

滿分追擊模擬試題

( ) 1. _____ a creative scientist he was to have come up with such a solution to the problem.

    (A) What   (B) How   (C) So   (D) Such

( ) 2. Sue is _____ clumsy that she always breaks something when she is shopping at a store. 【學測】

    (A) so   (B) such   (C)how   (D)what

( ) 3. _____ considerate a gentleman he is to have thought of that in advance!

    (A) How   (B) What   (C) So   (D) Such

( ) 4. However, candy and other things that children like are on lower shelves _____ children can see them easily and ask their parents to buy them.

    (A) so as for   (B) as far as   (C) so that   (D) as long as

( ) 5. The low-pressure center of a tornado is _____ a powerful vacuum _____ it can tear the roofs from houses or suck the corks from bottles.

    (A) so; that   (B) so; enough that

    (C) such; enough that   (D) such; that

( ) 6. _____ agreeable a weather is it that I would like to take a stroll for a while.

    (A) How   (B) What   (C) So   (D) Such

( ) 7. We _____ the importance of punctuality.

    (A) cannot hardly emphasize   (B) cannot over-emphasize

    (C) cannot emphasize   (D) cannot too emphasize

( ) 8. This machine is _____ complex _____ be used every day.

(A) too; to   (B) X; enough   (C) too; enough   (D) X; to

( ) 9. Steve's description of the place was _____ vivid that I could almost picture it in my mind. 【學測】

(A) how   (B) what   (C) so   (D) such

( ) 10. Celebrities in the rally probably have no idea about _____ a CD of their music albums costs. 【指考】

(A) so much   (B) how much   (C) what much   (D) that much

( ) 11. _____ smart boys they are to be able to answer such difficult questions!

(A) How   (B) What a   (C) What   (D) How a

( ) 12. _____ sight I saw!

(A) How terrible   (B) What terrible a

(C) How terrible a   (D) What terrible

( ) 13. He studies _____ hard _____ get the highest score in every exam.

(A) so; to   (B) so; enough to   (C) so; that   (D) so; as to

14. 你開車時應格外小心。

15. 夜晚來臨了，天氣太冷而使得Soapy無法在中央公園睡覺。 【指考】

16. 我們在巴黎觀光時，天氣是多麼好呀！

1. (A) 一個多麼有創意的科學家，用what修飾。

2. (A) clumsy是形容詞，其前方只能用so或 how，但此處只是修飾後面的 clumsy，並不是感嘆句，因此選(A)。

3. (A) 修飾considerate用how。

4. (C) 空格之後是有主詞（children）與動詞（can see）的子句。(B) as far as S be concerned 就……而言；(D) as long as 只要（表條件）。此處文意為：因為孩子喜歡的東西在下層，所以他們可以輕易地看到這些商品。是因果關係，所以選(C) 如此一來；所以。

5. (D) such...that 如此……以至於

6. (C) 此處是so/such...that 句型的倒裝句，原句應為It is so agreeable a weather that I would...。因為空格後是agreeable，為形容詞，故選(C)。

7. (B) 我們再怎麼強調準時也不為過，是否定字與over-V的連用，故選(B)。

8. (A) too...to 太……以至於

9. (C) so...that

10. (B) 這裡是問音樂專輯的CD花費多少錢，所以選(B)。

11. (C) what修飾smart boys

12. (C) How＋adj.＋冠詞＋N → What＋（adj.）＋N。故選(C)。

13. (D) so as to表示目的。

14. You cannot be careful enough when driving.

15. The night came, and it was too cold for Soapy to sleep in Central Park.

16. What lovely weather we had while we went sight-seeing in Paris.

Part 6

形容詞變化法

Part6
形容詞變化法

　　國中就學過初階的形容詞變化法則，但此章節必須要了解的是跟比較級或最高級相關的句型變化。閱讀文章時，讀懂這些句型可以明白作者的弦外之音，寫作時使用這些句型，可以較婉轉，或是多變化的表達自己的想法。

規則形容詞比較及與最高級字形變化

❶ 規則形容詞變化：

　　(1) 單音節字及有些字尾為-er, -ow, -y的兩音節字，後面加-er變成比較級，加-est變成最高級。而需要注意的是，最高級的形容詞或副詞前方要加上定冠詞the或是所有格。

原級	比較級	最高級
old	older	oldest
soft	softer	softest
strong	stronger	strongest
narrow	narrower	narrowest
busy	busier	busiest
pretty	prettier	prettiest

　　(2) 大多數的兩音節字，及三音節以上的字，前面加more變成比較級，加most 變成最高級。概念：因字制宜。

原級	比較級	最高級
interesting	more interesting	most interesting

reliable	more reliable	most reliable
plentiful	more plentiful	most plentiful
likely	more likely	most likely
selfish	more selfish	most selfish
famous	more famous	most famous

❷ 不規則形容詞的變化：

原級	比較級	最高級
good well	better	best
bad ill	worse	worst
many much	more	most
little	less	least
far	farther（距離） further（程度）	farthest furthest
late	later（時間） latter（順序）	latest last

❸ 絕對形容詞（Absolute Adjective）：沒有比較級與最高級

定義：這類形容詞具有絕對性，不宜劃分刻度，造成等級或程度上的對比。

true	真實的	ready	準備好的	false	假的
right	正確的	correct	正確的	wrong	錯誤的
round	圓的	unique	獨特的	empty	空的
perfect	完美的	absolute	絕對的	vertical	垂直的

主題一 | 形容詞變化概念：三級互通

❶ 三級是可以互通的。

- **He is the tallest boy in his class.**
= **He is taller than anyone else in his class.**
= **He is taller than any other boy in his class.**
= **No one else is as tall as he (is) in his class.**
  他是班上最高的男孩。

❷ 在使用比較的句型時，要注意到**數目**與**人稱**的一致。

(1) **同類型的事物**才能比較。

(2) 兩所有物的比較，後者以**所有格**直接代替。

- **After my brother entering college, his allowance is more than mine.**
  哥哥上大學後，他的零用錢比我的還多。

(3) 要比較的對象，單數或不可數名詞用that，複數名詞用those來替換前面提過的同概念名詞。

- **Jackson insists that the moon he saw in the States is rounder than that in Taiwan.**
  傑克森堅持他在美國看到的月亮比台灣的月亮要圓。

- **According to the research, children taking care of pets tend to more responsible than those who don't have any pets.**
  根據研究，照顧寵物的孩子比起沒有寵物的孩子要有責任感。

❸ 比較級的用法中，若要強調「比……多得多」，可在比較級的形容詞或副詞前加上much、even、still、far及a lot等副詞來修飾。

❹ 最高級可直接修飾名詞，形成S＋V＋**最高級**adj.＋N＋介系詞片語的句型。

例句講解

- **Nothing is better than this.**（比較級）
= **This is the best.**（最高級）
= **This is as good as good can be.**（對等比較）
= **What is better than this!**（比較級）
= **Nothing is so good as this.**（對等比較）

　沒有什麼比這個東西好（這個是最棒的）。

- **The climate of Taiwan is as humid as that of India.**
（→that代指the climate）

　台灣的天氣比印度來的潮溼。

- **The ears of a hare are longer than those of a fox.**
（→those代指the ears）

　野兔的耳朵比狐狸來得大。

- **A chimpanzee has as much IQ as a child of six does.**
（→as...as 意指跟……一樣，兩動作的比較，後者以助動詞代替，does代指has much IQ）

　黑猩猩的智商相當於六歲小孩的智商。

- **Bob is the most industrious student in his class.**
（→最高級adj.＋N）

　鮑伯是他們班上最用功的學生。

- **Oranges are the most popular fruit of the year.**
= **Of all the fruit of the year, oranges are the most popular.**
（→最高級adj.＋N）

　今年的水果裡，柳橙是最受歡迎的。

隨堂測驗

(　) 1. Solar energy are highly valued partly because they are _____
　　than any other source of energy.

　(A) cheapest　　　　　　(B) the cheapest
　(C) cheap　　　　　　　(D) cheaper

(　) 2. The tail of my dog is longer than that of _____.

　(A) you　　　　(B) your　　　　(C) yours　　　　(D) yourself

(　) 3. It is _____ to set up a large business these days than it was two decades ago.

　(A) much harder　　　　　　(B) much hard
　(C) more harder　　　　　　(D) more hard

(　) 4. Of all the countries in the world, Canada is the _____ to the United States.

　(A) close　　　(B) closest　　　(C) closed　　　(D) closer

(　) 5. Pollution all over the world has been becoming progressively _____.

　(A) worse　　(B) bad　　　(C) the worst　　(D) worst

解答：1. (D) 2. (C) 3. (A) 4. (B) 5. (A)

解析：
①以太陽能跟其他的能源作比較，故使用比較級。
②yours代指「你」的狗的「尾巴」。
③修飾比較級harder可以用much，此處使用比較級則是現在和20年前做比較。
④譯：在全世界的所有國家當中，加拿大是離美國最近的。
⑤此處探討的是全世界汙染情況日益變嚴重，故使用比較級。

主題二 | 對等比較句型 as...as...的用法

❶ 意思為「和……一樣」時

(1) as...as...中第一個as為副詞，第二個as為連接詞。中間須接形容詞或副詞原級，或者是不定詞數量詞（如much、many、little等），是句子所要表達的意思而定。

(2) 這個句型中，如果動詞為及物動詞，則形容詞與受詞須一起放在as...as... 中間。

- **Warm waters are not as rich in food as cold waters.**　【三民B2 L7】
  溫暖的水域並不像寒冷的水域一樣富涵食物。

❷ 意思為「盡可能地……」時，此句型的as...as＋S＋can可換成as...as possible

- **To gain knowledge, Students are supposed to read as many books as possible.**
- **= Students are supposed to read as much as you can.**
  為了增進知識，學生應該盡可能多讀書。

 例句講解

- **He is as old as I. = He and I are of the same age.**
  他跟我同年。

- **It is just as cold today as it was yesterday.**
  今天跟昨天一樣冷。

- **The computer is as important an invention as the telephone.**
  電腦的發明跟電話一樣重要。

- **She doesn't practice playing the piano as often as she used to.**
  她不像過去一樣常常彈鋼琴了。

- **Living in a highly competitive society, you definitely have to arm yourself with as much knowledge as possible.**

  活在這個高度競爭的社會，你必須讓自己盡可能地多具備一些知識。

★延伸學習

由as...as衍生出來的兩個常用句型

❶ as long as或so long as，有三種句意

(1) 一樣長

- **My hair is as long as yours.**

  我的手跟你的一樣長。

  (2) 只要

- **Detergents cannot harm a fabric, so long as it has been properly dissolved.**

  只要適當地溶解的話，清潔劑並不會傷害布料。

  (3) 長達

- **He stays at home as long as winter lasts.**

  他在家裡待了長達一個冬天的時間。

  ❷ as far as或so far as，有三種句意

  (1) 一樣遠

- **The distance from here to the bus terminal is as far as to the school.**

  從這裡到公車總站的距離跟到學校一樣遠。

  (2) 就……而言

- **So far as I have read, I think this is the best novel he has ever written.**

  就目前我所讀到的部份來説，我認為這是他所寫過最好的小説。

  (3) 遠至

- **The desperado was out of bullets and food, so he ran as far as he could, trying to get to the border.**

  那亡命之徒已經彈盡糧絕，所以他盡可能的跑遠，想辦法要到邊境去。

 隨堂測驗

( ) 1. When he saw the destination only five meters in front of him, he ran _____ in an attempt to win first prize.

(A) as quick as possible
(B) as fastly as he can
(C) as possible as he could
(D) as fastly as he could

( ) 2. However busy you may be, you can manage to spare time to read a good many books, _____ you feel inclined to do so.

(A) as much as
(B) as many as
(C) so far as
(D) so long as

( ) 3. The woman seized _____ possible to be with her husband for fear that he might pass away in the next moment.

(A) as many as chances
(B) as many chances as
(C) as much as
(D) as a lot as

( ) 4. Eat _____ if you want to stay healthy.

(A) as few meat as you can
(B) as some meat as you can
(C) as little meat as possible
(D) as more meat as possible

( ) 5. _____ grammar is concerned, this article leaves nothing to be desired.

(A) As soon as
(B) As long as
(C) As possible as
(D) As far as

6. 只要保持安靜，你就無須離開這裡。

_____ you keep _____, you don't have to leave here.

7. 依我所知，他是無辜的。

_____ I know, he is _____.

8. 請儘早到校打掃教室。

_____

解答：1. (A) 2. (D) 3. (B) 4. (C) 5. (D)
6. As/So long as; silent
7. As/so far as; innocent
8. Please come to school as early as you can to clean the classroom.

解析：

①當他看見目標離自己只差五公尺遠，他盡全力跑已嘗試拿下冠軍。

②So long as在此處有「只要」之意。

③As+S+as有盡可能的意思。

④Meat為不可數名詞，修飾時用little。

⑤As far as意思為「就……而言」。

178

❶ 若表達「如果……越……，就會越……」之意，則屬於**條件句**用法，此時句型的前半句用簡單現在式，而後半句用未來式。

- **The faster you drive, the more dangerous it will be.**
  你車開得越快，就越危險。

❷ 比較級形容詞，若不是當補語，而是**修飾名詞**時，則名詞應接在形容詞之後。

- **The harder you study, the better grades you will get.**
  你越用功讀書，你的分數就會越好。

例句講解

- **The more haste, the less speed.** 欲速則不達。

- **The more one knows, the more ignorant he finds himself.**
  一個人知道得越多，就越覺得自己無知。

- **The older you grow, the more experienced you will become.**
  你的年紀越大，你就會越老練。

- **The higher you climb, the farther you see.**
  爬得越高，看得越遠。

- **The fresher the produce is, the higher the value of nutrition is.**
  產品越新鮮，它的營養價值就越高。

隨堂測驗

(　) 1. _____ you climb, _____ you may fall.

(A) The high; harder　　　　(B) Higher; harder

(C) Higher; the harder　　　(D) The higher; the harder

(   ) 2. The more generous you are, _____.

(A) the more you have friends   (B) you will have more friends

(C) the more friends you have   (D) you have many friends

(   ) 3. The _____ you practice, the _____ mistakes you will make.

(A) more; fewer   (B) less; more

(C) more; less   (D) less; fewer

(   ) 4. _____ the pause, _____ the heart pulse will be, causing

more severe pain. 【學測】

(A) Longer; stronger   (B) The long; the strong

(C) The longer; the stronger   (D) The longest; the strongest

5. 你書讀的越多，就越有智慧。

The _____ you read, the _____ you will have.

6. 你越足不出戶，認識的朋友就越少。

_____ you go out, _____ you will make.

7. 一個人擁有的越多，想要的就越多。

解答：1. (D) 2. (C) 3. (A) 4. (C)
5. more books; more wisdom
6. The less; the fewer friends
7. The more one has; the more he wants.

解析：
①譯：你爬得越高就可能摔得越重。
②譯：你越慷慨，朋友就可能越多。
③譯：你越努力練習，就可能犯越少錯誤。
④譯：停得越久，脈搏就越強，就會越痛苦。

主題四 | 倍數比較法

句型：S＋V＋（1. 倍數用法）＋（2. 比較用法）表示「……是……的幾倍」

倍數＋比較級＋than

倍數＋ as＋adj.（＋N）＋as...

倍數＋ the＋N＋of...

❶ 倍數用法

(1)小數	(2)分數
0.5 : half	1/2 : half
1 : as adj. as	1/3 : one-third
1.5 : one time and a half	2/3 : two-thirds
2 : two times	3/4 : three fourths
2.5 : two times and a half	

❷ 比較用法:as+adj.+as= the+N+of

大:large= the size of 小:small=the size of 長:long=the length of 短:short=the length of 數:many=the number of 量:much=the amount of	快:fast=the speed of 慢:slow=the speed of 深:deep=the depth of 淺:shallow=the depth of 寬:wide=the width of 窄:narrow=the width of 遠:far=the distance of 近:near=the distance of	高:tall=the height of 矮:short=the height of 胖:fat=the weight of 瘦:thin=the weight of 輕:light=the weight of 重:heavy=the weight of 長:old=the age of 幼:young=the age of

❸ 其他用法

(1) half as （many/much/old/long）...as... （……的一半）

(2) half as （many/much/old/long）...again as... （……的一倍半）

(3) again as （many/much/old/long）...as... （……的兩倍）

(4) X as （many/much/old/long）...again as... （……的兩倍）

例句講解

- **My study is half as large as yours.**
  我的書房是你的**一半**。

- **My study is half as large again as yours.**
  我的書房是你的**一倍半**

- **My study is as large again as yours.**
  我的書房是你的**兩倍**。

- **The earth is forty-nine times as large as the moon.**
- = **The earth is forty-nine times the size of the moon.**
- = **The earth is forty-nine times larger than the moon.**
  地球是月亮的四十九倍大。

- **Women employees are still being discriminated by male officials, and they still have to fight twice as hard as men do to get fair treatment.**
  在男性辦公室裡，女性員工仍然是被歧視的，她們必須比男性加倍努力才能得到公平的待遇。

- **The amount of time I spent on this project is one third of a month. That is, it took me ten days to accomplish it.**
  我花在這項計畫上的時間是三分之一個月。也就是說，我用了十天完成它。

- **Only half of the population went to vote in the election.**
  只有一半的人參與了這次的選舉投票。

隨堂測驗

( ) 1. The bedroom of this house is _____ as _____ as the kitchen.

    (A) twice; size   (B) twice; large

    (C) two times; far   (D) two times; far

(　) 2. On the surface of the earth, the water is three times _____ the land.

(A) the size in
(B) as large to
(C) more large than
(D) the size of

(　) 3. This university is ten times _____ that elementary school.

(A) larger than
(B) more large than
(C) as large of
(D) the size to

(　) 4. I have three times _____ you have.

(A) the number in books
(B) much books than
(C) as more books as
(D) as many books as

(　) 5. About _____ of the students had trouble communicating with their family, including their siblings.

(A) one-second
(B) one half
(C) second
(D) the half

6. 這部筆記型電腦的價格是那部數位相機的四倍。（中翻英）

7. 這位丈夫的年紀是他太太的兩倍。（中翻英）

解答：1. (B) 2. (D) 3. (A) 4. (D) 5. (B)
6. This notebook computer is four times the price of that digital camera.
7. The husband is twice the age of his wife's.

解析：
①twice表示「兩倍」大；而large則用來講大小。
②在地球表面，水的面積是陸地的三倍。
③此題比較的是大學和小學兩者的面積差異。
④As+S+as、book為可數名詞用many。
⑤One half在此表示一半。

❶

用法	中譯
more than	多餘、非常
less than	少於、很不
more A than B less B than A	1. 多／少於 2. 與其説A不如説B

- If you give me your Teddy Bear, I am more than willing to help you in the exam.

  如果你給我你的泰迪熊娃娃，我就十分樂意在考試時幫你忙了。

- The department of archeology is less than perfect.

  考古部門十分不完美。

- Some people think much more about their right than (they do) about their duties.

  有些人考慮他們的權利多過於思考他們的義務。

- So far heat pollution has been more a threat than a fact.

  目前為止熱污染與其説是一個事實，更不如説是一種威脅。

- David is known less as an professor than as a tutor.

  大衛與其説是一個教授，更不如説是個家教老師。

❷

用法	中譯
no more than=only no less than=as many/much as not more than=at most not less than=at least	跟……一樣少；只有 跟……一樣多；多達 至多 至少

- **What he desires is** no more than **someone to rely on.**

  他只不過是渴望能有人依賴。

- **Poor as he is, he donates** no less than **three thousand dollars to the orphanage every month.**

  儘管他很窮，他每個月還是捐出多達三千元到孤兒院去。

- **Since he had tight schedule, he will stay in Taiwan for** not more than **two days.**

  由於他的行程很滿，他在台灣最多只會待兩天。

- **These foreign tourists decided to stay in Taiwan for** not less than **five days.**

  這些外國觀光客決定在台灣至少待五天。

❸

用法	中譯
no more A than B	A和B一樣→都不
no less A than B	A和B一樣→都是

- **Absolute justice is indeed** no more **attainable than absolute truth.**

  絕對的正義和絕對的真實一樣都是達不到的。

- **She is** no less **busy than a bee.** 她和蜜蜂一樣忙碌。

❹

用法	中譯
nothing more than	僅僅、只不過
nothing less than	簡直就是

- **This was** nothing more than **a false alarm.**

  這不過就是個假的警報。

- **He saved three people from the building on fire. He was** nothing less **than a hero.**

  他從失火的大樓裡救出了三個人。他簡直就是個英雄。

 隨堂測驗

( ) 1. What he said and did was _____ a fraud.

    (A) nothing more than   (B) no less than

    (C) nothing than   (D) more than

( ) 2. In order to pass the test, I will review for _____ three times.

    (A) not more than   (B) no more than

    (C) nothing less than   (D) as much as

( ) 3. I can barely make both ends meet, so I can lend you _____ one thousand dollars.

    (A) not less than   (B) no less than

    (C) not more than   (D) nothing than

( ) 4. The air crash left _____ 400 passengers dead.

    (A) no more than   (B) nothing more than

    (C) no less than   (D) nothing less than

( ) 5. This painting is _____ a copy of the other.   【學測】

    (A) nothing than   (B) not more than

    (C) anything more than   (D) nothing more than

解答：1. (A) 2. (B) 3. (C) 4. (C) 5. (D)

解析：

①nothing more than表示「僅僅、只不過」。

②no more than表示「only」。

③「最多」只能借你1000元。

④No less than表示「多達」。

⑤同第一題。

主題六 ┃ 其他強調語句的比較級用法

S＋V＋the last＋(N)＋to VR「絕非、最不可能……」

＋that cl.

- **The author is the last person to talk about his work.**

  這個作者是最不可能去談論他的作品的。

- **Her sudden disappearance from home was the last thing that we had dreamed of.**

  她突然從家裡消失，對我們來說是絕對想像不到的事。

  ❶ 用adv.＋比較級來強調「更不用說、更何況」。

  句型：

  肯定句＋much more＋N

  否定句＋much less＋N

  ❷ 比較級的修飾種類

  (1) very/really/so...＋原級

  (2) far/much/even/still/a lot/a little/a great deal＋比較級

  (3) the very/much the/by far the＋最高級

- **I like mathematics, much more English.**

  我喜歡數學，更別說是英文了。

- **I don't like English, much less mathematics.**

  我不喜歡英文，更別說是數學了。

- **James ran a good deal faster than I.**

  詹姆士跑得比我快多了。

- **James is the very most handsome teacher that I have ever met.**

= **James is much the most handsome teacher that I have ever met.**

= **James is** by far the most handsome **teacher that I have ever met.**

詹姆士是我遇過最帥的老師。

❶ 以more/less的句型強調「更加、更不」。

❷ 相關片語列表

(1) all the more （**更加**）

(2) all the less（**更不**）

(3) none the more（沒有比較好=**一樣**）

(4) none the less（沒有比較差=**一樣**）

• **I am** all the more **nervous because there is a mirror opposite me.**

我感到更緊張了，因為有面鏡子對著我。

• **His success was** all the less **praiseworthy because he made it in some indecent way.**

他的成功根本不值得誇獎，因為他是以不光彩的方式做到的。

• **She was** none the less **beautiful although she didn't wear any makeup.**

雖然她沒有上任何妝，但仍然很美。

• **He is** none the happier **for his wealth.**

他沒有因為他的富有而更高興。

🕐 隨堂測驗

(　　) 1. I like music, _____ dancing.

　　(A) much less　　　　　　(B) much more

　　(C) all the less　　　　　(D) all the more

(　　) 2. James is the _____ person to find fault with others.

　　(A) good　　　　　　　　(B) better

　　(C) worst　　　　　　　　(D) last

(　) 3. He drove his car_____ carefully because the road was frozen.

    (A) none the more   (B) none the less

    (C) all the more   (D) all the less

(　) 4. The girl is _____ talented kid in my piano class, so I suggest her parents to send her to Vienna.

    (A) most   (B) the best

    (C) by far the   (D) very

(　) 5. She looks _____ happier although she seems to own the whole world.

    (A) none the more   (B) none the less

    (C) much   (D) all the more

6. 正因她有缺點，我才更喜歡她。（中翻英）

I like her _____ because of her demerits.

7. 他不愛朋友，更不必別說陌生人了。（中翻英）

_____

解答：1. (B)　2. (D)　3. (B)　4. (C)　5. (A)

6. all the more

7. He doesn't love friends, much less strangers.

解析：

①我喜歡音樂，更別説跳舞了。

②The last有最不可能、絕非的意思。

③No the less 字面意思為「沒有比較差」，有一樣的意思。

④By far有「最」的涵義，表示其他人事物跟其差距很大。

⑤No the more 字面意思為「沒有比較多」，有一樣的意思。

(　　) 1. In the past three decades, I spent _____ of it in Africa, and I traveled to Italy during the other ten years.

(A) a half

(B) two thirds

(C) some

(D) two third

(　　) 2. Mia went shopping _____ get some new clothes as to release some stress.

(A) more than to

(B) in order to

(C) not so much to

(D) none the more to

(　　) 3. Usually an adult doesn't pick up a new language _____ a child does.

(A) as early as

(B) the same as

(C) as much as

(D) as quickly as

(　　) 4. He eats _____ three bowls of rice per meal, or he will feel hungry.

(A) no more than

(B) as much as

(C) no less than

(D) not more than

(　　) 5. He still keeps exercising, but it is _____ for losing weight _____ for maintaining his health.

(A) no more; than

(B) not so much; as

(C) not more; than

(D) no much; as

(　　) 6. Any book will do _____ it is interesting.

(A) so long as

(B) so far as

(C) as well as

(D) as good as

( ) 7. They spent much time practicing their speeches. Therefore, their performance was better than _____.

(A) we

(B) us

(C) our

(D) ours

( ) 8. He doesn't love friends, _____ strangers.

(A) much less

(B) much more

(C) no more

(D) no less

( ) 9. The contributions of the electric light to human welfare is far greater than _____ in history.

(A) that of any other invention

(B) any other invention does

(C) those of any other invention

(D) these of any invention

( ) 10. His salary as a bus driver is much higher _____.

(A) as that of a teacher

(B) as a teacher

(C) than that of a teacher

(D) than a teacher

( ) 11. Knowing his father was in a critical condition, he left his work behind and went to the hospital _____ he could.

(A) as much as

(B) as possible as

(C) as soon as

(D) as high as

( ) 12. The temperature in Kenting is usually higher than _____.

(A) that in Taipei

(B) which in Taipei

(C) Taipei

(D) which in Taipei

( ) 13. As far as baseball is concerned, Taiwan is _____ Mainland China.

(A) prior than

(B) superior than

(C) prior to

(D) superior to

(   ) 14. My sister earns about three times _____ I every month.

    (A) as much as   (B) much more than

    (C) the number as   (D) as more as

(   ) 15. Health is the _____ that wealth can buy.

    (A) less thing   (B) last thing

    (C) best thing   (D) more thing

(   ) 16. The boy's face is _____ under medical treatment.

    (A) none the more   (B) none the better

    (C) all the more   (D) all the worse

(   ) 17. The father can't discipline himself, _____ set a good example for his children to follow.

    (A) as possible as   (B) much more

    (C) so as to   (D) much less

(   ) 18. I have three times the _____ of your books.

    (A) many   (B) amount

    (C) size   (D) number

(   ) 19. It is reported that young visitors get more out of a visit in museum if they focus on _____ nine objects. 【指考】

    (A) no better than   (B) nothing less than

    (C) no more than   (D) no sooner than

(   ) 20. The product was put on the market _____ 1990. 【指考】

    (A) no later than   (B) no less than

    (C) no more than   (D) nothing later than

解答

1. (B) 「在過去三十年中，我花了三分之二在非洲，然後在另外十年間，我去了義大利。」這一題主要是考驗three decades（三十年）的文意，以及the other ten years（剩下的十年）的了解。別忘記分數表示法中，先寫分子（用基數），後寫分母（用序數），如果分子大於一時，則分母後要加s。

2. (C) 「Mia去購物與其說是為了買些新衣服，不如說是為了紓解壓力。」本題是考：not so much to＋VR/adj./N as to＋VR/adj./N 與其說是……不如說是……的句型。

3. (D) 此題探討的是成人與小孩學習新語言的速度。

4. (B) no less than「至少」。

5. (B) 此句型中，依文意，運動目的是減重，更是維持健康。所以選擇與其說是……，不如說是……的句型。記得not so much A as B的A與B必須要相同。

6. (A) so long as「只要」。

7. (D) 此處比較的是他們的表演跟我們的表演比，所以要用所有代名詞。

8. (A) 更不用說。

9. (C) 電燈對人們福祉的貢獻比起歷史上任何一個發明的貢獻要大。所以對等的結構是 the contributions of any other invention，故用複數的代名詞，選(C)。別忘記在比較級用法中，單數用that，複數用those來代替前面提過的名詞。

10. (C) 比較級用than，而且比較的是薪水，不是老師，所以選(C)。

11. (C) 盡可能的去做某事，用as...as one can/possible，但絕不可用as possible as one can的寫法，故選(C)。

12. (A) 是墾丁的溫度跟台北的溫度比，是以單數相比，故選(A)。

13. (D) superior to有「優於」之意。

14. (A) as much as有一樣多的意思。

15. (B) 「絕非、最不可能」

16. (B) 沒有比較好=一樣差。

17. (D) 更不用說。

18. (D) 以我和你的書籍「數量」做比較。

19. (C) 博物館裡有很多的陳列品，但是年輕的參觀者只能欣賞不多於九件物品。這樣是很少的，所以用強調少量的no more than。

20. (A) no later than是不晚於，也就是要早於1990年的意思。而(D)的用法不符合此處文法。

Part 7

假設語氣

—— Part7 ——
假設語氣

　　假設語氣在閱讀上會出現的難題在於「敘述的狀況與事實相反」，也就是說，你看到的"would have won"是贏了，但其實是"didn't win"沒贏。而句子時態的呈現，也跟事實多有不同。同學請記得，不要死背公式，因為假設語氣只是一種說話的語氣，請用理解的方式去解讀你看到的句子喔。

❶ 假設語氣的定義
　　表達與事實不符的假定、想像、願望等，要將動詞加以變化，這種特殊的用法稱為假設語態。

❷ 假設語氣相關句型分類

基本句型	
(1)和現在事實相反的假設	→過去式
(2)和過去事實相反的假設	→過去完成式
(3)和未來相反的假設	→絕對相反
	→萬一相反
	→條件句型
	→特殊句型
應用句型	
(1)彷彿	→as if/though
(2)但願	→if only/I wish
(3)若非	→but for/that;only for/that; without
(4)該是……的時候了	→it's time
(5)意志動詞+意志形容詞	→S1+意志動詞that S2+(should)+VR
(6)以免	→lest/for fear that
(7)助動詞與假設語氣	→should/would/could/might

主題一 | 與現在事實相反的假設

❶「與現在事實相反的假設」句型如下：

副詞子句　　　　　　　　主要子句

If＋S＋　V-p.t./過去式助V/were　　，S＋would/should/could/might＋VR

❷「與現在事實相反」if引導的子句，**若是be動詞，一律用**were，若是一般動詞，則用**過去式**，而主要子句動詞則為could/would/should/might＋VR。

❸ if 子句的 be 動詞用were，但口語中第一人稱和第三人稱單數用was。

例句講解

• **If I had wings, I would fly to you.**
　如果我有翅膀，我就會飛向你。

• **If he were on the crime scene, you could find his fingerprints all over the room.**
　如果他在犯罪現場，你可以發現他的指紋到處都是。

• **If I was/were cold, I could cover myself with a blanket.**
　如果我冷，我可以拿毯子來蓋。

• **If the television were in the corner of the room, we all could see the screen clearly.**
　如果電視是在房間角落，我們就都能清楚看到螢幕了。

　注意要點 if 子句中的 if 若省略，were 或助動詞必須提到句首形成倒裝。

• **If James were fast, he could join the track team.**
= **Were James fast, he could join the track team.**
　如果詹姆士跑得快，他就可以參加田徑隊。

• **If my sister could sew, she could fix the hole in my shirt.**

= Could **my sister sew, she could fix the hole in my shirt.**

如果我妹妹會縫紉，她就可以幫我修補衣服上的破洞。

隨堂測驗

( ) 1. I would call him if I _____ his phone number.

    (A) knew   **(B)** know   **(C)** had known   **(D)** would know

( ) 2. You would be less tired if you _____ to bed early enough each night.

    (A) go   **(B)** went   **(C)** had gone   **(D)** will go

( ) 3. Mary would make better progress if she _____ hard.

    (A) studied   **(B)** study   **(C)** studies   **(D)** would study

( ) 4. If I _____ a millionaire, I would buy a luxurious villa.

    (A) was   **(B)** am   **(C)** had been   **(D)** were

解答：1. (A) 2. (B) 3. (A) 4. (D)

解析：
①和現在事實相反，子句使用過去式。
②和現在事實相反，子句使用過去式。
③和現在事實相反，子句使用過去式。
④和現在事實相反，子句使用過去式。

主題二 與過去事實相反的假設

❶ 與「過去事實相反的假設」句型如下：

If+S+had+V-p.p., S+would/should/could/might+have+V-p.p.

❷ 「與過去事實相反」，if引導的子句動詞須用had＋V-p.p.，而主要句動詞則為could/should/might＋have＋V-p.p.

例句講解

- **If you had come earlier, you could have witnessed this accident.**
  你若早一點來，就會目擊這場意外。

- **If you had asked, I would have told you the truth.**
  若你當時有提問，我早就告訴你實情了。

- **If I had had enough money, I could have studied abroad.**
  當時我若有有足夠的錢，早就能到國外進修了。

★延伸學習

❶ 若if子句是「與過去事實相反」，而主要句是「與現在事實相反」，則全句意指「假如當時……，現在就……」。

❷ 此種句型中，if子句常有then、before等表示過去時間的字詞，而主要句常有now、today等表示現在時間的字詞。

- **If he had studied medicine in college, he would become a doctor now.**
- → **He didn't study medicine in college, and he is not a doctor now.**
  若他大學時讀醫科，現在就是醫生了。
  （→他大學時沒讀醫科，現在不是醫生）

( ) 1. If I had known his address, I _____ to him.

    (A) will write   (B) would write

    (C) had written   (D) would have written

( ) 2. If it had not rained so hard yesterday, we _____ fishing.

    (A) went   (B) would go

    (C) should go   (D) would have gone

( ) 3. If John had left earlier, he _____ able to arrive in London.

    (A) will be   (B) would be

    (C) were   (D) would have been

( ) 4. If you had done those exercises, you _____ from them.

    (A) might benefit   (B) might have benefited

    (C) had benefited   (D) have benefited

解答：1. (D) 2. (D) 3. (D) 4. (B)

解析：

①「與過去事實相反」，if引導的子句動詞須用had＋V-p.p.，而主要句動詞則為could/should/might＋have＋V-p.p.。

②「與過去事實相反」，if引導的子句動詞須用had＋V-p.p.，而主要句動詞則為could/should/might＋have＋V-p.p.。

③此為與過去事實相反之假設語氣，主要子句用過去式。

④「與過去事實相反」，if引導的子句動詞須用had＋V-p.p.，而主要句動詞則為could/should/might＋have＋V-p.p.

主題三 | 對未來事情的推測

❶ 與「未來預測之完全相反」→ 0%，句型為：

　　　副詞子句　　　　　　　　主要子句

　If＋S＋were to＋VR, S＋would/should/could/might＋VR

= Were＋S＋to＋VR

❷ 此句型強調未來事情發生的可能性近乎零，if子句**不分人稱**動詞**一律**用were to＋V，而主要子句動詞則為could/would/should/might＋VR，表示與未來事實相反。

• **If I were to rule the world, I would destroy all nuclear weapons.**
→**It is impossible for me to rule the world, and I don't have the ability to destroy all nuclear weapons.**

　若我未來能統治全世界，就要摧毀所有核子武器

　　❸ 此假設句用以表示和未來事實相反的情況。

• **If her son were to come back to life, she would become more stable emotionally.**

　如果她兒子活過來，她的情緒就會比較穩定。

　　❹ 此句型強調可預見的未來。

• **If photosynthesis（光合作用）were to stop, all the living things in the world would become extinct（滅絕）in a few years.**

　如果光合作用停止了，那麼世界上的所有生物都會在若干年內滅絕。

　　❺ 此句型可用於提議，語氣比直接建議來得客氣。

• **If the document were to be edited in the office, our team could make it perfect before it goes to the client.**

　如果這份文件能在辦公室裡先編輯過，我們團隊就能在把文件交給客戶前做得更完善。

❶ 與「未來預測之**萬一相反**」→0.0001%，句型為：

副詞子句　　　主要子句

If＋S＋should＋VR，　　┌ S＋will/shall/can/may＋VR

＝ Should＋S＋to＋VR　├ S＋would/should/could/might＋VR

　　　　　　　　　　└ **命令句**

❷ 若表達對未來發生的可能性「強烈懷疑」，但不排除其發生的可能性，則if子句動詞一律用should＋VR，表示「萬一」，而主要句動詞則用would (will)/ could (can)/should (shall)/might (may)＋VR。

- **If an asteroid（行星）should hit the earth, man could die out.**
  萬一有顆行星撞到了地球，人類就有可能全部死亡。

- **If he should come, tell him I don't want to see him.**
  萬一他來了，告訴他我不想見他。

❸ 本句型用於未來假設，表示發生的可能性雖然不大但有可能，所以用if＋S＋should 表示「萬一」，主要子句的動詞也可用**祈使句**。

- **If the box should open, use this tape to close it.**
  萬一這只箱子會開的話，就用這膠帶來封貼。

- **You should/must/have to correct me if I should pronounce your name incorrectly.**

=**Please correct me if I should pronounce your name incorrectly.**
  如果我把你的名字唸錯，你得糾正我。

❶ 描述「未來有**可能改變**的事實」⇨50%，句型為：

副詞子句　　　主要子句

　If＋S＋**現在式**V（代替未來），　　S＋will/shall/can/may＋VR

- **If it rains tomorrow, we will not go on a picnic.**
  如果明天下雨的話，我們將不會去野餐。

- **If we don't start now, we will be late.**
  如果現在不出發的話，我們會遲到。

❷ 條件句常用if、when等連接詞，而且連接的子句中，雖然是未來可能發生的事，但動詞需用**簡單現在式**，而主要句的動詞，則用**未來式**。

• **If metal（金屬）gets hot, it will expand.**

金屬一旦遇熱，就有可能延展。

• **If the weather is fine tomorrow, we will go mountain-climbing.**

假如明天天氣好的話，我們就會去爬山。

❸ if所引導的子句，若表達未來可能發生，則稱為**條件句**，雖然中文說成「假使……；假設……」，但不是英文文法中的「假設語氣」句型。

• **If he passes the exams, he can enter an ideal university.**

假如通過考試，他就能上理想的大學。

描述「條件與過去事實相反，結果與現在事實相反」的特殊句型為：

副詞子句主要子句

If＋S＋had＋V-p.p., S＋would/should/could/might＋VR

（與過去相反）　　　　　　（與現在相反）

• **If you hadn't gone to bed so late last night, you wouldn't look so tired now.**

你如果昨天沒有那麼晚睡的話，現在看起來就不會那麼累了。

• **If I had studied harder in school, I could qualify for（勝任）the job now.**

如果我在學校裡更用功讀書的話，現在就能勝任這份工作了。

隨堂測驗

（　）1. Although I already had the script carefully checked, if there _____ any mistakes, please inform me.

(A) were to

(B) are

(C) have

(D) should be

(　) 2. Jasmine would not suffer that much now if you _____ her earlier.

(A) could have warned
(B) couldn't have warned
(C) could warned
(D) couldn't have

(　) 3. If females _____ disappear in the world, could males live alone?

(A) will (B) would
(C) were to (D) should to

(　) 4. It is unlikely that this typhoon will strike Taiwan, but if it _____ Taiwan, it would cause great damage.

(A) strikes (B) had stricken
(C) should strike (D) were to strike

解答： 1. (C)　2. (C)　3. (B)　4. (A)

解析：

①條件句常用if、when等連接詞，連接的子句中，雖然是未來可能發生的事，但動詞需用**簡單現在式**。

②句型為If＋S＋<u>had＋V-p.p.</u>, S＋<u>would/should/could/might＋VR</u>

③譯：如果女性消失在這世界上，男性可以獨自存活嗎？

④請參考第一題之解析。

主題四 | 「彷彿」的表示法

❶ 以as if/though 表達「彷彿」的句型：

主要子句　　　　　　　　　　　副詞子句

S+V+as if/as though, S+ {
were/V-p.t.（與現在事實相反）
should/would/could/might have V-p.p.
　　　　　　　　　　（與過去事實相反）
直述句
}

❷ 本句型的子句不是單純的「與現在事實相反」或「與過去事實相反」。

(1) as if假設句若與主要子句（不論現在式或過去式）**同一時間**發生，則子句動詞用**過去式動詞**。

(2) as if假設句比主要子句（不論現在式或過去式）**更早發生**，則子句動詞用 had＋V-p.p.。

(3) as if後的子句有時會省略主詞與動詞，而成為片語。

例句講解

• **He talks as if he were a doctor.** （→副詞子句動詞were，與事實相反）
  他現在講話的樣子彷彿是個醫生。（他其實不是醫生）

• **He talked as if he were a doctor.** （→副詞子句動詞were，與事實相反）
  他當時講話的樣子彷彿是個醫生似的。（他其實不是醫生）

• **They all thought the two boys had been dead but they walked into the church as if they had returned from the dead.** （→與過去事實相反）
  他們都認為那兩個男孩死了，但他們走去教堂裡彷彿他們死而復生一樣。

- **He stood up as if to speak.** （→省略as if後的he was to）
  他站起來，彷彿有話要說似的。

★注意要點

　　as if引導的子句也可描述「**可能發生的事實**」，此時動詞依照直說法規則即可，不需做變化。

- **It looks as if the typhoon will hit Taiwan next week.**
  看來颱風下星期會侵襲台灣。

 隨堂測驗

(　) 1. Falling in love is always magical. It feels eternal as if love _____
    last forever. 【學測】

   (A) will last
   (B) should last
   (C) would have lasted
   (D) have lasted

(　) 2. He describes the Hell vividly as if he _____ there before.

   (A) were   (B) was
   (C) had been (D) is

(　) 3. He ran away as if _____ my appearance.

   (A) frightened by
   (B) he had been frightened by
   (C) he were frightened by
   (D) he frightened by

(　) 4. He lives as if he _____ a millionaire and talks as if he _____ a
    rich man.

   (A) is; were   (B) is; is
   (C) were; is   (D) were; were

(   ) 5. James walked in the classroom, lecturing as if he _____ a bad cold, though he insisted he didn't. Then he just fainted away on the platform.

(A) had caught   (B) would have caught

(C) caught   (D) might catch

(   ) 6. Sean looked into my eyes as if he _____ too much to say. However, he just didn't know how to tell me that my fly was open

(A) would have   (B) had

(C) would have had   (D) had had

(   ) 7. Eric is chatting as if nothing _____ before. However, they had a serious fight a week ago.

(A) happened   (B) could happen

(C) had happened   (D) might have happened

8. 我看著她，彷彿這事從未發生過。

解答：1. (C) 2. (C) 3. (A) 4. (D) 5. (A) 6. (B) 7. (C)
8. I looked at her as if it had never happened.

解析：

①as if假設句若與主要子句（不論現在式或過去式）**同一時間**發生，則子句動詞用**過去式動詞**。

②as if假設句比主要子句（不論現在式或過去式）**更早發生**，子句動詞用 had＋V-p.p.。

③子句省略了he was。

④與現在事實相反，用過去式。

⑤as if假設句比主要子句（不論現在式或過去式）**更早發生**，子句動詞用 had＋V-p.p.。

⑥與現在事實相反，用過去式。

⑦as if假設句比主要子句（不論現在式或過去式）**更早發生**，子句動詞用 had＋V-p.p.。

主題五 「但願」的表示法

❶ 以 If only 等表達「但願」的句型：

(1) if only	could/would+VR（表未來但願）
(2) S+wish/would rather that	+ S+ were/V-p.t.（與現在事實相反）
(3) How I wish　　　　　that	had V-p.p.（與過去事實相反）

❷ if only 用來表示與現在、過去、未來不同的希望，意思相當於 I wish（但願、要是……就好了）。

❸ if only 用來表達和**過去**不同的希望，動詞用**過去完成式**；表達和**現在**不同的希望，子句動詞用**過去式**；表達和**未來**不符的希望時，動詞用could/might/ would/should＋VR。

❹ wish表不可能發生的願望，若「與現在事實相反」，子句動詞用**過去式**；若與「過去事實相反」，子句動詞則用had＋V-p.p。此句型前常加上how，強調整個句子。本句型的I wish可替換成If only或Would that，用法及意思皆不變。

例句講解

• **Holy shit! I'm going to be late again. If only I had woken up on time.**
（→與過去事實相反）

　糟了，我又要遲到了。要是我準時起床就好了。

• **If only Mia were two years older, she would be able to drive a car.**
（→與現在事實相反）

　要是米亞再多個兩歲就好了，她就能開車了。

• **If only she would marry me, I would be the happiest woman in the world.**（→對未來推測）

　但願她會嫁給我，我就是世界上最幸福的人。

- I wish **I could go to the party, but I have to study.**
（→與現在事實相反）

  真希望我能去參加派對,但是我得唸書。

- **The lost man** wishes/wished **that he had brought some food along in his backpack.**
（→與過去事實相反）

  迷路的男子希望自己要是有在背包裡帶些食物就好了。

- How I wish **I hadn't made this mistake.**
（→與過去事實相反）

  多麼希望我沒有犯下這個錯。

- I wish **you had told the truth earlier. =** If only **you had told the truth earlier.**
= Would that **you had told the truth earlier.** （→與過去事實相反）

  若是你早一點說實話就好了。

★延伸學習

	使用時機	例句
wish	與事實相反的假設或事實;表示「祈求、祈願」。	The athlete wishes he could run just a little bit faster. 這名運動員希望自己能再跑快一點。 （→假設） We wish you a merry Christmas and a happy New Year. 祝你聖誕快樂,新年快樂
hope	表示可能實現的希望、希望未來會發生的事,後接直述句。	I hope I can study law and become a lawyer in the future. 我希望我能讀法律系,日後當個律師。（→希望）

( ) 1. _____ I were the king of this world!

   (A) How I wish   (B) What wish I have

   (C) How wish   (D) How do I wish

( ) 2. I wish I _____ more knowledge and experience when I was still young.

   (A) gained   (B) have had gained

   (C) were to gain   (D) had gained

( ) 3. _____ there were peace in the world forever.

   (A) Only if   (B) Would that

   (C) I hope   (D) What if

解答: 1. (A) 2. (D) 3. (B)

解析:

①與現在事實相反。

②與過去事實相反。

③與現在事實相反。

❶ 意志動詞列表

(1)表「建議」	move　advise suggest　propose recommend	
(2)表「堅持」	hold　urge insist　maintain	that S2+(should)+VR【要點】 (1)S1≠S2 (2)should可以省略
(3)表「要求」	ask　rule desire　provide request　demand require　stipulate	(3)意志動詞可以改成beV+意志形 容詞
(4)表「命令」	order direct command	

❷ 意志形容詞列表

It is	vital　imperative proper　advisable urgent　mandatory necessary　obligatory essential　important	+that+S+(should)+VR （should通常省略）

例句講解

• I insist **that he (should) pay the money at once.**

= I insist **on (/upon) his paying the money at once.**

= I insist **on (/upon) it that he (should) pay the money at once.**

　我堅持他要一次付清款項。

- **Mary** demanded **that he apologize to her.**
  瑪莉堅持要他道歉。

- **The manager** suggested **that we adopt a different policy.**
  經理建議我們採取不一樣的策略。

- **It is** urgent **that a new law (should) be enacted to protect children.**
  實行一條能保護孩童的新法律是很迫切的事。

- **It is** necessary **that the work (should) be done right off.**
  這件工作是必須立刻完成的。

- **It is** imperative **that all of us (should) tell the truth.**
  我們必須講實話。

★延伸學習

　　意志動詞也可改為名詞形式，並以作為強調的分裂句It beV...that來表現。

- **I suggest that he (should) give up his plan.**
= **It is** my suggestion that **he (should) give up his plan.**
  要他放棄他的計劃，是我的建議。

- **He insisted that we (should) be allowed to go picnicking.**
= **It was** his insistence that **we (should) go picnicking.**
  他堅持我們該去野餐。

 隨堂測驗

(　　) 1. Nobody suggested that the meeting _____ on the first day of the
　　　next month.

　　(A) held　　　　　　　　　　(B) should have held
　　(C) hold　　　　　　　　　　(D) be held

( ) 2. Physicians suggest that we _____ have a physical check-up every year.

  (A) will   (B) x

  (C) shall   (D) can

( ) 3. Since Jim did not feel well, his mother insisted that he _____ home.

  (A) stay   (B) stays

  (C) stayed   (D) staying

( ) 4. He is not supposed to play with us until the manager recommends that he _____ a member of this club.

  (A) be   (B) is

  (C) been   (D) being

( ) 5. The new governor gave the order that all drivers _____ their gas tanks only on even-numbered days.

  (A) must fill   (B) filled

  (C) fill   (D) filling

解答：1. (C) 2. (B) 3. (A) 4. (A) 5. (C)

解析：

①有省略一個should，故應使用原形動詞。

②完整句型為that S2+(should)+VR

③參考第一題。

④Be在此處有成為的意思。

⑤有省略一個should。

主題七 | 表達推測的助動詞

❶ 「過去式語氣助動詞＋have＋V-p.p.」亦可表示「過去該……，但是卻未如此」的意思，要根據上下文判定其義。句型為：

(1) $\left\{\begin{array}{l}\text{could} \\ \text{should} \\ \text{ought to} \\ \text{might} \\ \text{would}\end{array}\right.$ ＋have＋V-p.p.　「過去該……，但是卻如此」

(2) needn't＋have＋V-p.p. 「過去不必……，但是卻如此」

(3) must＋have＋V-p.p. 「過去一定……」，表對過去的猜測

❷ would/could/should＋have＋V-p.p.表示「與過去事實相反」，事情「本將／本可／本該做而沒有做」

例句講解

- **We had a great time last night. You should have been there, too.**
  我們昨晚玩得很盡興。你也應該在場的。

- **Helen didn't catch the bus. She might have overslept this morning.**
  海倫沒趕上公車。她今早應該是睡過頭了。

- **According to the report about the robbery, the doorman might have been killed.**
  根據關於搶案的報導，那個門房應該是被殺了。

- **My clothes were not totally dry. I guess it might have rained last night.**
  我的衣服還沒全乾。我猜昨晚應該下過雨。

★延伸學習

　　❶ must have＋V-p.p.表「對過去的強烈推測」，不是「本必須做而沒有做」。否定句用can't have＋V-p.p.。

　　❷「對現在的強烈推測」，則用must＋V，否定句用can't＋V。

- **The ground is wet now. It must have rained last night.**
  地面是溼的。昨晚必定下過雨了。（→對過去的推測）

- **James was on his way to Japan last night. They can't have met him at the party.**
  詹姆士昨晚啟程前往日本。他們不可能在宴會中看到他。（→對過去的推測）

隨堂測驗

(　　) 1. James is a workaholic. If he is not here, he ＿＿＿＿ in the office now.

　(A) must have been
　(B) can have been
　(C) must be
　(D) can be

(　　) 2. The twins knew that genetics ＿＿＿＿ a role in their condition.
　　　　　　　　　　　　　　　　　　　　　　　　【學測】

　(A) might have played
　(B) can't play
　(C) must play
　(D) play

(　　) 3. John ＿＿＿＿ well in the exam, but he didn't. He was too nervous.

　(A) could do
　(B) must do
　(C) could have done
　(D) must have done

(　) 4. When you saw the superstar in person, you _____ hands with him. I envy you!

   (A) must have shaken

   (B) might have shaken

   (C) could have shaken

   (D) should have shaken

(　) 5. The baby is crying for an hour. She _____ hungry because she just changed the diaper.

   (A) must be

   (B) must have been

   (C) can be

   (D) can have been

解答：1. (C)　2. (A)　3. (C)　4. (A)　5. (A)

解析：

①「對現在的強烈推測」，用must＋V。

②「過去該……，但是卻如此」

③「過去該……，但是卻如此」

④must have＋V-p.p.表「對過去的強烈推測」

⑤「對現在的強烈推測」，用must＋V。

❶ 以would rather等字表示「寧願……而不願……」的句型如下：

(1) S＋would rather VR than VR

　　S＋would sooner VR than VR

　　S＋would VR rather than VR

(2) S＋prefer to VR rather than VR

　　S＋prefer to VR instead of V-ing

　　S＋prefer V-ing/N to V-ing/N

❷ would rather...than...的注意要點如下：

(1) would rather...than 中的 than 為連接詞，連接對等的結構，動詞須用**原形**，若前後動詞相同時，可省略後面的動詞。

(2) 本句型would rather為固定用法，用法等於would sooner，後接**原形**動詞。

(3) 本句型也可將rather置於than之前，成為would...rather than...。

❸ would rather...than...也可用prefer to...rather than...代替。

(1) prefer to...rather than...中 rather than 為連接詞，前後須連接VR。

(2) rather than的意思等於instead of，所以prefer to V1 rather than V2 的句型可寫成prefer to VR rather than VR。但要留意的是，instead of須加V-ing。而prefer...to...的句型意為「喜歡……勝過……」，不同的是prefer及to之後接須接**名詞**或**動名詞**。

❹ instead of 的注意要點如下：

(1) instead 作副詞用，可置於**句首**或**句尾**，置於句首要用逗號與句子分開。

(2) instead of 與rather than為介系詞片語，之後接**名詞**或**動名詞**，表

示「不……而是……；代替……」的意思，與 rather than意思相同。rather than 作連接詞用時，前後詞語的詞性必須對等。

(3) 這裡的rather than 連接不定詞片語時，後面的不定詞 to 常會省略。

例句講解

- **He** would rather **travel around the island** than **go abroad.**
- = **He** would **travel around the island** rather than **go abroad.**
- = **He** prefers to **travel around the island** rather than **go abroad.**
- = **He** prefers to **travel around the island** instead of **going abroad.**
  他寧可環島旅行，也不願出國。

- **James would rather die than surrender.**
- = **James** prefers to **die** rather than **surrender.**
- = **James** prefers **dying** to **surrendering.**
- = **James** prefers to **die** instead of **surrendering.**
  詹姆士寧死也不願投降。

- **Tim** would rather **eat at home** than **spend his money in restaurants.**
  提姆寧可在家吃飯也不要花錢去餐廳。

- **I** prefer **action movies** to **romance ones.**
  我喜歡動作片勝過文藝片。

- **What children need is love** instead of **pocket money.**
  孩子所需要的是愛而非零用錢。

- **When we told him about his fault, he didn't apologize, but blame on others** instead.
  當我們告知他的錯誤時，他沒有道歉，反而怪罪他人。

- Rather than/Instead of **spending money playing video games, you should find fun things that are free to do.**
  你應該找些不花錢、有趣的事情做，而不是花錢打電動。

滿分追擊模擬試題

( ) 1. "Why are you in such a hurry?" "The librarian said it was important that I _____ this book immediately."

(A) returned   (B) had returned

(C) was returning   (D) return

( ) 2. _____ the man warned her, she could have been cheated.

(A) Without   (B) Had   (C) As if   (D) But that

( ) 3. If the shrinking continues, India _____ in 200 million years.

【96學測】

(A) disappears   (B) will disappear

(C) would disappear   (D) would have disappeared

( ) 4. Egyptian culture _____ so well-known if the museums had not put Egyptian mummies on show. 【學測】

(A) would not have become   (B)would have become

(C) would not become   (D)would never become

( ) 5. If I _____ the fact, I would have taken action right away. 【學測】

(A) know   (B) knew

(C) had known   (D) would have known

( ) 6. The chairman insisted that we all _____ to him before ten o'clock.

(A) reported   (B) report

(C) will report   (D) must report

( ) 7. _____ my parents, I couldn't have a comfortable life now.

(A) Without   (B) With   (C) But if   (D) But that

( ) 8. Bag-matching would invade passengers' privacy _____ ensure their security. 【學測】

(A) sooner than　　(B) prefer to　　(C) rather than　　(D) instead of

( ) 9. Whenever I set foot on the soil of Rwanda, a country in eastcentral Africa, I feel _____ I have entered paradise: green hills, red earth, sparkling rivers and mountain lakes. 【學測】

(A) as if　　　(B) even if　　　(C) even though　　(D) as although

( ) 10. The ancient civilizations would not be so deeply admired today if these ancient artifacts（手工藝品）_____ so widely available to an international public in major museums throughout Europe and America. 【學測】

(A) were not　　(B) are not　　　(C) had not been　　(D) would not be

( ) 11. _____, tell me the results as soon as you get them.

(A) If it possible　　　　　(B) If possible

(C) Were it possible　　　　(D) Had it been possible

( ) 12. The reincarnated leaders were always "discovered" in the households of lowly families _____ noble ones. This was to ensure that no single and powerful noble family could seize the title and pass it to the next generation. 【學測】

(A) relative to　(B) rather than　　(C) as a result of　　(D) with regard to

( ) 13. It is time _____ with this problem. 【指考】

(A) that we dealt　　　　(B) for us dealing

(C) that we deal　　　　(D) to dealing

( ) 14. Even today, visitors to the park marvel at how such a road _____ built. 【學測】

(A) must have been　　　(B) must be

(C) could have　　　　　(D) could have been

假設語氣

(   ) 15. It was the judge's order that he _____ the money.

    (A) returned   (B) return   (C) returns   (D) must return

(   ) 16. _____, I would be more considerate.

    (A) Were I you   (B) If I am you

    (C) Were I to be you   (D) If were I you

(   ) 17. A case of museum feet makes one feel like saying. "This is boring. I _____ the painting myself. When can we sit down? What time is it? 　　　　　　　　　　　　　　【指考】

    (A) could done   (B) could have done

    (C) had done   (D) should do

(   ) 18. If we used more of this source of heat and light, it _____ all the power needed throughout the world. 　　　　【指考】

    (A) supplies   (B) has supplied

    (C) was supplying   (D) could supply

(   ) 19. With a DJ playing various kinds of music rather than just rap, and a mix of clothing labels designed more for taste and fashion than for a precise age, department stores have managed to appeal to successful middle-aged women _____ losing their younger customers. They have created a shopping environment where the needs of both mother and daughter are satisfied.

    (A) in   (B) while   (C) after   (D) without

(   ) 20. If you've ever seen the Sean Connery movie Medicine Man, then the annual convention of wizards and witches will be familiar to you. _____, get prepared for the overwhelming attack of wizards and witches here. 　　　　　　　　　　　　　　【指考】

    (A) If any   (B) If not   (C) If even   (D) If only

解答

1. (D) 有省略了should。

2. (D)「若非」。

3. (B) If後用現在式continues，所以此句為未來的推測，所以選(B)。

4. (A) 與過去事實相反。

5. (C) 主要子句用would have＋V-p.p.表示與過去事實相反，用過去完成式。依照公式，答案選(C)。

6. (B) 省略should。

7. (A)「沒有」我的父母的話。

8. (C) rather than有而不是的意思。

9. (A) 我踏上盧安達時，我覺得彷彿進到了天堂。依照文意用彷彿，答案選(A)。

10. (A) 主要子句用would not be，表示與現在事實相反，用過去式。所以if後子句也用過去式，依據公式，選(A)。

11. (B) 譯：如果可能的話，你一拿到結果就盡快告訴我。

12. (B) 依照文意，轉世者投胎至低階的家庭，而不是貴族世家。所以選(B)。

13. (A) 該是我們處理這個問題的時間了。

14. (D) 此處依文意，路竟然能夠（不是必定）被建造得如此美麗。選(D)。

15. (B) 有省略should。

16. (A) 主要子句用would be表示與現在事實相反，選過去式。原為If I were you，此處用倒裝句。選(A)。

17. (B) 首先，畫作已經陳列，所以要用與過去事實相反的表述用法，此處為主要子句，根據公式選(B)。

18. (D) 與過去事實相反。

19. (D) 成功吸引中年婦女顧客群，同時不「失去」年輕客群，故用without。

20. (B) 前面說你會對巫婆巫師的傳統聚會很熟悉。後面文意應為：「如果沒有，那就要準備面對許多巫婆巫師的景象了。」選(B)。

Part 8

倒裝句型

—— Part8 ——
倒裝句型

　　倒裝句型中，倒裝的莫過於(1)主詞與動詞調換位置，或是(2)疑問句式的倒裝，換句話說，就是調換be動詞的位置或加入助動詞，使其看起來像是疑問句。

　　所以，每次看到倒裝句型，要注意，調換位置的方式是屬於以上哪一種喔！而倒裝句的出現，大多是用在閱讀時，要能看懂文意。再者，就是用在寫作中，以強調文意了。

　　倒裝句 (inversion) 就是正常詞序顛倒的句子，其中以主詞和動詞順序對調的情況最為普遍。英文中最常見的倒裝句型是問句，其次就是下列三種倒裝句型：否定副詞、以Not做開頭的詞句、Here和there。不管是哪一種倒裝句，主要子句的主詞和動詞詞序都要對調，而其目的都是在加強特定字詞的語氣或起強調作用。

❶ 否定副詞（或具否定意義的片語）放句首時，其後子句需用倒裝句。

(1) 若原子句是主詞加be動詞時，直接把主詞與be動詞對調成倒裝。

句型：**否定副詞＋beV＋S**

(2) 若原子句是主詞加一般動詞時，則在主詞前面加上助動詞，形成倒裝。

句型：**否定副詞＋助V＋S＋VR**

(3) 請注意，若原子句是完成式，原是S＋have/has/had＋V-p.p.，其倒裝句型為：**否定副詞＋have/has/had＋S＋V-p.p.**

❷ 常用的否定副詞列表

(1) hardly/barely/rarely/scarcely/seldom 幾乎不

(2) few（可數）/little （不可數）幾乎沒有

(3) no sooner/no more/no longer 不再

(4) never (again) 再也不；never (before) = not for a moment 從來沒有

(5) not until 不……直到

(6) without effect/without avail/in vain 沒有用

(7) not a/not an/not any 沒有任何一個

(8) not at all/not in the least 一點也不

(9)in no way/on no account/in no case/on no condition/by no means/under no circumstances/to no purpose 絕不

- It is seldom **wise to answer back your boss.**
= Seldom is it **wise to answer back your boss.**（→保留be動詞is）

   對你的老闆回嘴不是一個明智之舉。

- He rarely comes **to visit us. = Rarely does he come to visit us.**
（→動詞為第三人稱現在式，用助動詞does）

   他很少來見我們。

- I have never met **such a person as you in my whole life.**
= In my whole life I have never met **such a person as you.**
= Never **in my whole life** have I met **such a person as you.**
（→動詞為第一人稱完成式，用完成式have）

   我從來沒遇過像你這樣的人。

- Hardly was he（→原句：he was）**ready when the chairman announced**
（宣布）**the winner.**

   當主席宣布獲勝者的時候，他幾乎沒有準備。

- Never have clothes been seen before（→原句：Clothes have never been
   seen before）**so stylish**（流行的）**, well-made, and wearable as those of**
   today. 以前的服飾從來沒有像今天的這麼流行、作工良好又耐穿。

★注意要點

　　表達「絕對不允許」或「絕對不能」的否定詞，置於句首時，後面引
導的句子需倒裝，倒裝的結構和疑問句的結構一樣；即「助V＋S＋V...」
或「BeV＋S...」，完成式則用「has/have/had＋S＋V-p.p.」。和by no
means（絕不）同義的否定詞尚有：in no way/on no account/in no case/on
no condition/under no circumstances/to no purpose。

- **By no means** did my parents **read my diary without my permission.**
   沒有我的允許，我父母絕對不能閱讀我的日記。

- **On no account did this woman allow her husband to stay out overnight.**
   這個女人絕不允許他的丈夫在外過夜。

主題二 | Only的倒裝句型

only的意思為「只有」，若接**副詞子句**或**副詞片語**，其後之主要子句需倒裝。 only之後引導的副詞子句不需倒裝。

句型：

$$
\text{only+} \left\{ \begin{array}{l} \text{介系詞片語} \\ \text{副詞子句} \\ \text{副詞} \end{array} \right. \text{+} \left\{ \begin{array}{l} \text{be+S} \\ \\ \text{助V+S+VR} \end{array} \right.
$$

 例句講解

• **Only <u>in my own country</u> do I feel happy.**
（→only＋介系詞片語）

　只有在我自己的家鄉我才會覺得快樂。

• **Only <u>if the prices come down</u> will I buy a house in the downtown.**
（→only＋副詞子句）

　只有當價格下跌時，我才會在市中心買房子。

• **You can succeed only <u>by working hard</u>.**
　Only <u>by working hard</u> can you succeed. （→only＋介系詞片語）

　唯有透過努力工作，你才會成功。

• **You can fulfill（達成）your dreams only <u>by burning the midnight oil</u>.**
　Only <u>by burning the midnight oil</u> can you fulfill your dreams.
（→only＋介系詞片語）

　唯有熬夜你才能夠實現你的夢想。

• **Only <u>when a young bird becomes strong enough</u> can it leave the nest
　to look for food by itself.** （→only＋副詞子句）

　只有在年輕的鳥兒變得夠強壯時，牠才能離巢去獨立找尋食物。

★注意要點

only置句首時，後面不是接副詞子句或副詞片語，則主要子句不需倒裝。

- **Only you can help me.**
  只有你能幫助我。

★延伸學習

「Only＋副詞子句＋助動詞＋S＋V...」句型可替換為「not...until...」。有關「not...until...」的句型，請參考【主題四】。

- **I began to enjoy the results of my hard work only after the whole year.**
- = **Only** <u>after the whole year</u> **did I begin to enjoy the results of my hard work.**
- = **Not until** <u>the whole year</u> **did I begin to enjoy the results of my hard work.**
  我只會在這一整年過完後才會享受我辛苦工作的成果。

隨堂測驗

( ) 1. Only when all attempts had failed _____ to depose the president.

     (A) the man decides   (B) did the man decide

     (C) the man decided   (D) the man would decide

( ) 2. Only _____ all this world seem right.

     (A) can you make   (B) you make

     (C) makes you   (D) you can make

( ) 3. Only when one loses freedom（自由）_____ its value（價值）.

     (A) one know   (B) one doesn't know

     (C) does one know   (D) one will not know

(   ) 4. _____ the objects be fully appreciated by the world. 【學測】

    (A) Only can in the leading museums

    (B) Only is in the leading museums

    (C) Only in the leading museums are

    (D) Only in the leading museums can

(   ) 5. German police could take action against Michael Jackson
_____ an official complaint was made against him. 【指考】

    (A) only by   (B) only when

    (C) if only   (D) when only

解答： 1. (B) 2. (D) 3. (C) 4. (D) 5. (B)

解析：

①此處要使用倒裝句。

②只有你能讓這個世界看起來正常。

③此處要使用倒裝句。

④此為ony之倒裝句型。

⑤only when意為「只有」。

主題三 | No sooner 的倒裝句型

❶ no sooner為否定詞，置於句首時其後引導的句子需用倒裝句。整個句型表示「一……就……」。句型為：No sooner had S＋V-p.p. than S＋V-p.t.

❷ 連接詞than所引導的子句不需倒裝，子句裡的動詞用**過去簡單式**。

❸ 此句型描述兩動作發生的先後次序，主要子句的動作**先發生**，用過去完成式 (had＋V-p.p.)，than引導的子句動作**後發生**，用過去簡單式 (V-p.t.)。

❹ 同義句型列表

(1) The moment/minute/instant S＋V-p.t...., S＋V-p.t....

(2) Once/Directly/Instantly/Immediately S＋V-p.t...., S＋V-p.t....

(3) On/Upon＋V-ing, S＋V-p.t.

(4) As soon as S＋V-p.t., S＋V-p.t.

　　= S＋had no sooner＋V-p.p. than S＋V-p.t.

　　= No sooner had S＋V-p.p. than S＋V-p.t.

(5) S＋had hardly/scarcely＋V-p.p. when/before S＋V-p.t.

　　= Hardly/Scarcely had＋S＋V-p.p. when/before S＋V-p.t.

例句講解

陣雨一過，就出現美麗的彩虹。

• The moment **the shower passed, a beautiful rainbow appeared.**

= Directly **the shower passed, a beautiful rainbow appeared.**

= On/Upon **passing the shower, a beautiful rainbow appeared.**

= As soon as **the shower passed, a beautiful rainbow appeared.**

= The shower had no sooner **passed than a beautiful rainbow appeared.**

= **No sooner** had the shower passed than a beautiful rainbow appeared.

= The shower had hardly passed before a beautiful rainbow appeared.

= Hardly had the shower passed before a beautiful rainbow appeared.

● As soon as James finished washing his car, it began to rain.

= James had no sooner finished washing his car than it began to rain.

= No sooner had James finished washing his car than it began to rain.

詹姆士一洗完他的車就開始下雨。

● The moment Jack heard the news that Rose had passed away, he burst into tears.

= On hearing the news that Rose had passed away, Jack burst into tears.

傑克一聽到蘿絲去逝的消息，就突然哭了起來。

● I had scarcely arrived when I had a new problem to cope with.

= Scarcely（幾乎不）had I arrived when I had a new problem to cope with.

= I had a new problem to deal with as soon as I arrived.

我才剛抵達就有個新問題要處理。

隨堂測驗

( ) 1. Our instructor had no sooner _____ baseball than we _____ excited about it.

(A) mentioned; had became   (B) spoken of; become

(C) has spoken of; became   (D) mentioned; became

( ) 2. No sooner _____ the news than they rushed out into the street.

(A) they heard   (B) they had heard

(C) did they hear   (D) had they heard

( ) 3. _____ had she heard the news than she wept（哭泣） aloud.

(A) No sooner   (B) Never

(C) Not only   (D) Hardly

( ) 4. Hardly _____ when a quarrel（爭吵）broke out.

    (A) I had arrived   (B) I arrived

    (C) had I arrived   (D) I did arrive

( ) 5. Scarcely _____ home when he turned on the TV.

    (A) did he arrive   (B) he arrived

    (C) had he arrived   (D) he had arrived

( ) 6. _____ had he left the house than the storm broke.

    (A) Scarcely   (B) No sooner

    (C) The moment   (D) As soon as

解答： 1. (C) 2. (D) 3. (A) 4. (C) 5. (C) 6. (B)

解析：

②此為no sooner之倒裝句型。

③no sooner之倒裝句型。

④倒裝句型，hardly表示「幾乎不」

⑤倒裝句型

⑥解析同第二題。

主題四 | Not until 的倒裝句型

❶ 此句型「S＋助動詞＋not＋V...＋until＋子句／時間副詞」，為「直到……才……」的加強語氣句型。因為否定字not至句首，後之主要子句需倒裝，形成「Not until＋子句／時間副詞＋助動詞＋S＋V...」的句型。

❷ until以及not...until的差別

(1) till = until：（表示動作、狀態的持續）一直……為止

(2) not... until：直到……才……

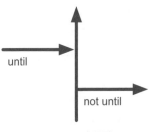

until + 時間點

例句講解

- **She stayed awake until midnight.**
- = **She did not go to bed until midnight.**
- = **Not until midnight did she go to bed.**

  她直到午夜才就寢。

- **He lived with his parents until he got married.**
- = **He did not leave his parents until he got married.**
- = **Not until he got married did he leave his parents.**

  他直到結婚前，都還和爸媽住在一起。

- **Not until he told me did I know the news.**

  直到他告訴我，我才知道這個消息。

- **Not until she failed in exams did she realize that she had neglected her schoolwork for too long.**

  直到考試失敗，她才了解到她已經忽略學校課業太久。

★延伸學習

　　「Not until＋子句／時間副詞＋助動詞＋S＋V...」也可以分裂句「It＋be動詞＋not until＋子句／時間副詞＋that＋S＋V...」的形式呈現，強調用法。此句型裡連接詞that引導的子句**不須倒裝**，until引導的子句為副詞子句，也**不須倒裝**。而主要子句倒裝的結構和疑問句的結構一樣。

- **He did not know who his parents were until he was 18.**
- = **Not until he was 18 did he know who his parents were.**
- = **It was not until he was 18 that he knew who his parents were.**

  他直到18歲才知道雙親是誰。

- **I don't realize how nice home is until I am away from it.**
- = **Not until I am away from home do I know how nice it is.**
- = **It is not until I am away from home that I know how nice it is.**

  直到離開家，我才知道家是多麼好！

🕐 隨堂測驗

(　　) 1. Jerry _____ recognize his primary school classmate Mary _____ he listened to her self-introduction.

    (A) not until; did　　　　　　(B) didn't; until

    (C) did; until　　　　　　　　(D) would; until

(　　) 2. Not until the doctor was sure everything was all right _____ the emergency room.

    (A) he left　　　　　　　　　(B) left he

    (C) did he leave　　　　　　　(D) he did leave

( ) 3. Not until you paint your first oil color _____ the difference between theory（理論）and practice.

(A) you find out
(B) and find out
(C) finding out
(D) do you find out

( ) 4. _____ the invention of the movable print can ordinary people afford to buy one.

(A) After
(B) Until
(C) Not until
(D) Because of

( ) 5. _____ she got rid of the watch she had found _____ she felt happy.

(A) It is not until; that
(B) Not until; does
(C) It was not until; that
(D) Not until; did

( ) 6. You _____ realize what you have _____ it is almost taken away.

(A) don't; when
(B) will; when
(C) don't; until
(D) will; until

7. 直到報紙揭露，這件醜聞才曝光。

_____ the scandal（醜聞）come to light _____ the newspaper disclosed（揭發）it.

8. 直到午夜十二點，我才回家。

_____ did I get home.

9. 直到失去健康我們才了解它的重要性。

_____

解答： 1. (B) 2. (C) 3. (D) 4. (C) 5. (A) 6. (C)
7. Not until;did=It was not until; that.
8. Not until 12 o'clock at midnight
9. We do not know the importance of health until we lose it.
=Not until we lose health do we know the importance of it.
=It's not until we lose health that we know the importance of it.

解析：
①not until「直到」
②not until之倒裝句型。
③解析同上題。
④not until之倒裝句型。
⑤「Not until＋子句／時間副詞＋助動詞＋S＋V...」也可以分裂句「It＋be動詞＋not until＋子句／時間副詞＋that＋S＋V...」的形式呈現，強調用法。
⑥not until「直到」

主題五 | As..., so...的倒裝句型

說明 此句型用來表示「A之於B猶如 C之於D」。

有下列同義句型：

A is to B as/what C is to D

= As C is to D, so is A to B

= As C is to D, so A is to B

= What C is to D, so A is to B

= What C is to D, (that) A is to B

例句講解

• **Reading is to the mind as/what food is to the body.**

= **As food is to the body, so is reading to the mind.**

= **What food is to the body, reading is to the mind.**

= **What food is to the body, that reading is to the mind.**

讀書之於心靈猶如食物之於身體。

• **The skin is to a man as the bark is to a tree.**

= **The skin is to a man what the bark is to a tree.**

= **As the bark is to a tree, so is the skin to a man.**

= **As the bark is to a tree, so the skin is to a man.**

= **What the bark is to a tree, the skin is to a man.**

皮膚之於人猶如樹皮之於樹。

( ) 1. _____ the spirit is exhausted by overwork, so it is destroyed by idleness.

(A) If   (B) As   (C) X   (D) What

( ) 2. As fire tries gold, so _____ adversity try courage.

(A) do   (B) does

(C) as   (D) that

( ) 3. _____ air is to men, _____ water is to fish.

(A) What; X   (B) As; X

(C) What; so is   (D) As; so is

( ) 4. As rust（鐵鏽）eats iron（鐵）, so _____ care eat the heart.

(A) like   (B) as

(C) does   (D) is

( ) 5. New York is to America _____ Taipei is to Taiwan.

(A) what   (B) as

(C) like   (D) but

解答：1. (D) 2. (B) 3. (A) 4. (C) 5. (B)

解析：
②這邊要使用倒裝句型。
③as/what...so...的倒裝句型。
⑤as在這表示「如同」。

主題六 | not only 的倒裝句型

❶「not only A but (also) B」的句型表示「不只……還有……」，A和B須連接**性質相同**的字詞。

❷ not為否定字詞，置於句首時，後面引導的子句倒裝。but之後的動詞片語或子句皆不須倒裝，但**時態須與前面動詞一致**。

❸ 句型中only可替換為just或merely。

例句講解

- She not only sings like an angel, but also dances divinely（似神仙地）.
= Not only does she sing like angel, but she also dances divinely.
  她不僅唱歌像個天使，舞也跳得如仙子一般。

- Yo Yo Ma plays not only the cello（大提琴）, but also the violin.
= Not only does Yoyo Ma play the cello, but he also plays the violin.
  馬友友不只會拉大提琴，也會拉小提琴。

- Rose not only made promise, but she also kept it.
= Not only did Rose make a promise, but she also kept it.
  蘿絲不僅許下了諾言，還實現了它。

★注意要點

連接句子時，also 必須置於動詞之前、be 動詞之後。

- The students not only studied hard, but they also played hard.
  學生們不但用功唸書，也認真玩樂。

- James is not only my teacher, but also my benefactor.
= Not only is James my teacher, but he is also my benefactor.
  詹姆士不僅是我的老師，還是我的恩人。

★延伸學習

❶ 在同一個子句中，not only A but (also) B的**語意重點在B**，故動詞以**主詞B 為主**。句型為：Not only A but (also) B＋V (視B決定)

• **Not only Joyce but also <u>her parents</u> are coming.**

  不只喬伊絲，連她的父母都來了。

• **Not only he alone but <u>we</u> are your great supporters.**

  不只有他一人，還有我們，都是你最佳的支持者。

❷ not only A but (also) B也等同於A as well as B（A以及B），但A as well as B的**語意重點在A**，故動詞以**主詞A為主**。句型：A as well as B＋V（視 A決定）

❸ 在句意上，as well as = along with = together with。

• <u>James</u> as well as I **is trying very hard to enhance the student' knowledge.**

  詹姆士以及我，正努力嘗試增進學生的知識。

• <u>My teacher</u> as well as my parents **set great example for me.**

  我的老師以及我的父母都為我樹立了好的榜樣。

• <u>I</u> as well as my brother **sing well, so we plan to join the singing contest.**

  我還有我的弟弟歌都唱得好，所以我們打算要去參加歌唱比賽。

隨堂測驗

( ) 1. _____ to obtain, but it also is a solution to environmental pollution（污染）.

  (A) Solar energy（太陽能）is not only easy

  (B) Solar energy is easy not only

  (C) Not only easy is solar energy

  (D) Not only is solar energy easy

( ) 2. Not only _____ his girlfriend help him cook dinner but also cleaned his house.

  (A) did   (B) has   (C) X   (D) does

( ) 3. Not only _____ advantage of my kindness but his brother has set my family up.

  (A) had Nick taken   (B) has Nick taken
  (C) did Nick take   (D) does Nick take

( ) 4. Not only the students but also the teacher _____ to turn off their cell phone during class.

  (A) have   (B) did have   (C) has   (D) does have

( ) 5. This actress not only stays fit but also _____ in shape.

  (A) she keeps (B) keeps   (C) her keeps   (D) keeping

( ) 6. Not only _____ instructions but also recognizes shapes, colors and words－and remembers. 【學測】

  (A) she follows   (B) does she follow
  (C) she does follow   (D) does follow she

解答： 1. (D) 2. (A) 3. (B) 4. (C) 5. (B) 6. (B)

解析：

①此處為not only...but also...的倒裝句型。

②解析同上題，此處要倒裝。

③此處要倒裝。

④此處性處變化要搭配the teacher。

⑤性數變化與主詞the actress相同。

⑥此處為倒裝句型。

主題七 So, Neither, Nor 作為附和的倒裝句型

★ POINT 7-A so的倒裝句型

❶ so表示**贊同**的附和句，就是「也」的意思。

- A: I enjoy watching romance movies. 我喜歡看愛情片。
  B: I do, too./So do I. 我也喜歡。

❷ neither和nor的用法一樣，都是表**否定**的附和句，是「也不」的意思。

- A: I am not reading a comic book. 我沒有在看漫畫書。
  B: I am not, either. 或 Neither/Nor am I. 我也沒有。

❸ so/neither（也／也不……）在此為副詞，句子之間需用連接詞and或分號 (;)或句點隔開，之後的句子**須倒裝**，助動詞／be動詞用**肯定**。句型為：

肯定句, and so＋助動詞／be動詞＋S（皆為也……）
= 肯定句, and＋S＋助動詞／be動詞, too.

 例句講解

- A: I like classical music. 我喜歡古典音樂。
  B: I like classical music, too. 我也是。
= I do, too.
= So do I.

- You are a student, and Jack is, too. → and so is Jack.
  你是學生，傑克也是。

- Sue can speak German, and Mary can, too. → and so can Mary.
  蘇會說德文，瑪麗也會。

- I was tired, and so were the other classmates.
  我累了，其他同學也一樣。

- I like singing; so does my husband. 我喜歡唱歌，我先生也喜歡。

★ POINT 7-B neither的倒裝句型

❶ neither用來表達「附和」之意時，句型和so相同。句型為：

否定句，and neither＋助動詞/be動詞＋S（……也不……）

否定句，and＋S＋助動詞/be動詞＋not, either.

其中neither可替換為nor，但nor是**連接詞**，句與句之間用逗點(,)隔開。

❷ 「neither A nor B」的句型則是表達「既不……也不……」，連接兩個子句，A和B須詞性相同。若主詞相同時，則nor引導的子句中，「助動詞＋主詞」可以省略。neither或nor為否定字詞，置於句首時，後面引導的句子須倒裝。

 例句講解

• A: I don't like the teacher who is fond of telling dirty jokes in class.

  B: I don't like the teacher who is fond of telling dirty jokes in class, either.

= I don't, either.

= Neither do I.

  A: 我不喜歡那個在上課時講低級笑話的老師。

  B: 我也是（我也不喜歡）。

• He can't speak German, and I can't, either. →and neither can I.

→and nor can I.

  他不會說德文，我也不會。

• He is not the man stealing the money; neither am I.

  他不是偷錢的人，我也不是。

• My brother doesn't like getting into trouble, nor do I.

  我弟弟不喜歡惹麻煩，我也是。

• I like neither apples nor oranges.

  我既不喜歡蘋果，也不喜歡橘子。

- **Neither did James want to figure out this affair nor want to get involved.**
  詹姆士既不想要理解這件事，也不想和它有所牽扯。

★注意要點

　　neither A nor B（既不……也不……）或其類似句型either A or B（不是……就是……）的句型中，A和B須對等，亦即連接性質相同的字詞，動詞以最靠近的**主詞**B為主。句型為：(1) Neither A nor B＋V(視B決定)... (2) Either A or B＋V(視B決定)...

- **Neither I nor <u>my friend</u> has thought to betray you.**
  我和我的朋友都沒有背叛你的想法。

　　延伸學習雖然「either A or B」類似句型「neither A nor B」，但either並非否定字詞，置於句首時，後面引導的子句不須用倒裝句，or之後的子句也不須倒裝。

- **A newborn baby either drinks milk or falls asleep every day.**
  新生兒每天不是喝牛奶就是睡覺。

- **Either her father gives her money for lunch every morning or her mother brings her a lunch box at noon.**
  不是他父親每天早上給她錢買午餐，就是她的母親中午幫她送便當。

隨堂測驗

(　　) 1. The largest television network in America is not ABC, or Fox. _____ one of the cable networks such as CNN, which carries only news and news stories. 【學測】

　　(A) So does it　　　　　　　(B) So is it
　　(C) Nor is it　　　　　　　　(D) Nor it is

(　　) 2. Good health is not something you are able to buy, _____ get it back with a quick visit to a doctor. 【學測】

　　(A) nor can you　　　　　　(B) nor are you
　　(C) and neither are you　　(D) and nor you can

(　) 3. So, if you need money now, you should try _____ finding a job
_____ cutting down on your expenses. 【學測】

(A) neither; nor　　　　　(B) both; but also
(C) either; or　　　　　　(D) as; as

(　) 4. I am not the kind of person bullied without getting angry, and I think
_____.

(A) my friends are, too　　(B) neither my friends do
(C) neither are my friends　(D) neither do my friends

(　) 5. My father doesn't understand me _____ my mother.

(A) , and neither　　　　(B) ; neither does
(C) , neither　　　　　　(D) ; and neither does

解答： 1. (C)　2. (A)　3. (C)　4. (C)　5. (B)

解析：
①nor的倒裝句型。
②同上題。
③either...or...「不是……就是……」。
④我的朋友也不是，此處否定要用neither。
⑤此處否定要用neither+倒裝句型。

主題八 | So...that.../ Such...that...的倒裝句型

❶ so...that及such...that的句型，原本結構為

S＋beV＋so＋adj.＋that＋S＋V...

S＋beV＋such＋名詞＋that＋S＋V...

動詞為be動詞，so＋adj. 及such＋名詞為主詞補語，若為了強調此補語而將補語放句首，其後引導的子句則須用倒裝結構。

❷ 倒裝的是主要句，連接詞that所引導的子句，則不須用倒裝形式。

例句講解

• James is so kind that everyone is his friend.
= So kind is James that everyone is his friend.
= Such is James's kindness that everyone is his friend.
（→補語為adj. kind時，搭配副詞so；補語為N kindness時，搭配形容詞 such）

　　詹姆士是那麼仁慈以至於每個人都是他的朋友。

• He studied so hard that he won the first prize.
= So hard did he study that he won the first prize.
（→補語為adj. hard，搭配副詞so）

　　他那麼用功因此得到第一名。

• She felt so embarrassed that she could not say a word.
= So embarrassed did she feel that she could not say a word.
（→補語為分詞embarrassed，搭配副詞so）

　　她尷尬得連一句話都説不出來。

• Such is Sam's politeness that his future mother-in-law likes him a lot.
（→補語為Sam's politeness，搭配形容詞such）

　　山姆很有禮貌，所以他的未來岳母很喜歡他。

- **Such a good girl was she that Ms. Lin chose her to be the model student.**

（→補語為a good girl，搭配形容詞such）

她是一個好女孩，所以林老師選她當模範生。

🕐 隨堂測驗

( ) 1. Snow White has _____ white skin that she is hardly recognized in a snow-covered forest.

(A) so   (B) such   (C) very   (D) too

( ) 2. _____ that whoever knew it felt sorry for him.

(A) Such a sad story did he share   (B) He shared a sad story

(C) It was a sad story he shared   (D) Such a story he shared

( ) 3. They are _____ energetic kids that they bring joy to everyone.

(A) so   (B) how   (C) what   (D) such

( ) 4. "So delicate _____," Dr. Lee said, "that they cannot be satisfactorily smeared for three days."

(A) the cells are   (B) that the cells are

(C) are the cells   (D) looks the cells

( ) 5. _____ strong is the sunlight _____ it tanned my skin.

(A) How; that   (B) So; as   (C) How; as   (D) So; that

解答：1. (B) 2. (A) 3. (D) 4. (C) 5. (D)

解析：①such用以修飾white skin。
      ②此為such...that之倒裝句型。
      ③such用以修飾energetic kids。
      ④此處為倒裝句型，so用以修飾delicious。
      ⑤so...that之倒裝句型。

主題九 | 方位副詞的倒裝句型

❶ 將**地方副詞**（片語）**置句首**，是加強語氣的用法，目的在強調句子中的地方副詞（片語），其後之句子須將主詞和動詞的位置互換，不須用助詞來形成倒裝句（亦即非問句式倒裝）。

❷ 常用的地方副詞除了there、here外，還有表示地方的介副詞，如：in、out、up down、off、way等，以及表示位置的副詞片語，如：near my house、on the tree、in the church等。

例句講解

- <u>An old house</u> <u>stood</u> <u>at the side of the hill</u>.
  　　　S　　　　V　　　　地方副詞

= <u>At the side of the hill</u> <u>stood</u> <u>an old house</u>.
  　　地方副詞　　　　　V　　　　S

山腰上矗立著一座舊屋子。

- <u>A pile of paper cups</u> <u>stood</u> <u>next to the table</u>.
  　　　S　　　　　　V　　　　地方副詞

= <u>Next to the table</u> <u>stood</u> <u>a pile of paper cups</u>.
  　　地方副詞　　　　V　　　　S

桌子的鄰近處擺著一堆紙杯。

- <u>When she opened the box,</u> <u>out</u> <u>leaped</u> <u>a frog</u>.
  　　　時間副詞　　　　地方副詞　V　　S

當他把盒子打開時，一隻青蛙跳了出來。

★注意要點

在此句型中，若主詞為代名詞，則地方副詞（片語）之後不需倒裝。

- **Come on! There you go again.** 拜託，你老毛病又犯了。
- **Here you are.** 給你。
- **Here we are.** 我們到了。
- **There she goes.** 她走了。
- **There goes the bell.** 鈴響了。

★延伸學習

有時也會將句子中的**時間副詞**移置句首，時間副詞之後亦須將主詞和動詞的位置互換，不需用助動詞來形成倒裝句。

- <u>Then</u> came the age of science and technology.
  然後科技的時代來臨了。
- <u>After the storm</u> comes a calm.
  否極泰來。

隨堂測驗

( ) 1. Along the river bank _____ taking part in the marathon race.

   (A) did the athletes run   (B) ran the athletes
   (C) the athletes ran   (D) the athlete did run

( ) 2. In your hands _____.

   (A) the future of our country lies
   (B) does the future of our country lie
   (C) lies the future of our country
   (D) the future of our country does lie

( ) 3. _____ the flock of birds.

   (A) Fly away   (B) Flying away are
   (C) Away flying are   (D) Away are flying

(　　) 4. Beside the door _____ angrily with her arms folded in from of her chest.

(A) did she stand   (B) stood she

(C) she stood   (D) did she stood

(　　) 5. _____ perched（棲息）a large black bird.

(A) Often   (B) Suddenly   (C) On the wire (D) It

(　　) 6. Across the street from the station _____.

(A) stood an old drugstore

(B) it stood an old drugstore

(C) where an old drugstore stood

(D) which stood an old drugstore

(　　) 7. _____ the group of astronauts（太空人）who are to lead in man's exploration（發現）of outer space.

(A) Here come   (B) Here comes

(C) Here are coming   (D) Here coming are

8. 我家附近有一家超市。（中翻英）

解答：1. (B) 2. (C) 3. (B) 4. (B) 5. (C) 6. (A) 7. (B)
8. A supermarket is near my house.
=Near my house is a supermarket.

解析：
①此為地方副詞片語置句首倒裝之加強語氣用法。
②同上題。
③原句為The flock of birds are flying away.
④同第一題。
⑤同第一題。
⑥原句為An old drugstore stood across...。
⑦同第一題。

主題十 | 假設語氣的倒裝句型

❶ 假設語氣的倒裝常出現在文學作品中,因為順序有變,又省略掉關鍵字if,所以閱讀時需要仔細判讀。

❷ 句型變化如下:

If+S+were... → Were+S...

If+S+V... → Do/Does/Did+S+VR...

If+S+助V+VR... →助V+S+VR...

例句講解

• **If I were a millionaire, I could grant(答應)your request(要求).**

= **Were I a millionaire, I could grant your request.**

如果我是個百萬富翁,我就可以答應你的要求。

• **If he had followed my advice(忠告), he would have succeeded.**

= **Had he followed my advice, he would have succeeded.**

如果他有聽我的忠告,他本來是能成功的。

• **If she should come, I will dissuade(勸阻)her from going abroad(出國).**

= **Should she come, I will dissuade her from going abroad.**

如果她有來,我會勸阻她不要出國。

隨堂測驗

(　　) 1. Mia would cry louder _____.

(A) were it not for your joke　　(B) if there were a joke

(C) were there a joke　　(D) if there were for it

( ) 2. They should have arrived earlier _____ no accident.

    (A) were there   (B) had there been

    (C) were it   (D) had it been

( ) 3. _____ it not been for this test, Yuki wouldn't be so hardworking.

    (A) If   (B) Were

    (C) Had   (D) Would have

( ) 4. _____ too noisy, I could have a sound sleep

    (A) Were the kid not

    (B) Were not the kid

    (C) Had not been the kid

    (D) Had the kid not been

( ) 5. _____, what would happen?

    (A) The earth were to stop revolving

    (B) If the earth stops revolving

    (C) Were the earth to stop revolving

    (D) If The earth is to stop revolving

解答：1. (A)　2. (B)　3. (C)　4. (A)　5. (C)

解析：

①此為假設語氣之倒裝句型。

②同上題。

③同第一題。

④同第一題。

⑤假設語氣倒裝句型。

滿分追擊模擬試題

( ) 1. The boys were thrilled, for _____ believe that they were being paid to do something they enjoyed. 【學測】
(A) hardly can them
(B) hardly does it
(C) hardly do they
(D) hardly could they

( ) 2. Rarely _____ a house constructed by using mostly recyclable materials _____ environmental pollution.
(A) ×; causes
(B) does; cause
(C) ×; to cause
(D) has; to cause

( ) 3. Not for a single moment _____ giving light.
(A) the sun has stopped
(B) stopped has the sun
(C) has the sun stopped
(D) has stopped the sun

( ) 4. By no means _____ his mind after he made up his mind.
(A) he would change
(B) he wants to change
(C) does he change
(D) did he change

( ) 5. Someone's biography is nonfiction; _____. 【學測】
(A) so is your autobiography
(B) so does your autobiography
(C) so your autobiography is
(D) neither is your autobiography

(　) 6. The city is incredibly urbanized, but beneath its modern appearance _____. 　【學測】

    (A) does an unmistakable Thai-ness lie

    (B) an unmistakable Thai-ness lies

    (C) does lie an unmistakable Thai-ness

    (D) lies an unmistakable Thai-ness

(　) 7. Most amazing _____ they can be viewed only from the air. 　【學測】

    (A) that is the fact   (B) is that the fact

    (C) is the fact that   (D) the fact that is

(　) 8. Neither flashlight fish nor fireflies _____ out light to find their way home. 　【學測】

    (A) send   (B) sends

    (C) has sent   (D) has been sent

(　) 9. I have cheated in exams. No matter what I say, on no account _____ that I get good grades by myself in this exam.

    (A) believe my mother not

    (B) but my mother believes

    (C) will my mother believe

    (D) my mother is going to believe

(　) 10. Only just now _____ to him about the things to heed while riding a motorcycle.

    (A) I talked   (B) was I talking

    (C) talked I   (D) I was talked

(　) 11. Only where there is a will _____.

    (A) there is a way   (B) there as a way

    (C) is there a way   (D) has there a way

(　) 12. This international recognition highlights the important of this area, ＿＿＿ to the United States and Canada, ＿＿＿ to the entire world.　【學測】

(A) both; but

(B) not just; but

(C) together; with

(D) not only; and

(　) 13. Memory is to experience as regret is to ＿＿＿.

(A) sorrow

(B) problem

(C) recollection

(D) mistake

(　) 14. Just across the border, in Canada, ＿＿＿ the Western Lakes National Park.　【學測】

(A) here is

(B) there has

(C) is

(D) is there

解答

1. (D) 此處為倒裝句型。

2. (B) Rarely否定字放句首，後面就要用倒裝句。此句還原：A house constructed by using mostly recyclable materials rarely causes environmental pollution. 所以可知，本句動詞為causes，故改成倒裝用 does...cause。

3. (C) 時間副詞置首的加強語氣用法。

4. (D) 倒裝句，強調By no means。

5. (A) 這一句是附和句的倒裝，前句用肯定句，所以後句用so來寫。需注意 nonfiction為非虛構，雖有「非」意，但仍為肯定句。

6. (D) 倒裝句，強調beneath its modern appearance。

7. (C) 原句為The fact that they can be viewed only from the air is most amazing.

8. (A) Neither A nor B 中，動詞跟接近的主詞一致，此處以fireflies為主詞，選(A)。

9. (C) on no account的倒裝句。

10. (B) I was talking to him only just now，此處強調only just now。

11. (C) 此處要使用倒裝句。

12. (B) not just...but...有「不只……還……」意。

13. (D) 記憶之於經驗，就如同遺憾之於錯誤。（有經驗即有記憶，有錯誤就有遺憾。）

14. (C) 這句是地方副詞放句首的倒裝句，原句是The Western Lakes National Park is just across the border, in Canada.

Part 9

It的相關句型

　　每當看到it的出現，但是前文又沒有很明確的指出it所代稱的字，那麼我們就可以推斷，it為虛主詞或虛受詞了。It的出現，是為了讓句子避免頭重腳輕的現象。所以要想找出it所代表的真正文意，就要往其後去尋找真主詞或真受詞的to＋VR或that＋Cl的結構，以正確判讀文意。

　　it 的題型其實本身不難，但是因為it充斥在文章中各個地方，又不一定都是當虛主詞或虛受詞，所以作答時常被忽略。每次在選代名詞時，請小心觀察題目的結構。

例句講解

● **That you saw your ex-boyfriend in the office was embarrassing!**
　你在辦公室裡看到前男友還真是尷尬！

　　前面主詞That you saw your ex-boyfriend in the office很長，為了要改掉者個句子頭重腳輕的問題，我們可以把這個主詞移到後面，並在前面加上一個虛主詞it，變成：It was embarrassing that you saw your ex-boyfriend in the office.

主題一 | it作虛主詞與補語

★ **POINT 1-A** **It is＋adj.＋(for sb.)＋to V**

❶ 當虛主詞 it 代替真主詞不定詞片語、不定詞片語作主詞用時，須搭配**單數動詞**。句型為It is＋adj.＋(for sb.)＋to V，表示「**對某人而言，做某件事情是……的。**」

❷ 此句型中的形容詞，是所謂的「非人形容詞」，用來修飾後面的不定詞，而不是修飾人，所以不可以改成用人做主詞。

❸ 這類形容詞有：

(1)（重要的）important/crucial/significant

(2)（必要的）necessary/imperative/essential

(3)（不必要的）unnecessary

(4)（困難的）hard/difficult

(5)（容易的）easy

(6)（方便的）convenient

(7)（不方便的）inconvenient

(8)（緊急的）urgent/emergent

例句講解

• **It is necessary for young people to read as many good books as possible.**

年輕人需要盡量多讀好書，這是必要的。

• **It is important for you to get to work on time.**

你上班要準時，這是重要的。

- **It is crucial for you to fill out the application form according to facts.**
  你要根據事實來填申請表，這是重要的。

- **It is convenient for students to gather information online.**
  學生在網路上蒐集資料很方便。

★注意要點

　　本句型也可以與It is important/necessary...＋that＋S＋(should)＋V的句型互換。

- **It is essential for each of us to hand in our homework on time.**
- = **It is essential that each of us (should) hand in our homework on time.**
  我們每個人都必須要準時交作業，這是基本而必要的。

- **It is urgent that you (should) send her to the hospital at one.**
  你應該要馬上送她去醫院，這是很緊急的。

隨堂測驗

(　) 1. It is not easy _____ old people to scratch their backs.

　　(A) of 　　　　　　　　　　**(B)** for

　　(C) as 　　　　　　　　　　**(D)** than

(　) 2. It is not uncommon nowadays _____ women working outside their homes.

　　(A) finding 　　　　　　　　**(B)** for finding

　　(C) to find 　　　　　　　　**(D)** as to find

(　) 3. It's _____ to cling to that belief.

　　(A) hardness 　　　　　　　**(B)** hard

　　(C) exhausted 　　　　　　　**(D)** exhaustedly

(　) 4. _____ never too late to apologize for what you had done.

　　(A) You are 　　　　　　　　**(B)** It is

　　(C) That is 　　　　　　　　**(D)** This is

( ) 5. It is _____ that Daniel should make a choice between studying abroad or taking over his family business.

(A) clever   (B) stupid

(C) necessary   (D) careless

( ) 6. After a long discussion, we all agreed that it was hard to _____ the win-win situation.

(A) be reached   (B) reach

(C) be solved   (D) solve

7. 醫生們刊登未出生的嬰兒照片是不對的。（中翻英） 【指考】

解答： 1. (B) 2. (C) 3. (B) 4. (B) 5. (C) 6. (B)

7. It is wrong for doctors to publish pictures of unborn babies.

解析：

①此句型為It is＋adj.＋(for sb.)＋to V

②for後要接人，此處應為省略for sb直接接to V。

③本題談論的是堅守信念很「艱難」，故選B。

④此為it作為虛主詞置於句首強調用法。

⑤此處談論的是「必須」在後面提到的兩件事中做出選擇，C符合文意。

⑥解析參考第一題。

★ POINT 1-B It is＋adj.＋of sb.＋to V

❶ 此類的形容詞是用來**修飾人**的，而不是修飾事物，所以可以把整句改成人作主詞。

❷ 這類形容詞有：凡是可以修飾人的形容詞，都可以如此使用。

(1)（好心的）good/kind/kind-hearted、（有同情心的）sympathetic

(2)（殘忍的）cruel

(3)（有禮貌的）polite/well-mannered、（無禮的）impolite/rude

例句講解

* It is kind of **her** to **give a helping hand to the poor and needy.**
= She is kind to **give a helping hand to the poor and needy.**
  她對窮苦的人伸出援手，真是好心。

* It is unkind of **him** to **insult you to your face.**
= He is unkind to **insult you to your face.**
  他這樣當面羞辱你，真是很壞心。

* It is cruel of **parents** to **abuse their children.**
  虐待小孩的父母，真是殘忍。

★注意要點

注意下面兩句中，因不同的介系詞而讓good有不同含意。

* It is good **for you to take regular exercise.** （→ good**修飾事物**）
  定期做運動對你是很好的。

* It is good **of you to give me a hand when I am in trouble.**
（→ good**修飾人**）
  你真是心地善良，當我有麻煩時就會對我伸出援手。

 **隨堂測驗**

( ) 1. It is kind-hearted _____ her to visit the old lady who lives alone.

   (A) of   (B) for   (C) to   (D) with

( ) 2. It was dishonest _____ him to cheat on the exam.

   (A) of   (B) to   (C) from   (D) as

( ) 3. It is rude _____ to speak ill of others behind their backs.

   (A) of she   (B) for she
   (C) of her   (D) of her

( ) 4. It is so _____ of Sean to remind his girlfriend that she is overweight.

   (A) foolish   (B) crucial
   (C) important   (D) useful

5. 她在公車上讓座給老人，真是好心。（中翻英）

解答： 1. (A) 2. (A) 3. (C) 4. (A)
5. It is kind of her to give her seat to the elderly man on the bus.

解析：
①句型為It is＋adj.＋of sb.＋to V。
②參考上一題。
③同第一題。
④譯：Sean提醒他女朋友她超重真的很「蠢」。

★ **POINT 1-C** It is＋a/the/one's＋N＋that...

❶ 本章到此為止的句型中，it都做虛主詞，有時是指後面的不定詞片語，有時是指that子句。在本句型中，that後面所加上的子句，其實就是用來說明前面名詞的**補語**，因此，that後面是一個完整的子句。

❷ 在這個句型中，that是用來引導後面補充說明that之前的名詞子句，所以不能用其他關係代名詞替代。

• It was **a surprise** that <u>my parents came visiting on Christmas Eve</u>.

（→這裡的that之後，是一個完整子句。用來補充說明前面的驚喜。）

我爸媽在聖誕夜來看我，真是驚喜。

❸ 另外，常混淆的是分裂強調句，請看以下句子：

• It was **a surprise** that <u>my parents gave me on Christmas Eve</u>.

（→這裡的that是代替前面的a surprise。that之後的句子應該是my parents gave me (a surprise) on Christmas，於是可以知道是分裂強調句的寫法，這裡的that之後的子句是形容詞子句。）

這是我爸媽在聖誕夜給我的驚喜。

📝 例句講解

• It was **his discovery** that <u>the rays can penetrate solid walls</u>.
他發現這種光線可以穿透過堅硬的牆壁。（→名詞子句）

• It is **an established fact** that **those with a high EQ are more likely to succeed.**
EQ高的人比較可能成功，這是個既定的事實。（→名詞子句）

• It was **a great discovery** that <u>he made in the lab at that time</u>.
= It was **a great discovery** which <u>he made in the lab at that time</u>.
當時他在實驗室中所做出的，是個大發現。（→強調句型）

• It is **a scientific breakthrough** that <u>scientists can clone animals in the lab</u>.
科學家們可以在實驗室裡複製動物，這是科學上的突破。（→強調句型）

★注意要點

若是為that引導補語的句型，可與下列句型互相替換。

• It is our belief **that he is a charismatic leader.**

= We believe **that he is a charismatic leader.**

= It is believed **that he is a charismatic leader.**

= He is believed **to be a charismatic leader.**

我們相信他是個很有領袖魅力的領導人。

 隨堂測驗

( ) 1. It is his commitment _____ he should contribute something to humanity.

(A) for which
(B) which
(C) because
(D) that

( ) 2. It is my observation _____ girls are better at communicating with others.

(A) that
(B) which
(C) in that
(D) in which

( ) 3. It is an undisputed fact that the earth _____ around the sun.

(A) is revolving
(B) revolves
(C) is to revolve
(D) would revolve

(　) 4. It was a self-evident fact _____ the professor is trying to convey to the public.

(A) what

(B) how

(C) that

(D) whether

(　) 5. It was the final conclusion _____ everyone in this team should be responsible for the failure of the experiment.

(A) which

(B) how

(C) why

(D) that

(　) 6. It is the book _____ Dr. Lin explained how to solve the crisis.

(A) how

(B) what

(C) that

(D) if

7. 我相信只有在努力之後才會有成功。（中翻英）

解答：1. (D) 2. (A) 3. (B) 4. (C) 5. (D) 6. (C)

7. It is my belief that success comes only after hard work.

解析：

① so as to表示「為了」。

② so as not to表示「為了不要」。

③ 譯：他這樣說話真的很失禮。

④so修飾elegantly，as to表示為了。

⑤so修飾much noises，as to用來表示目的。

主題二 | 分裂強調句型

❶ 句型要點：為加強句中某部份語氣而使用之結構

It is/was＋**被強調結構**＋that＋子句

          sth.   → that/which

          sb.   → who/whom

          地方副詞→ where

          時間副詞→ when

   It is/was...that...屬於分裂句，可以強調主詞、受詞、時間副詞、地方副詞等。另外，除了用that之外，也可以依據前面強調的語詞，使用適當的關係代名詞(who/whom/whose/which)，或關係副詞(when/where)等。

❷ It is a＋N that...這種句型，後面的句子為完整的子句，用來作為前面名詞的補語，相當於名詞的同位語。

例句講解

• <u>Mr. Tang</u> broke <u>a vase</u> <u>in the living room</u> <u>yesterday</u>.
    1   2   3   4

→It was <u>Mr. Tang</u> that broke a vase in the living room yesterday.
   昨天是譚先生在客廳打破花瓶的。

→It was <u>a vase</u> that Mr. Tang broke in the living room yesterday.
   昨天譚先生在客廳打破的是花瓶。

→It was <u>in the living room</u> that Mr. Tang broke a vase yesterday.
   昨天譚先生是在客廳打破花瓶的。

→It was <u>yesterday</u> that Mr. Tang broke a vase in the living room.
   譚先生是昨天在客廳打破花瓶的。

- It was <u>on a hot summer day</u> when/that he arrived at the harbor.
  就在一個炎熱的夏日，他到了港口。

- It was <u>John</u> who/that gave me a hand when I was in great trouble.
  當我陷入麻煩時，是約翰幫了我的忙。

- It was <u>not until two hours later</u> that electricity was restored. 【學測】
  直到兩個小時後，電力才恢復。

★注意要點

　　動詞不可以用分裂句強調，而是要用**助動詞＋原形動詞**來強調。

- His insulting remark did embarrass me at that moment.
  他羞辱人的話，在當時的確使我感到很尷尬。

- What is reported on cover the magazine did shock the public.
  在雜誌封面報導的內容的確使大眾震驚。

隨堂測驗

(　　) 1. It was _____ kept encouraging me and never gave me up.

  (A) my father that

  (B) yesterday when

  (C) my father whom

  (D) yesterday in which

(　　) 2. It is _____ he made up his mind to go abroad for further studies.

  (A) the reason that   (B) for the reason that

  (C) the reason because   (D) in the reason which

(　　) 3. It is not exactly what a child eats _____ truly matters, but how much time it stays in his mouth. 【學測】

  (A) to   (B) for   (C) that   (D) who

( ) 4. It is when these behaviors are inappropriate for their age and affect different areas in their lives _____ the disorder is diagnosed（診斷）. 【指考】

(A) which   (B) whose   (C) that   (D) what

( ) 5. It is the seven dwarves in the woods that _____ the Snow White from being eaten by bears.

(A) saves   (B) save
(C) to save   (D) will save

( ) 6. It is the little boy holding a ball in his hands that _____ me I can park here.

(A) telling   (B) tell
(C) he tells   (D) tells

7. 溫室氣體造成全球暖化，這是個既定事實。（中翻英）

解答：1. (A) 2. (A) 3. (C) 4. (C) 5. (B) 6. (D)
7. It is an established fact that greenhouse gases contribute to global warming.

解析：
①從後面「不斷鼓勵我而且從不放棄我」可以看出要強調的應該是人，此處關代應使用who/that，故選A。
②此句型為t is/was＋被強調結構＋that＋子句。
③可參考上一題。
④可參考第2題。
⑤此處動詞變化應搭配the seven dwarves。
⑥此處動詞變化應搭配the little boy。

★ **POINT 3-A** that子句為真主詞的基本概念

❶ 在這個句型裡，it為虛主詞，真正的主詞為that引導的名詞子句。主詞為名詞子句時常以虛主詞it代替，把名詞子句置於形容詞後面以**避免頭重腳輕**。 that不可省略。

❷ that子句中的主詞可移到句首，之後接**不定詞**來描述現況或事實。若that子句的時間早於主要子句表示事情已發生，則要用不定詞完成式。

❸ 除了不定詞和不定詞完成式，表示動作正在進行要用 to＋be＋V-ing，表被動語態時則用 to＋be＋V-p.p. 或 to＋have＋been＋V-p.p.。

例句講解

- <u>That someone had been sleeping on the bed</u> was obvious, because it was all messed up.（→無虛主詞it情況）
= It was obvious <u>that someone had been sleeping on the bed</u> because it was all messed up.（→有虛主詞it情況）
  顯然有人睡過這張床，因為床上亂七八糟的。

- <u>That they will win the championship</u> is apparent.（→無虛主詞it情況）
= It is apparent <u>that they will win the championship</u>.（→有虛主詞it情況）
  顯然他們將會贏得冠軍。

- It turned out <u>that Ed was the person</u> who played the joke on me.
（→有虛主詞it情況）
= <u>Ed</u> turned out <u>to be the person</u> who played the joke on me.
（→無虛主詞it情況）
  原來艾德就是那個捉弄我的人。

- It seems <u>that Mia left home without locking the door.</u>
= <u>Mia</u> seems <u>to have left home without locking the door.</u>
  米亞似乎出門沒鎖門。

- It seemed <u>that Sean was playing bowling with students.</u>
= <u>Sean</u> seemed <u>to be playing bowling with students.</u>
  尚恩似乎跟學生在打保齡球。

- It seemed <u>that all the work had been finished by James alone.</u>
= <u>All the work</u> seemed <u>to have been finished by James alone.</u>
  似乎全部的工作都被詹姆士一個人完成了。

★注意要點

　　此句型的主詞除了名詞外，也可用 it 來代替名詞子句（that 子句、wh-子句、whether/if 子句）。也可用 a big、a great、a little、little、some 等取代 no，表示影響的程度。

- <u>Whether the flight will be cancelled</u> has a lot to do with the weather.
= It has a lot to do with the weather <u>whether the flight will be cancelled.</u>
  班機是否取消與天氣大有相關。

- It made little difference <u>that the team scored a goal now</u> because they were already so far behind.
  這支隊伍因為已經落後太多，所以達陣得了分也沒什麼差別。

★延伸學習

　　❶ 在此句型裡，除了 be 動詞、become 外，也可用 seem、appear（似乎）等動詞，表示語氣不是十分肯定。

- It seems obvious <u>that more time is needed when the due date approaches.</u>
  截止日期逼近，似乎需要更多的時間是很顯然的。

- **With the evidence collected by the police, it** appeared **apparent** that Thomas had stolen the car.

  有了警方收集的證據，似乎很明顯就是湯瑪士偷了車子。

  ❷ It matters/doesn't matter (to sb.) that/whether/if＋子句（有關係／沒關係）與此句型有類似的意思。

- **It doesn't matter** if you forgot your camera **since I brought mine.**

  你是否忘了帶相機沒關係，因為我帶了我的。

- **Does it matter** that I didn't turn in the form on time?

  我沒有準時繳交表單有關係嗎？

- **It matters a lot to me** whether my parents feel proud of me.

  我父母是否以我為傲對我很重要。

隨堂測驗

( ) 1. It matters _____ the professor that students turn in essays late.

    (A) for

    (B) from

    (C) with

    (D) to

( ) 2. The lock appeared _____ broken, so the woman called the police.

    (A) to have had

    (B) that it has been

    (C) to be

    (D) that it was

( ) 3. Parents know that it makes no difference to young children _____ they wear the latest styles.

    (A) that

    (B) whether

(C) what
(D) which

( ) 4. It seems true that the tycoon _____ a child with his secretary twenty years ago.

(A) to have had
(B) has
(C) to have
(D) had

( ) 5. _____ agreed that passengers should fasten the seatbelt.

(A) They are
(B) He is
(C) It is
(D) What is

解答：1. (D) 2. (C) 3. (B) 4. (D) 5. (C)

解析：

①..."for sb"+that子句，故選(D)。

②此處使用appear表示語氣不是十分肯定。

③「無論」小孩是否依潮流打扮對父母來說沒有差，(B)符合文意。

④此處描述過去發生的事，直接使用過去式即可。

⑤這裡的it是虛主詞。

★ POINT 3-B 表示「很奇怪……竟然……」的句型

❶ 一個句子的主詞若過長時，可用虛主詞it代替，並以that子句為真正的主詞。 that子句中的主詞可移到句首，之後接**不定詞**來描述現況或事實。若 that 子句的時間早於主要子句表示事情已發生，則要用不定詞完成式。

❷ 本句型要以形容詞表示「令人驚訝的、怪異的、奇異的」。句型為：
It is surprising/strange/unbelievable＋that＋S＋should＋VR

❸ 適用於這種句型的相關形容詞：queer（奇怪的）、astonishing（令人驚訝的）、incredible（令人難以置信的）、stunning（令人目瞪口呆的）等

❹ 本句型的should是表示「竟然」，不可省略。

例句講解

● **It is strange that he should leave so soon.**
他竟然會這麼早離開，真是奇怪。

● **It is queer that he should mistake his classmate for the professor.**
他竟然把同學誤認為教授，也太奇怪了。

● **It was strange that he should be absent from her birthday party.**
很奇怪，他竟然沒參加她的生日舞會。

★延伸學習

這個句型可以替換成to one's＋情緒性名詞，意為「令（人）……的」。

● **It is astonishing that he should hit the jackpot.**
= **To our astonishment, he hit the jackpot.**
令人驚訝地，他竟然中頭彩了。

隨堂測驗

(　　) 1. It is _____ that he should win first place in the speech contest.

(A) surprisingly
(B) surprised
(C) surprise
(D) surprising

( ) 2. It is stunning that he _____ such rude words.

(A) could say (B) have to say

(C) should say (D) would say

( ) 3. It is incredible _____ he should ask the charming girl out for a date.

(A) when (B) which (C) that (D) what

( ) 4. It is bizarre that _____ should appear at the fashion party.

(A) such sloppy man

(B) so sloppy man

(C) such sloppy a man

(D) so sloppy a man

( ) 5. It was unbelievable that Mia _____ lose 20 pounds in three days.

(A) could (B) might (C) would (D) should

( ) 6. _____ everyone's relief, Sean came back safe and sound.

(A) At (B) With (C) For (D) To

解答: 1. (D) 2. (C) 3. (C) 4. (D) 5. (D) 6. (D)

解析:

①surprising有「令人驚訝的」之意。

②在此處should有「竟然」之意。

③此句型為It is incredible＋that＋S＋should＋VR。

④such a sloppy man/ so sloppy a man是此處可以填入的。

⑤參考第二題。

⑥to one's＋情緒性名詞,意為「令(人)……的」。

★ POINT 3-C 表示「……是很重要的」的句型

❶ 表示「……是很重要的」的句型為：It is important/essential/crucial ＋that ＋S＋(should)＋VR。本句型是由It is＋adj.＋for＋sb.＋to＋V演變而來的。也可以代換成：It is important for＋sb.＋to＋V

❷ 適用於這種句型的相關形容詞常表「重要的、急迫的、必須的、義務的」等意思，如：crucial、essential、imperative、important、necessary、obligatory、urgent、vital 等。

例句講解

• It is **important** that <u>he stay away from all the distractions</u>.
= It is **important** for <u>him to stay away from all the distractions</u>.
　他必須要遠離那些讓他分心的事，這是很重要的。

• It is **vital** that <u>a beginner keep these formulas in mind</u>.
　初學者要背這些公式，這是很重要的。

• It is **important** that <u>everyone dress up for such a formal occasion</u>.
　為了這麼正式的場合，每個人都要盛裝，這是很重要的。

★注意要點

It is＋adj.＋of＋sb.＋to＋V的句型則**不可以改成**It is adj.＋that＋S (should)＋V的句型。

• It is **kind of you to give a hand to the beggar**.
=You are **kind to give a hand to the beggar**.
　你真是好人，願意對乞丐伸出援手。

★延伸學習

在現代英文中，that 子句也常用直述句來表示。

• It is **imperative** that <u>our department cooperates with the government in finding the criminals</u>.
　我們部門必須與政府合作找出罪犯。

• It is **obligatory** that <u>the security system is turned on by the last person to leave the office each night.</u>

每天晚上最後離開公司的人有義務啟動保全系統。

隨堂測驗

( ) 1. It is urgent that you _____ Martha to the hospital.

   (A) have to send   (B) should send
   (C) can send   (D) sent

( ) 2. It is _____ that everyone (should) fill out all of the forms completely.

   (A) interesting (B) ready   (C) essential   (D) normal

( ) 3. It is crucial _____ an old person have regular physical examinations.

   (A) that   (B) which   (C) when   (D) for that

( ) 4. It is important that Eric _____ the starter in this game.

   (A) be   (B) should   (C) were   (D) was

( ) 5. It is necessary that Daniel _____ leave the key to the doorman before he flies to China.

   (A) could   (B) would   (C) might   (D) should

解答：1. (B) 2. (C) 3. (A) 4. (A) 5. (D)

解析：
①此處的should可以省略，後面接原形動詞，完整句型為It is important/essential/crucial＋that ＋S＋(should)＋VR。
②參考上一題。
③參考第一題。
④此處省略了should，be的意思則是「成為、當」。
⑤完整句型參考第一題。

★ POINT 3-D 表達「據說」的句型

❶ 表示「據說……」的句型為：

It is said/believed/reported/rumored...that＋S＋V

據説／一般相信／據報導／謠傳……等

❷ 此句型用來表達**客觀**的立場，代替其後之名詞子句，that**不可省略**。

❸ 其他可用的動詞包括：said、believed、thought、reported、expected、rumored 等，須注意文意差異。

❹ 這個句型有幾種變化，要特別注意。

(1) 如果用it做虛主詞時，要用**被動**，表示後面那件事是被説／被報導／被謠傳等。

(2) 如果用人如: people或they作主詞需用**主動**。

(3) 若後子句中主詞做真主詞時，則其後要使用**不定詞**，不可加that子句。

❺ 上述的句型變化，轉換時要注意前後子句的**時態**是否一致。如果後面的事實時代比較早，則變成不定詞時，需使用to have＋V-p.p.的型態。

❻ 除了用虛主詞It代替that 子句外，也可將子句中的主詞移到句首接不定詞，即：S＋be reported/said＋to＋V。

🖋 例句講解

• **People say that he is rich.**

= It is said **that he is rich.**

= He is said **to be rich.**

　聽説他很有錢。

• **People say that he was rich.**

= It is said that **he was rich.**

= He is said **to have been rich.**

　聽説他曾經很有錢。

- It is reported that **global temperature is getting higher.**

= Global temperature is reported **to be getting higher and higher.**

  據報導全球的溫度越來越高。

- It is said that **he was a wealthy man when he was young.**

= He is said **to have been a wealthy man when he was young.**

  據說他年輕時是個有錢人。

- It is said that **it took James nearly two hours to figure out the math formula.**

  據說詹姆士花了將近兩小時來理解這個數學公式。

- It was expected that **the football team would remain a national champion since it had the country's best coach.**

  這支橄欖球隊預期會保持冠軍，因為它有全國最棒的教練。

★延伸學習

　❶ that 子句為 it 的同位語，word、rumor、legend、tradition要用單數，且不加冠詞。

- Word has it that **the opera house will be performing "The Miserable."**

  據說歌劇院將上演《悲慘世界》。

- Legend has it that **on moonlit nights, ghosts walk along the halls of the castle.**

  傳說月夜裡鬼魂會在城堡的走廊上四處徘徊。

　❷ It is rumored that...也可代換為Rumor has it that...，表示「據說；傳聞」。

- Rumor has it that **the tycoon was abducted by the terrorists.**

  謠傳該大亨被恐怖分子綁架了。

- **Rumor has it that the superstar has undergone several cosmetic surgeries.**

謠傳那個巨星做過好幾次整形手術。

❸ it 為虛主詞代替 that 子句，可改成 S＋be well-known＋for sth. 的形式。It is a well-known＋N＋that＋S＋V 亦是常見的句型。

- **It is well-known that kangaroos carry their babies in a pouch.**

= **Kangaroos are well-known for carrying their babies in a pouch.**

大家都知道袋鼠把小袋鼠裝在育兒袋裡。

- **It's a well-known fact that planes can travel faster than cars.**

飛機行進的速度比汽車快是大家都知道的。

❹ 類似的句型 It is universally/widely/generally acknowledged 表「普世公認的」。

- **It is universally acknowledged that dinosaurs roamed the Earth many years ago.**

恐龍在很多年前在地球上到處走動是大家都知道的。

隨堂測驗

( ) 1. It is _____ that he was killed by his rival.

(A) rumored

(B) rumoring

(C) rumors

(D) rumor

( ) 2. _____ the fire started because some children were playing with matches.

(A) It is a report which

(B) It is report that

(C) It is reported which

(D) It is reported that

( ) 3. _____ that the company is going out of business soon.

(A) Rumor with it

(B) Rumors of it

(C) Rumor has it

(D) Rumor admits it

( ) 4. This kind of medicine is believed _____ the 4th century B.C. 【學測】

(A) that it dates

(B) that it traces back to

(C) to date from

(D) to be dated from

解答：1. (A) 2. (D) 3. (C) 4. (C)

解析：

①此處要使用被動式，以表示是「被謠傳」。

②此處使用被動式表示「被報導」，that後面子句則是被報導之內容。

③that 子句為 it的同位語，word、rumor、legend等要用單數，且不加冠詞。

④此處為後子句中主詞做真主詞，其後要使用**不定詞**，不可加that子句。

★ POINT 3-E 表達「的確……但……」的句型

❶ It is true that..., but用來前後語意相反的句子，可用yet代替，表示「的確……但……」，此句型較常用於口語中。

❷ It is true that 亦可用肯定副詞如 surely、certainly、indeed 代替。

❸ 此句型可改成 the truth is that..., but... ，but 前會用逗號與前面句子隔開。

例句講解

• Certainly I'd like to help you, but I have to clean my room.

= Indeed, I'd like to help you, but I have to clean my room.

= It is true that I'd like to help you, but I have to clean my room.

= The truth is that I'd like to help you, but I have to clean my room.

　我的確很樂意幫你，但我必須打掃我的房間。

• It is true that he's a talented writer, but he's not dedicated to writing.

　他是個有天份的作家沒錯，不過他不熱愛寫作。

隨堂測驗

(　　) 1. It is true that the painting is expensive, _____ we are still interested.

(A) yet
(B) as
(C) because
(D) so

(　　) 2. It is true that the book was written for young readers, _____ we think people of all ages will like it.

(A) however
(B) but
(C) while
(D) then

( ) 3. Certainly, you have some prime commitment. _____, it's your job to finish the work before the due day.

(A) But
(B) Still
(C) Otherwise
(D) And

( ) 4. The truth is that the government did whatever they could, _____ the press still put great pressure on them.

(A) but
(B) and
(C) or
(D) however

( ) 5. It's certain that the police have found something weird, _____ they still need some further investigation.

(A) as
(B) so
(C) but
(D) when

解答：1. (A) 2. (B) 3. (A) 4. (A) 5. (C)

解析：
①很貴但仍然有興趣，要使用有轉折語氣的連接詞，故選A。
②此處句型為It is true that..., but。
③It is true that 亦可用肯定副詞如 surely、certainly、indeed 代替。後面要表示轉折語氣要使用but。
④句型參考解析第二題。
⑤此句型裡的true也可以用certain代替。

主題四 | 其他It為虛主詞的句型

★ POINT 4-A 表達「……是值得的」句型

要表達「……是值得的」有主要下列句型

(1) It pays to VR...

在此句型中，it為虛主詞，且是固定的用法，不能將to＋VR挪前成為主詞。

- **It pays to studying and doing part-time at the same time.**
  半工半讀是值得的。

(2) worth＋N/V-ing

之後接名詞或V-ing，接名詞表示「值多少金錢或所花的代價（時間或努力）是值得的」，而 V-ing 的用法，**不分主被動**，都直接加V-ing。

- **If you get the chance, the pyramids in Egypt are worth seeing.**
- **= If you get the chance, the pyramids in Egypt are worth a visit.**
  如果你有機會，埃及的金字塔值得去看看。

- **It is absolutely worth your effort/time to learn a second language.**
  學習第二語言絕對值得你投入心力／時間。

(3) worthy＋of N/to V

worthy之後可接 of＋N 或 to V，表示「值得……的；配得上」的意思。

worthy 之後表主動用 of＋V-ing 或 to＋V，表被動用 of＋being＋V-p.p. 或 to be＋V-p.p.，不過**這種用法複雜且少見，不建議使用**。

- **He has no experience. He isn't worthy of being given the job.**
- **= He has no experience. He isn't worthy to be given the job.**
  他沒有經驗，他配不上接受這份工作。

- **The town is worthy of note because a famous author was born here.**
  這個城鎮值得注意，因為曾有一名著名的作家出生在這裡。

(4) It is worthwhile＋to V/V-ing

本句型還可以It is worthwhile＋to V表示。worthwhile 之後可接 to＋V或 V-ing，It 用來代替真正的主詞 to＋V 或 V-ing。

• It is worthwhile **to stop at the bookstore, as it has a great selection of travel guides.**

= It is worthwhile **stopping at the bookstore, as it has a great selection of travel guides.**

那家書店值得你駐足，因為它有很棒的旅遊指南叢書。

• It is worthwhile **for young people like you to read as many good books as possible.**

= It is worthwhile **for young people like you reading as many good books as possible.**

= **Reading as many good books as possible** is worthwhile **for young people like you.**

像你們這樣的年輕人，多讀好書是很值得的。

★延伸學習

❶ pay除了用於上面的句型以外，也常用來指「付錢」。注意下面的分別：

    (1) pay＋sb.　付錢給……

    (2) pay for＋sth.　付錢買（某物）

    (3) pay the bill/tuition/rent　付帳／學費／租金

    (4) pay one's way through college 半工半讀唸完大學

• **To my embarrassment, when I got out of the taxi, I forgot to pay the cabbie.**

令我很尷尬的事，當我下計程車時，我忘了付錢給司機。

• **How much did you pay for the fantasy novel?**

你花了多少錢買那本奇幻小說？

❷ worthwhile 可寫作 worth one's while 來強調「值得某人……」，one's 可省略。

- **It is worth your while to bring sunscreen when you go to the beach.**
  去海邊帶防曬乳是值得的。

  > ❸ 本句型也可以替換成：It is rewarding＋to V。

- **It is rewarding to give a hand to the poor and the needy.**
  對窮困的人伸出援手是值得的。

  > ❹「值……時間、金錢」也可用「數量所有格＋worth of sth.」來表示。

- **The robber got away with five million dollars' worth of jewels.**
  這名搶匪搶走了價值五百萬的珠寶。

隨堂測驗

(　　) 1. It is _____ to visit the aquarium in Pintung.

    (A) worth   **(B)** worthy of   **(C)** worthy   **(D)** worthwhile

(　　) 2. That dress is not _____ NT$5,000, so don't buy it.

    (A) worth   **(B)** worthy of   **(C)** worthy   **(D)** worthwhile

(　　) 3. Not every musician–only the best – is _____ to play with us.

    (A) worth   **(B)** worthy of   **(C)** worthy   **(D)** worthwhile

(　　) 4. This speech is worth _____. I felt refreshed because of it.

    (A) listening   **(B)** listening to   **(C)** of listening to **(D)** of listening

解答： 1. (C)　2. (A)　3. (C)　4. (A)

解析：
①此處使用worthy＋to V，故選(C)。
②可以後面接名詞的有worth和worthy of，其中worth接名詞表示「值多少金錢或所花的代價（時間或努力）是值得的」。
③worthy之後可接 of＋N 或 to V，表示「值得……的；配得上」的意思。
④此處用法為worth＋N/V-ing。

一的相關句型

★ POINT 4-B 表達「……是無用的」句型

❶ It is (of) no use＋V-ing.= It is useless＋to V. 表示「做某件事是無用的」，其中的of可省略。不論是It is no use或It is of no use，後面都可以加上動名詞或不定詞，兩者都正確。

❷ 此句型還可代換為There is no use＋(in)＋V-ing，其中的 in 可省略。

 例句講解

• It is (of) no use **trying to change his mind.**
想改變他的心意是沒有用的。

• It is no use **crying over spilt milk.**
覆水難收。（後悔無用）

• There is no point/use in **worrying about tomorrow.**
= It is pointless/useless to **worry about tomorrow.**
擔心明天是沒有用的。

• There is no use (in) **looking for stars on a cloudy night.**
在多雲的夜晚尋找星星是徒勞無功的。

• There/It is no use in **thinking that you will get a good grade without studying.**
認為不用念書就可以得到好成績是沒有用的。

★延伸學習

there is no＋V-ing 表示「……是不可能的；無法……」，與 it is impossible to＋V 意思相同。

• There is no **knowing whether grandpa will get well.**
爺爺是否能痊癒根本無從得知。

• There is no **denying that Ken's photos were the best in the exhibit.**
= It is impossible to **deny that Ken's photos were the best in the exhibit.**
不可否認，肯恩的相片是展覽中最棒的。

❷ 注意以下的區別：

(1) There is no use＋to V = It is (of) no use＋V-ing/to V ……是沒有用的

(2) There is no need＋to V 沒有必要去做……

(3) It is no wonder that... 難怪……

(4) It goes without saying that...=It is needless to say that... 不用說，……

(5) There is no doubt that... 無疑地，……

(6) There is no point in＋V-ing ……是沒意義的

❸ 禁止標語常用 no＋V-ing 或 no＋N 來表示，如：No Smoking、No Parking。

- **James didn't see the "No Smoking" sign and lit his cigarette inside the restaurant.**
詹姆士沒看見「禁止抽煙」的標誌，在餐廳裡點了根煙。

🕐 隨堂測驗

(　) 1. Since he has been working so hard, there _____ to worry about whether he can pass the exam.

(A) isn't need
(B) is no need
(C) isn't use
(D) is no use

(　) 2. It is no use _____ to talk him into buying our product.

(A) to try
(B) for trying
(C) trying
(D) being trying

288

( ) 3. There is no _____ when the restaurant will be open, as the owner only serves customers when he is in a good mood.

(A) needing
(B) telling
(C) wondering
(D) looking

( ) 4. _____ of no use to apologize for the terrible mistake, although we all know that you didn't do it on purpose.

(A) There is
(B) There was
(C) It was
(D) It is

( ) 5. There was _____ in blaming the accident on the train conductor. I think the truck driver is to blamed.

(A) not point
(B) not pointing
(C) no point
(D) of no point

解答：1. (B) 2. (C) 3. (B) 4. (D) 5. (C)

解析：

①There is no need＋to V 意思為「沒有必要去做……」。

②此處句型為It is (of) no use＋V-ing.＝ It is useless＋to V. 表示「做某件事是無用的」。

③There is no telling表示「無法判斷……」。

④完整句型參考第二題。

⑤完整句型為There is no point in＋V-ing 表示「……是沒意義的」。

★ POINT 4-C 表達「花費了⋯⋯」句型

❶ 花費的對象，一個是錢，一個是時間，以下是相對應的句型：

(1) It takes (sb.) time＋to V　花時間／勞力等

(2) It costs (sb.) money＋to V　花錢

(3) sb. spend time/money on＋N/(in)＋V-ing

❷ spend 之後可接「in＋動名詞」或「on＋名詞」，介系詞 in 可以省略。

	動詞三態	使用時機	主詞
spend	spend/spent/spent	金錢、時間	人
cost	cost/cost/cost	金錢	人／事
take	take/took/taken	非金錢可計價的花費	人／事

例句講解

- **It will cost you about NT$30,000 to buy a notebook computer.**
  買台筆記型電腦大約要花台幣三萬元。

- **The villa cost him a fortune.**
  那棟別墅讓他花了一大筆錢。

- **It takes most people an hour each day to get to work.**
- **= It takes an hour for most people each day to get to work.**
  大多數的人每天上班要花一個小時。

- **She spent all her pocket money on cosmetics.**
  她把零用錢全花在化妝品上。

- **In college, students spend a lot of money (in) buying books each year.**
- **= In college, students spend a lot of money on books each year.**
  大學生每年都要花很多錢買書。

- **Getting to the airport took James hours because of the traffic.**
  詹姆士因為交通花了幾個小時才抵達機場。

★延伸學習

waste的用法和spend相同，意思是「浪費」。

- **You are not supposed to waste too much money on such luxuries.**
  你不應該浪費太多錢在這種奢侈品上。

- **You are wasting your breath trying to change his mind.**
  你想要改變他的心意，根本是白費力氣。

隨堂測驗

( ) 1. Many teenagers _____ too much time _____ online games.

    (A) spend; playing

    (B) spend; to play

    (C) take; playing

    (D) take; to play

( ) 2. Paul _____ half of his paycheck _____ a gift for his girlfriend.

    (A) cost; in

    (B) cost; on

    (C) spent; in

    (D) spent; on

( ) 3. It _____ the architect almost two years _____ the building.

    (A) spent; designing

    (B) took; designing

    (C) spent; to design

    (D) took ;to design

( ) 4. James _____ hours _____ to the airport because of the traffic.

(A) spent; to get

(B) spent; getting

(C) took; to get

(D) took; on getting

( ) 5. _____ cost an arm and a leg for Mia to get the lost package back.

(A) What

(B) She

(C) It

(D) This

( ) 6. Daniel bought a pet dog for Mia. It _____ the whole morning getting used to its new home.

(A) spent

(B) took

(C) paid

(D) cost

解答：1. (A) 2. (D) 3. (D) 4. (B) 5. (C) 6. (A)

解析：

①主詞為人用spend，spend後面可以接N/Ving。

②主詞為人用spend，搭配介系詞用on。

③It takes/took...to V表示「某事花費…」

④參考第一題。

⑤It在此處為虛主詞。

⑥spend完整用法參考第一及第二題。

主題五 | **It為虛受詞的句型**

❶ 虛受詞的出現，常與S＋V＋O＋OC連用，其實與虛主詞有異曲同工之妙。當受詞太長，會使得受詞補語的位置拖到太後面而模糊焦點，所以用虛受詞的句型，以方便判讀受詞補語。

❷ 以it為虛受詞的句型之一，用來表示「使人……覺得某事」的句型：

S.（人）＋believe/consider/find/prove/think＋it＋adj.＋to＋V

❸ 句型中的 it 為虛受詞，代替真正受詞的不定詞片語，這類動詞含有「認為」的意思，包括：believe、consider、find、prove、think 等。欲表明對象時，則在不定詞前加上 for sb./sth.。這個句型中的形容詞，就是前面所提到的「非人形容詞」，所以句中的it是代替後面不定詞的虛受詞。真正的受詞，是後面不定詞所說的事。

• **Most people find it annoying to <u>wait in line for a long time</u>.**
  多數人覺得長時間排隊是很煩人的。

• **I think it rude for people to <u>chew with their mouths open</u>.**
  我認為人咀嚼時張開嘴巴是很粗魯的。

❹ 句型中的受詞補語可用名詞，不定詞也可改成 that 子句，that 可省略。

• **Scientists have proven it unhealthy to <u>eat too much meat</u>.**
= **Scientists have proven (that) it is unhealthy to eat too much meat.**
  科學家證明吃太多肉是不健康的。

❺ 此句型中的主詞不明確或不重要時，亦可改成被動語態。

• **In the West, it is considered (that) <u>healthy and sexy to have a nicely tanned body</u>.**
  在西方，將身體曬成漂亮的古銅色才被認為是健康、性感。

以it為虛受詞的句型之一，用來表示「注重……、養成……的習慣」的句型：

(1) S（人）＋make it a rule＋to V＝S（人）＋make a rule of＋V-ing

(2) S（人）＋make it a point＋to V＝S（人）＋make a point of＋V-ing

- I make it a rule to <u>keep ten new words in mind</u> every day.
= I make a rule of <u>remembering ten new words</u> every day.

我養成每天都背十個單字的習慣。

- We should make it a point to <u>keep our surroundings clean and tidy</u>.
= We should make a point of <u>keeping our surroundings clean and tidy</u>.

我們應該養成習慣，將四周環境保持整齊清潔。

- I make it a rule that <u>the first thing I do every morning is listen to English radio program</u>.

我養成一個每天起床第一件事就是聽英語廣播的習慣。

以it為虛受詞的句型之一，用來表示「促成……」的句型：

S＋make it possible (for＋sb.)＋to V＝S＋make＋N＋possible

- TV sets make it possible for people to <u>stay home watching TV programs</u>.

電視的發明讓人們可以待在家裡收看電視節目。

- The invention of the airplane makes it possible to <u>fly from Taipei to America in a day</u>.

飛機的發明使得一天內從台北到美國成為可能。

- Your financial support made <u>my dream</u> possible.

你在財務上的支持使我夢想成真。

❶ 以it為虛受詞的句型之一，用來表示「把某人或事物為理所當然，忘了去珍惜或愛護」的句型：S＋take it for granted that...

❷ 這個句型，是從take＋O＋for granted來的。如果只要說一個簡單的事物，可以用名詞來表達的，就用take...for granted。但是，如果需要講到一個子句才能表達的概念，則用take it for granted that＋子句，也就是先用it做虛受詞，再加上後面的that子句做真受詞。

❶ take it for granted that＋S＋V 中的it為虛受詞，用來代替that子句，it 可省略。

❷ 受詞不是子句時，可用 take sb./sth. for granted 來表達；受詞過長 時，亦可移到 granted 之後。

• **Don't take it for granted that <u>I will help you</u>.**
不要以為我會幫你是理所當然。

• **Experts warn us not to take it for granted that <u>food prices are low</u>.**
專家警告我們不應該再將食物價格低廉視為理所當然。【指考】

• **The company takes <u>its employees</u> for granted.**
這家公司把員工視為理所當然。

• **People often take <u>friendship</u> for granted and seldom take it seriously.**
人們常視友誼為理所當然，而很少認真看待它。

隨堂測驗

(　) 1. Good luck makes _____ to become a millionaire.

　(A) it possible for him
　(B) him possible
　(C) him to be possible
　(D) that he is possible

(　) 2. I find _____ to get along with him.

　(A) it's hard
　(B) it hard
　(C) hard
　(D) hard it

(　) 3. I consider _____ to show up for work on time.

　(A) it my duty
　(B) my duty is to
　(C) my duty
　(D) it is my duty

(　) 4. Bob _____ it for granted that his classmates should help him.

    (A) asked

    (B) made

    (C) saw

    (D) took

(　) 5. He is often _____ for an Americans.

    (A) believed

    (B) mistaken

    (C) proven

    (D) found

(　) 6. What made _____ necessary to build a road through the Glacier National Park? 【學測】

    (A) that

    (B) it

    (C) which

    (D) its

解答： 1. (A)　2. (B)　3. (A)　4. (D)　5. (B)　6. (B)

解析：

①完整句型為S＋make it possible (for＋sb.)＋to V。

②it為虛主詞，真主詞為to get along with him。

③完整句型為S.（人）＋believe/consider/find/prove/think＋it＋adj.＋to＋V。

④take for granted表示「把…視為理所當然」。

⑤mistaken在此有「被誤認」之意。

⑥It在此處為虛主詞，真正的主詞為to build a road through the Glacier National Park。

滿分追擊模擬試題

( ) 1. It was cruel _____ him to beat the dog like that.

(A) for   (B) with   (C) of   (D) on

( ) 2. One day, an idea _____ Art Fry. 【學測】

(A) threw at   (B) occurred to

(C) looked down upon   (D) camp up with

( ) 3. It is astonishing that he _____ nominated（提名）for the best acting.

(A) will be   (B) had to

(C) should be   (D) has to be

( ) 4. Athletes _____ many hours each day practicing skills and improving teamwork under the guidance of a coach or a sports instructor. 【指考】

(A) take   (B) waste   (C) spend   (D) cost

( ) 5. _____ to attract new employees if it has a casual dress code. 【學測】

(A) A company is easier

(B) What is easier for a company

(C) It is easier for a company

(D) It is easier of a company

( ) 6. The conflicts（衝突）between John and his teacher made _____ difficult for the teacher to judge his performance objectively（客觀地）. 【學測】

(A) that   (B) it   (C) what   (D) which

( ) 7. Hard candies _____ a long time to consume and are a bad choice for Halloween treats. 【學測】

(A) take　　　(B) spend　　　(C) cost　　　(D) waste

( ) 8. It's a pity that you have to leave so soon. I _____ hope that you will come back very soon. 【學測】

(A) sincerely　(B) scarcely　(C) reliably　(D) obviously

( ) 9. Choose the correct sentence:

(A) The museum pays to be visited because there is a great collection of art objects.

(B) It pays to visit the museum, which is home to a great collection of art objects.

(C) It is worthy visiting the museum, which was founded three centuries ago.

(D) The museum is worth being visited for it is the temple of art and history.

( ) 10. Science _____ the use of new materials and new methods of producing objects. 【指考】

(A) makes possible　　　　(B) makes it possible

(C) makes us possible　　　(D) makes that possible

( ) 11. It is queer that he _____ leave without saying good-bye.

(A) may　　　(B) should　　　(C) must　　　(D) could

( ) 12. The delicate vision _____ decades to be fulfilled. 【指考】

(A) took　　　(B) spent　　　(C) cost　　　(D) wasted

( ) 13. It _____ to listen to his timely advice.

(A) takes　　　(B) pays　　　(C) is worth　　　(D) rewards

解答

1. (C) cruel是用來形容人的，要用of來連接。

2. (B) occur to表示「讓某人想起、想到」。

3. (C) should在此處有「竟然」之意。

4. (C) 主詞為運動員，依文意是指花費時間，故選(C)。

5. (C) It is easier for a company意為「對於一間公司來說很容易」，真主詞在後面。

6. (B) it為虛主詞。

7. (A) take在此處表示花費的時間。

8. (A) sincerely表示「誠摯地」。

9. (B) 正確的寫法應為：

(A) It pays to visit the museum...

(C) It is worthwhile visiting the museum...

(D) The museum is worthy of being visited...或 The museum is worth visiting...

10. (A) 虛受詞的句型要注意的地方是，後面的受主詞必須為to＋VR或that＋CI。但此處明顯皆非，所以可知是用受詞往後移動的寫法，選A。

11. (B) 同第三題。

12. (A) 主詞非人，且後面可知花的是時間，故選(A)。

13. (B) 譯：花時間聽他及時的建議划得來的。

NOTE

原來如此 系列 **E236**

我的第一本**完勝英文句型攻略**

收錄必考必學試題例句，補教名師帶你把英文句型一次學習到位！

作　　　者	李宇凡 ◎著
顧　　　問	曾文旭
社　　　長	王毓芳
編輯統籌	耿文國、黃璽宇
主　　　編	吳靜宜、姜怡安
執行編輯	吳佳芬、尤新皓
美術編輯	王桂芳、張嘉容
封面設計	阿作
法律顧問	北辰著作權事務所　蕭雄淋律師、幸秋妙律師

初　　　版	2020年10月
出　　　版	捷徑文化出版事業有限公司
電　　　話	（02）2752-5618
傳　　　真	（02）2752-5619

定　　　價	新台幣340元／港幣113元
產品內容	1書

總 經 銷	采舍國際有限公司
地　　　址	235 新北市中和區中山路二段366巷10號3樓
電　　　話	（02）8245-8786
傳　　　真	（02）8245-8718

港澳地區總經銷	和平圖書有限公司
地　　　址	香港柴灣嘉業街12號百樂門大廈17樓
電　　　話	（852）2804-6687
傳　　　真	（852）2804-6409

▶本書部分圖片由 Shutterstock、freepik 圖庫提供。

捷徑Book站

現在就上臉書（FACEBOOK）「捷徑BOOK站」並按讚加入粉絲團，
就可享每月不定期新書資訊和粉絲專享小禮物喔！

http://www.facebook.com/royalroadbooks
讀者來函：royalroadbooks@gmail.com

國家圖書館出版品預行編目資料

我的第一本完勝英文句型攻略 / 李宇凡著.
-- 初版. -- 臺北市：捷徑文化, 2020.10
　面；　公分. -- (原來如此：E236)

ISBN 978-986-5507-32-9(平裝)

1. 英語　2. 句法

805.169　　　　　　　　　　109009438